Dear heart,
I hate you

ELIAH
GREENWOOD

www.eliahgreenwood.com

This book is a work of fiction. Any references to historical events, real people, or real places are used fictitiously. Other names, characters, places, and events are products of the author's imagination, and any resemblance to actual events or places or persons, living or dead, is entirely coincidental.

Warning: This book contains topics which may be triggering to some readers (substance abuse, graphic mature scenes, foul language, violence.) Please proceed with caution.

ISBN: 978-1-7776223-3-6
Editing by One Love Editing
First printing edition 2022
Eliah Greenwood Publishing
Cover Photograph: Michelle Lancaster

For the people who save everyone...

I hope you remember to save yourself.

Playlist

Pretty Poison – Nessa Barrett

Dark Side – Bishop Briggs

As The World Caves In –Sarah Cothran's Version

Habits – Plested

I Don't Believe In Satan - Aron Wright

Prologue

Finn
Aged fifteen

Dear Mom,

I don't need therapy…

I wish you could tell that to Dad.

And the lady with the mustache.

While you're at it, tell her she smells like hobo socks and ask her what she's writing in that damn notebook of hers—I bet she's drawing bunnies and shit.

I'm currently stuck in some stupid office, on some stupid green couch, writing you stupid letters that you're never going to get.

I tried telling Hobo Socks that you're gone, but she

says that's the point of the exercise.

To *pretend.*

To talk to you like you're still here and not hanging out with the fish at the bottom of Lake Belmont…

And they say *I'm* out of touch with reality.

You haven't missed much, in case you were wondering. Dad still thinks I'm a nutcase, and he still secretly wishes Xavier was his son instead of me.

Apparently, my best friend is a "good kid" because he doesn't, *and I quote,* "go around stealing the neighbor's car and crashing it into a pole."

Big. Fucking. Deal.

He doesn't get it.

Xavier didn't lose you, Mom.

If he did, he'd want to set the world on fire, too.

Hobo Socks keeps saying I'm on a path to "self-destruction," whatever the fuck that means. Sounds fun, if you ask me. *Sign me up.*

It doesn't help that I should be in juvie right now. The car thing would've been strike three. Good thing Dad bribed the neighbor, huh? I guess money really can buy everything.

Wait, I take that back.

Money can buy everything *except* what matters.

It didn't give me super strength that day, did it?

It didn't stop your hand from slipping.

Because rich people don't float.

Not even people with hearts as big as the ocean.

"Look, but don't touch," you used to say about painful things. You said it only hurts if you let it. That the flame only burns if you get close enough.

And I promise you, Mom...

I'll never get burned again.

- Finley

One

Diamond

I once went on a date with a dog.

That's right… a *dog.*

It's one of those things you think will never happen to you. Until you show up on your crush's doorstep and find out your "date" is a border collie who can't tell the difference between your leg and a chew toy.

I know what you're thinking. How in the hell do you confuse a job offer with someone asking you out?

Well, it's simple, really.

Be a swooning idiot.

The day Everest Cahill came up to me, my brain cells shit the bed—plain and simple. I was so shocked to hear Hottie Cahill knew we inhabited the same planet that I might've missed a couple of sentences.

Or five.

I spent most of our conversation mentally planning our wedding before he said, "So, we're on for Saturday?" Too embarrassed to make him repeat himself, I assumed I'd hit the jackpot.

Boy, was I wrong.

I can still see his mom's confused smile when I turned up on her porch looking like a million bucks. She was quick to tell me that her son was out of town and the rest of the family was going away for the weekend.

Then she introduced me to their six-month-old puppy, Rio. You guessed it—I wasn't there for a date with Everest, but to take care of his dog.

And the crazy part?

I agreed.

It turns out my dad had told Everest's parents I was looking for work when they'd stopped by his restaurant a week prior. I couldn't believe it. My own *father* was to blame for the most embarrassing date of my life.

But I needed the money, so I swallowed my pride, slapped on a smile, and rolled with it. Little did I know my dad's stunt would lead to more job opportunities than I could ever want…

Word spread, and a week later, more furry-friend owners began requesting my services. Before I knew it, I was the town's "official" dog sitter—yep, as in people *pay* me to hang out with their dogs—and I was thrilled. I could never convince my parents to get a pet due to my dad's allergies.

Long story short, I was living the dream.

Until… *I wasn't.*

"Get on your fucking knees, prom queen," a deep voice says, jolting me awake.

Disoriented, I blink once.

Twice.

Where have I heard this voice before?

"Promise me he won't find out," a female croaks from the hallway, and I sit up in bed, clutching the blanket to my chest.

I'm not dreaming.

This is *real.*

There are people in the house.

And they're right outside my bedroom.

"I already told you I won't tell him shit," the masculine voice huffs, and I clench my eyes shut, preparing for impending death—*what?* Just because the people who broke into my boss's house at 3:00 a.m. are arguing like a married couple doesn't mean they're not serial killers.

"Just promise me, Finn," the girl insists.

That's when it all clicks.

Trembling, I loosen my grasp on the blanket.

Did she just say…

Finn?

"Nope, not doing this. Get on your knees, or get the fuck out," Mystery Guy snaps, his tone void of emotion.

Yep, that's Finn Richards, all right.

Good news: Mystery Guy is not a serial killer.

Bad news: he's a conceited asshole.

"You want me to leave?" The girl sounds indignant.

"I want you to *choose*, Randall."

My stomach drops.

Randall?

As in… cheerleader cliché *Brielle Randall?*

I don't even get the chance to let it sink in before I hear what sounds like a body getting shoved against the wall.

"So, what's it going to be, princess? Staying…" Silence lingers in the air, the tension palpable. "…or *leaving?*"

"I just… I feel so awful," Brielle bleats. "Do you think he'd ever forgiv—"

I'm positive he just smacked his hand to her mouth when he grits out an annoyed "Keep it the fuck down. My dad hired some cow to take care of the house for the summer. She's probably passed out somewhere."

I'll be damned.

He *knows.*

He knew I was starting the job today, and he still brought his booty call home in the middle of the night.

See? *Conceited asshole.*

"And I should care why?" Brie scoffs.

"Because I don't need her ratting me out when my dad's already pissed about basketball camp, that's fucking why. Now choose." Finn circles back to the point. "In or out?"

"I…" Brie falters.

"Maybe this will help."

The sound of a zipper is the only clue I need.

"*Fuuck.*" A raw moan rips from Brielle's throat, muffled by

Finn's palm, and I cringe deep in my bones.

"You hear that, cheat?" Finn taunts, his voice low and gravelly. "Your pussy's fucking begging you to stay."

My throat closes up at her arousal.

Someone get a mop because I'm not cleaning that up.

"It's… it's not cheating if he doesn't find out," Brielle squeaks in between moans.

I almost laugh.

The girl's been dating Xavier Emery, the school's star basketball player, for over a year now. Not only are these two Easton High's *IT* couple, but it's also common knowledge that her boyfriend and Finn Richards are practically brothers.

They grew up together.

Hell, they share everything—same basketball team, same goals, same inhuman good looks.

Same girl…

This is what I get for trying something new.

I could've stuck to dog-sitting on the weekends this summer, but no, I just *had* to take a house-sitting job for the most fucked-up family in Silver Springs.

In my defense, the gig sounded too good to be true—great money, room and board, two months living in a mansion. Not to mention the ad said *no* houseguests except a golden retriever named Lexie. My boss assured me his eldest son, Brody, had moved out and his youngest, Finn, was away at basketball camp for the summer.

Away for the summer, my ass.

"Bedroom. Now," Brie urges.

Dread claws at me.

Mr. Richards told me to treat myself to the biggest room in the house while he's away, but… there's just one problem.

I picked Finn's bedroom.

Shiiiiiit.

I consider sneaking out through the opened window before remembering that I'm on the second floor and have as much stealth as my deaf grandma trying to hear bingo numbers.

A plan.

I need a plan.

The door to the bedroom swings open the next second, and I opt for the only course of action I can think of: hide under the blanket and pretend I don't exist.

The cheaters stumble into the room, neither of them taking notice of my presence as they undress each other. It takes me a second to realize that I could go undetected all night. The room is pitch-black, and this bed could fit all of my imaginary boyfriends combined.

I'm not sure what's worse: getting caught half-naked in my boss's son's bed… or being forced to listen to the cool kids have scandalous sex.

I shouldn't have removed my shorts earlier, but it was as hot as the fiery pits of hell. Safe to say my see-through tank top and lace panties wouldn't make the best first impression? I worry my heart is going to tear through my chest when two tangled bodies sink down next to me.

This is it.

I'm going to witness a cheerleader deep-throat a jock.

Worst. First. Day. Ever.

Severing the kiss, Brie chokes out a weak "T-This is never happening again."

Finn cracks a low, deriding laugh. "Sure."

"I mean it, dickhead."

"You meant it last time, too."

Hold on…

This isn't the first time they've hooked up?

My throat aches.

Poor Xavier.

A long moment of silence ensues.

Normally, this would be when it sinks in.

The looming self-hatred that comes with betraying your oldest friend. If this Finn guy has even a *sliver* of humanity, he'll come around before betraying Xavier.

Again.

"Fuck the blowie. Lift up your skirt," Finn commands.

Nope, still a sociopath.

"God, you're so hot. I love a guy who takes charg—"

"I must've missed it," Finn cuts her off.

"Missed what?" she questions.

"The part where I tell you to fucking talk."

Holy shit…

I can't help laughing in my head.

"What the fuck?"

That's when I realize that I'm an idiot.

And what I did just now?

Definitely not in my head.

The lights come on immediately, and I wonder if I could get away with pretending to be asleep. Then I decide that if talking in your sleep is weird, *laughing* in your sleep is downright terrifying.

From the moment my sight adjusts to the light, I see Brie jolt to her feet, her dark red hair a tangled mess, followed by Finn, who leaps off the bed in a knee-jerk reflex.

Not a word is uttered for the next five seconds, but it feels like thirty. Brie and Finn don't move a muscle as they stare at me like I'm some feral creature waiting to pounce. Brie is wearing a black push-up bra and a short denim skirt while Finn…

Finn is just annoying.

I knew Finn Richards was hot from seeing him at school, but I didn't know *shirtless* Finn Richards was the kind of gorgeous you want to punch in the face on behalf of average-looking males everywhere.

I scan him from head to toe, starting with the silver chain hanging down his neck, the black jeans falling an inch too low around his hips, and the deep V-line pointing to his, *ahem*, downstairs neighbor.

And those abs…

Lord, have mercy.

Tousled brown hair drapes down his forehead, concealing sharp hazel eyes where pits of darkness are brewing. Sleeves of tattoos snake up his arms, the ink covering every inch of his biceps. Top that with a jaw so sharp it could draw blood and you have yourself a dirty, cruel temptation with a bow on top.

The big guy definitely worked weekends making this one.

"Who the hell is that?" Brie glowers at me, elbowing Finn in the ribs. Finn doesn't say a word, mouth hanging as he stares me up and down.

Anyone in their right mind would apologize in this scenario. Any smart house sitter would suck up to her employer's kid.

So, you can imagine my surprise when my mouth forms the words, "Hi, I'm Dia, the cow your dad hired for the summer. *Nice to meet you.*"

Finn's eyebrows lift to his forehead at my response. The shock in his gaze quickly morphs into something so cold it shoots shivers up my spine.

In his eyes… I see hate.

Not just your everyday dislike.

The real deal.

You know, the kind you save for someone who gave you an incurable STD?

So, why is he directing it at me? His hateful stare makes me so uncomfortable I lift the blanket higher up my chest as if to shield myself. He's about to speak when Brie beats him to it.

"You… I… how long has she been listening?"

Someone's worried about this getting back to her boyfriend.

"I woke up when you came into the room," I lie.

"Get out." Finn's harsh voice steals my breath.

I blink at him.

"Get the fuck out," he repeats, this time louder.

Brie lets out a small snicker. "You heard him, *cow*."

"I was talking to you," Finn shocks her by saying.

"You what?" she spits.

"Just fucking leave, Randall. I'll deal with her."

Deal with her?

What's he going to do?

Sell my organs to the highest bidder?

Brie picks her top off the bed, throws it back on, and makes a beeline for the door, only stopping to say, "You make sure she keeps her fucking mouth shut, or I'll come back and staple your balls to the wall, *we clear*?"

"I said leave." Finn doesn't even spare her a look, his focus drilled into my forehead. Offended, Brie intentionally slams the door. Her footsteps fade down the hall until there isn't a sound to be heard.

It hits me a second too late.

I'm all alone.

In the middle of the night.

With Easton High's delinquent—seriously, the guy was voted "most likely to end up in jail" by his own friends—with no witnesses around except a golden retriever who's sound asleep downstairs.

"What the actual fuck are you doing in my bed?" Finn accuses as soon as Brie's gone, and I curse every decision I've ever made for leading me here.

"Sleeping. Your dad said—"

He interrupts me. "My dad is a fucking moron for hiring you in the first place."

Stunned, I stare at him.

He looks like he's waiting for something.

"Translation, you're fired. *Scram.*" He jerks his head toward the door.

"E-Excuse me?" It comes out as a whisper, and I loathe the tremor in my voice.

"You. Are. Fired." He spells it out like I have a hunk of cotton balls for a brain. "We won't be needing your services anymore. Pack your shit and get out." He gives the overnight bag I left at the bottom of the bed a careless kick.

Anger roars within me.

Who does this guy think he is?

"Last I checked, you're not the one paying me. I'm not going anywhere unless your dad tells me to." I direct all of my energy into sounding confident.

Finn thinks on his answer for a long moment before saying,

"Suit yourself. He'll fire your ass tomorrow, anyway. Even better, *I'll get to watch.*"

Astounded by his cruelty, I keep up our staring contest.

"Pretty sure I told you to get the fuck out of my bed," he hounds when I don't move fast enough, and I snap out of it, starting to lift the blanket off my body.

Then I remember…

I'm still close to naked.

"I'm sorry, but I'm not leaving this bed—"

Until you turn around, I intend to say, but he's heard enough, and he's not having it. I let out a small yelp when Finn snatches the blanket off me in a single move and wraps his hand around my left ankle.

I wonder if I'm imagining the whole thing when he uses the hold he has on my ankle to yank me to the edge of the bed. There, in my panties, with my ass hanging off the bed, I realize something I'm in no way prepared for.

I'm scared of this boy.

Maybe it's the way he carries himself.

The nothingness seeping out of him.

There's no warmth, no kindness, no weakness to pick up on. I'm usually good at reading people, but I couldn't get so much as a hint on this motherfucker if I tried.

I plant my feet on the cold hardwood floor and shiver when he leans over me, leveling his hard stare with mine and placing his arms on each side of my body.

He's… breathtaking.

And not in a good way.

"You're not leaving this bed, huh?" he asks, eyes roaming down my chest. Slowly. Shamelessly.

I can't move.

Why can't I move?

His focus locks onto my tank top, and I'm mortified when I feel my nipples pebbling under his gaze.

And the worst part?

He seems to notice because he *smiles.*

The logical part of me wants to disappear, run back home, and never set foot in this house again, but the other… The other feels a pull in her stomach. The kind I shouldn't.

"Then what? What's the plan, sitter girl? Stay in my bed while I beat my cock?"

My mouth dips open.

"Watch me finish what you so *rudely* interrupted?" He presents me with a bunch of empty threats.

Only, they don't sound empty.

He leans even closer and whispers, "Because that's exactly what's going to happen if you don't get your tight little ass out of my bed in the next five seconds."

You'd think the bastard is hoarding every bit of oxygen in the room.

"Or… did you want to put that pouty mouth to use?" He stops, his focus aimed at my lips. "Can't promise you a raise, but you sure could get one out of me."

His eyes drift to his crotch for clarification, and my cheeks heat up. He's just putting on a show now. Trying to send me packing. To disgust me out of this job. *Whatever works.* Too bad I need the money more than this boy needs therapy.

My next move as clear as his superiority complex, I rise off the bed, guide my palms to his broad shoulders and smile at the question marks plaguing his eyes. His skin is flaming hot. Soft, too. And he smells good, but I'd rather drink toilet water than acknowledge it.

Then… I knee him in the balls.

Hard.

His groan of pain is nowhere near as satisfying as the look on his face when I push him off me and stuff my legs into my pajama shorts. He bends forward, holding his crotch and staring bullets through my skull as I pick up my bag of clothes.

"Let's make something clear." I look him dead in the eyes. "The only thing this mouth is ever going to do for you is telling you to *fuck off*."

With that said, I grab my phone on the nightstand and haul ass out of there. I'm sauntering to one of the many guest rooms in the Richardses' house when I realize…

I just did that.

I just kneed my boss's son in the balls on my first day on the job. My hands trembling, I lock myself into an empty bedroom three doors down and think back to the hatred in his eyes when

I walked out.

There isn't a doubt in my mind that I can kiss my quiet summer by the pool goodbye.

I know better than to think Finn Richards won't get me back twice as hard the moment I let my guard down. Because I didn't just put an asshole in his place.

No, what I did in there…

…was declare *war.*

Two

Finn

A house sitter.

A. Fucking. House sitter.

My old man's had his fair share of bad ideas in his days, but this one? This one takes the cake *by far.* I'm gone one week, and he lets a complete stranger into the house to watch Lexie while he's off sipping cocktails with some gold digger in Santa Monica.

"Dude, will you just get that broom out of your ass?" Axel, my moronic friend, drags a hit of the joint in his hand. "Worst-case scenario, the girl stays and you get a plaything for the summer. *Boo-fucking-hoo.*"

"That's not the point, shithead." I lean back into my driver's seat, kicking my feet up on the dash. "The point is my dad ran off to the beach house and left Lexie alone with some rando the first chance he got."

"Bro, you really need to see someone for your obsession with that dog. That shit can't be healthy." Axel snorts, guiding his lighter to the bong on his lap.

He seals the opening with his mouth and inhales a gust of

smoke. I smack him on the back of the head, sending him into a coughing fit. The guys love to say I'm too attached to my dog to mess with me, and, fine, maybe I am overprotective of Lexie. *So what?* It's not like Mom's around to take care of her.

Ignoring Axel's choking, I open the window on his side to release the smoke irritating my lungs. I scan the parking lot by the town's springs.

It's empty.

No surprise there.

Silver Springs isn't exactly famous for its entertainment, and *yes*, that's just a nice way of saying my hometown is fucking boring. It's even worse now that Xavier, the asshole I call my best friend, is off at basketball camp for the summer. Admittedly, I should be there, too.

Too bad they kicked me out.

It turns out giving wedgies to other players isn't the camp's definition of "*team spirit*."

Eh, it's probably for the best.

If I'd known Lexie was going to be stuck with the psycho in my house all summer, I would have ripped off Ridge Garcia's underwear from the get-go.

Letting my head droop against the headrest, I pluck my phone out of my pocket and select my dad's number. The faster he kicks this Gemstone girl—or whatever her name is—to the curb, the better.

The phone rings five times before he picks up.

"Hank's phone."

Either Dad got a voice transplant, or I'm talking to the blonde parasite leeching off him.

I cut to the chase. "I need to talk to my dad."

"Oh, hi, Xavier, is it? I'm Sonia. Your dad's told me so much about you."

I wish I was even the tiniest bit shocked, but I'm not. My dad talking some bimbo's ears off about my best friend instead of his own kid? *Sounds about right.*

"Wrong person."

"Shit, Brody, then?" she says nervously.

This is getting ridiculous.

"I'm Finn. Brody's my big brother."

The line goes quiet for a moment.

"Finn. Of course. Your father talks about you all the ti—"

I cut in. "Selma, just give him the fucking phone, will you?"

"It's Sonia," she corrects.

"Any day now."

Offended, she blows out a bitter "Just a minute."

Shuffling erupts down the line, followed by a marriage of distant voices. I hear what sounds like water, waves…

The sea?

He's out on a yacht, isn't he?

On some new boat with some new girl?

What's next?

Renaming Mom's boat after one of his whores?

"Hey, kiddo. Sorry, I was out swimming," Dad says on the other end. "Everything okay at home?"

"You mean apart from the raging bitch living there?"

A deep sigh flares down the line.

"I told you about the house sitter."

"You did, and it was fine when I wasn't home, but I'm back now. Feel free to fire her."

There's a beat of silence.

"That's not happening."

Did he just say…

"I'm sorry?"

"I'm not firing her, Finley."

"But you don't fucking need her. I'll take care of the house. Like I always have."

"And allow what happened last summer to happen again?"

Here we go.

"It was one party!"

Dismissing me, he continues, "Kid… you didn't even make it one week at basketball camp before starting shit. What am I supposed to do with that?"

Rage boiling in my stomach, I mutter, "Fine. What about Brody?"

"Your brother's taking summer classes."

"So, he can't come back on the weekends? Bullshit."

"And leave Lexie alone five days out of the week?"

"She won't be alone. She'll have me," I argue.

"Look, son, no offense, but you don't exactly have the best track record these days. Maybe if you knew better like Xavier, I—"

That's my snapping point. "When the fuck did this become about Xavier?"

"It's not." Dad sighs again. "It's about you not being ready to take on responsibilities."

"So, you don't trust me," I gather.

"That's not what I said."

"That's what you meant."

My accusations don't faze him.

"Listen, the Mitchells are good people. They raised their daughter right. And you'll have someone to take care of everything, so you can go out with the guys without having to worry about Lexie. It's a win-win."

"So, you've made up your mind?"

"I have. I'm sorry, bud, but she's not going anywhere. Not unless she quits."

I play his words on a loop, my brain swamped with the thousand ways I could make her suffer.

"Fine."

Just as I'm about to hang up, Dad stops me.

"Finn?"

"What?" I spit.

"Have you gone to see her yet?"

I immediately know what he means.

"My guys said she's as good as new," he adds.

A fire ravages my insides, burning the little respect I had left for my father to a crisp.

Some things never change.

Even when they should.

I squeeze my fists so hard I lose feeling in my joints.

"I told you the only way I'm ever getting on that fucking boat again is to sink it."

Then I hang up.

Silence fills the car, and I welcome the distraction of the springs gurgling in the distance. Anything to drown out the hurt little boy in my head. He remembers things I'd rather forget. Like a time where his own father didn't trust a complete stranger over him…

I want to break something.

Preferably something Daddy dearest doesn't want broken.

And I think I know exactly where to start…

"Well, that was intense," Axel quips from my passenger seat.

"Out of the car." I don't even spare him a look.

"Are you talking to me?"

"I sure as shit ain't talking to your mom."

"Dude, you're my ride," Axel laughs nervously like he's waiting for *me* to start laughing.

"Sucks to be you, then. Get out. There's something I have to do."

Irritated, Axel flings the car door open and climbs out.

"Take your shit with you." I throw him the bong and the bag of weed he left behind.

"You're going to leave me here? With a dick bong in the middle of a parking lot? Seriously, dude?"

In response, I push the gear into reverse, back out of the space, and drive away at full speed. I pick up on his last words through the opened window as I'm taking off.

"What could be so important that you have to go *right now*?"

Axel is nothing but a small silhouette holding a dick-shaped bong in my rearview mirror by the time the answer comes to me. Dad won't fire the Gemstone bitch?

Fine.

But that doesn't mean I can't get her to quit.

* * *

Diamond

Aveena: How's the first day going?

I quickly read my best friend's text as I hurry down the sidewalk with Lexie. One more walk down this block and the granny across the street might burst a blood vessel.

She's been giving me the evil eye from her porch for two hours now. *Two hours.* She's definitely one of those people who think dogs only exist to piss on their lawn.

Okay, I'm stalling.

I tiptoed down the stairs this morning, terrified that I'd find my housemate waiting for me in the kitchen.

With an axe.

Or a bar of gold.

Or whatever weapon rich people use.

I felt good about sticking up for myself last night, but daylight Dia? She isn't quite as confident. Especially after my phone call with Mr. Richards this morning.

He apologized for failing to warn me about his son's return, then offered me more money to keep working for him, no questions asked. You know you're in for one hell of a summer when even your *boss* knows his kid is a nightmare.

I couldn't turn him down. I need a car before the beginning of senior year—special mention to my big brother, Jesse, for plowing into my old one while drunk off his ass.

I already have the perfect car lined up.

Brenda, a waitress working at my dad's restaurant, is selling her bug car and promised to save it for me if I can make payment before the end of the summer. Hopefully, Mr. Richards keeps on raising my salary every time he feels guilty about his evil spawn.

Realizing I didn't text my best friend back, I shoot Aveena a message while Lexie does her business on the sidewalk.

Dia: Let's see. I haven't kicked anyone in the balls yet, so... it's going better than yesterday?

My phone dings with her response a nanosecond later.

Aveena: That was oddly specific?

Aveena: I'm going to need a full story with details and receipts, thank you.

I snort out a laugh.

My best friend's never been interested in school drama. Aveena's shy, keeps to herself, and wouldn't be caught dead gossiping about some cheerleader sleeping with her man's best friend—I'm looking at you, Brielle Randall—but when it comes to *my* drama?

Aveena Harper turns into a detective.

Dia: Remember when I said I was supposed to be alone with the Richardses' dog for the summer?

She knows right away.

Aveena: You're kidding.

Dia: Am not.

Aveena: Please don't tell me you're going to be spending the summer with Finn Richards.

Dia: Do you want me to lie to you?

Aveena: Girl, run! They don't pay you enough for this shit!

Dia: Actually, my boss just gave me a raise…

Aveena: See? Even he knows his son is crazy. What did your dads say?

Dia: I told Mr. Richards I'd ask them if it was okay, but I sort of… didn't.

Aveena: Do you think they'd let you work there?

Dia: And leave their little girl alone with a boy for two months? Are you high?

Aveena: Shit, D, what are you going to do?

Dia: No idea. Just avoid him for two months, I guess?

Lexie cuddles up to my leg before Aveena messages me back. I can't contain a smile, trying to pet the top of her head and laughing when she licks my hand instead.

I already adore Lexie.

She's sweet, loving, protective.

I hadn't even been here one day before the nine-year-old golden retriever started following me everywhere. She's the only silver lining to this job so far.

I clean up after Lexie and come to the conclusion that I can't avoid Finn forever. I'm going to have to go back to the house eventually. I might even try to make peace with him if he lets me.

The walk back to the Richards estate is a quick one. I catch myself dragging my feet every two steps, but Lexie won't let me off the hook, pulling on her leash when she feels me slowing down.

I prepare a speech as I amble up the long driveway, rehearsing a fake apology in the hope of restoring some civility between Finn and me.

Until I reach the top…

And I realize "restoring civility" was never an option.

The first thing I see is the duffel bag I use as a suitcase tossed into the water fountain in the center of the driveway.

Then I spot my T-shirts, shoes, swimsuits, shorts—even my goddamn underwear—littering the lawn to the million-dollar mansion. They're everywhere, every single piece of clothing I brought with me, dumped outside like garbage.

My makeup is smashed all over the concrete, including the liquid lipsticks I got for my birthday and the ninety-dollar eyeshadow palette I borrowed from my sister.

My phone charger and Kindle e-reader were also dropped at the bottom of the water fountain, but what truly enrages me... is the sight of the only shirt I'd run through fire to save.

My Radiohead T-shirt.

Finn left it in a puddle of foundation, the liquid spilling from the bottle onto the fabric. I've never been a violent person, but when I see Finn strolling out of the house, an infuriating grin on his face, I want to start a petition to set his junk on fire.

Blind to my destroyed clothes on the ground, Lexie charges toward Finn, tail swinging as she barks her head off.

"Down, girl," Finn commands, and Lexie stops on cue. "Sit." Lexie obliges, and Finn bends down on one knee to pet her. Lexie jumps at the chance to swipe her tongue across his cheek.

How could a dog so sweet... love a boy so *cruel?*

"Come here." Finn scratches Lexie under the chin and rubs her belly when she rolls over on her back to greet him.

Only then do I understand.

He's not cruel.

At least, not to her.

I stand there for a moment, watching them reunite, until Finn jerks the front door open to let his dog inside. As soon as Lexie bounds into the house, the ability to keep my cool leaves my body.

"What the *hell?*" I nearly shout. "Are you fucking crazy?"

I speed over to him.

Unbothered, Finn looks down at me and folds his arms over his chest.

"Oh, this?" He gives me a shit-eating grin. "Hope you don't mind. My dad said I was irresponsible, so I figured I'd prove him wrong and take out the trash."

My jaw crashes to the floor.

This motherfucker.

"You're way over the line!"

His grin doesn't waver one bit.

"Oh, sweetheart—" He surprises me by stepping closer and tilting my chin up with his index. "—I've been dancing with the line since before you had tits. *Bite me.*"

I swallow hard, deep diving into his eyes in search of a hint of humanity. For what it's worth, he *is* right about that last part. Everybody knows Finn Richards was forced to deal with adult realities way before his time.

He was eight when he lost his mother.

My family didn't even live in Silver Springs on that fateful day, but one week here and we knew all about what happened on Lake Belmont.

The details of Mrs. Richards's death are scarce in every article I looked up before taking the job—you don't agree to work for a widowed millionaire without doing some research first.

Most pieces on the web state there was a boating accident that ultimately led to Finn's mother drowning in the lake, but nothing specific. From what I could gather, the boat was named after her, too, which makes it that much worse.

The dive to recover her body lasted an eternity, but even after months of tireless efforts, she never turned up.

Her body remains unfound to this day.

"What do you say, Gemstone?" Finn jerks me back to earth, his gaze burning with loathing. "Ready to quit yet?"

Smacking his hand away, I push to the tips of my toes for credibility purposes, looking like a dwarf next to him.

Seriously?

Who gave him permission to be *this* fucking tall?

"First, the name is Diamond. And second… did you really think trashing my clothes would be enough to make me quit?" I scoff. "Oh, honey, that's embarrassing."

The smirk melts right off his face.

"You think I'm afraid of you, rich kid? I grew up with a big brother whose passion was making my life a living hell, so, this?" I gesture to the mess he made. "That's a fucking Tuesday to me."

In response, Finn steps forward, his imposing frame towering over me like it's nobody's business. He's such a poker face master that I barely notice the corners of his lips curling in anger.

I'm confident there's something wrong with my lungs when he tilts his head to the side, narrows his eyes at me, and grits out a threatening "Is that a challenge?"

Inhale, exhale.

"That's a warning." I inch closer. If this asshole thinks his chiseled jaw, ridiculous body, and deep hazel eyes are enough to throw me off my game, he's…

Absolutely right.

Abort the mission.

I distance myself from him as quickly as I moved in, clearing my throat and zooming in on the stained Radiohead T-shirt at my feet.

"You're paying for the dry cleaning," I say matter-of-factly.

He heaves a scoff. "Like hell I am."

There's no way I can afford to buy everything again or get my Radiohead T-shirt cleaned.

"How's Xavier doing, by the way?" I stoop down to his level. "I heard he was out of town for the summer. Must be really hard for Brie. It sure makes you wonder how she passes the time."

His face crumbles.

Surprise, asshat. I can play dirty, too.

I'm sure that clothes stunt would've worked on a lot of girls, but me? Not a chance. I'm part Spanish and Indonesian. I spent my *entire* childhood being reminded of my coal-black curls and darker skin. It turns out kids can be real assholes when they want to.

Don't even get me started on having *two* dads and all of my siblings being adopted—myself included. We'll be here until Finn grows a soul, and I don't have that long.

We stare each other dead in the eyes for a few seconds, his

jaw twitching as he resists the pressure of the walls closing in on him. I have him. He's stuck, and he knows it.

"Tenacious, aren't you?" he concedes.

"About time you noticed."

I know by the wince on his face that he can't stand the taste of his own medicine.

"I'll have the money tomorrow," he spits, jaw tight, and storms back inside the house.

I should be happy.

I stood tall when all I wanted to do was collapse, but I'm not nearly stupid enough to think the devil is done with me.

I might've won this round…

But the fight is just beginning.

Three

Diamond

"Seven weeks to go," I grumble under my breath as I jog down the stairs with the bag I packed with my clothes—and by "clothes," I mean the few outfits I was able to salvage after Finn's stunt last week.

My demonic housemate stayed true to his word and paid for the damage he caused, but I still have to go shopping and replace everything his fancy dry cleaner couldn't save.

Fortunately for Finn's genitals, my Radiohead T-shirt fully recovered. Bastard has no idea how *close* I came to dumping itching powder into his underwear drawer.

Barking travels through the first floor of the house when I reach the bottom of the stairs. Lexie comes running in my direction with a swinging tail. She's been greeting me this way for five days straight.

I might've had the weirdest first week at a new job in history, but I'm still going to miss her running to me every morning.

"Good morning to you, too." I chuckle, petting her behind the ears. "Who's a good girl?"

As if on a quest to prove herself, Lexie sits and holds out her paw. I've been practicing tricks with her all week. It sure didn't take her long to understand that shaking hands equals treats.

"Nice try." I squint at her, but she doesn't budge, ogling me with those big, adorable brown eyes.

I hate playing bad cop, but I'd rather Mr. Richards didn't come home to find his dog has gained thirty pounds.

Stay strong, Dia.

Resist.

Resist.

Resi…

Res…

Re…

Run to the kitchen and give her a treat.

I'm back to my feet in an instant and maneuvering my way to the kitchen to give her a goodbye treat. Mr. Richards suggested that I take my weekends off for the rest of the summer. He said his son could hold down the fort for two days out of the week, and I deserved a break from Finn.

Fine, he didn't say I deserved a break "*from Finn,*" but I can read between the lines.

He's been checking in nonstop, asking me how things are going like he half-expects me to cry him a river about his awful son. Worst part is, even if I wanted to snitch, I *can't.*

My silence is the only thing protecting me from Finn's cruelty. He read me loud and clear when I insinuated that I'd tell Xavier about his betrayal.

Finn lay low for the rest of the week, staying out all night, then grunting in disgust whenever I walked into the room. He's been avoiding me like the plague, but there haven't been any more "ruin your life" schemes…

Yet.

I put on coffee and grab Lexie's treats in the cabinet above the fridge.

"Last one. I'm serious," I fake-scold, and Lexie devours the treat off the palm of my hand.

"A pet rock has more authority than you."

I flip my head to see Silver Springs' killjoy standing in the doorway. Finn is shirtless, wearing gray shorts, and balancing a basketball against his hip.

We make eye contact for a second too long, and I lower my gaze, focusing on his shredded six-pack and his large fingers wrapped around the basketball.

He has big hands.

Dia, stop.

He's not even worth the calories *you're burning checking him out.*

"Hey, roomie." I flash a smile, which, to my disbelief, isn't forced. Knowing I won't have to see him for two whole days put me in a good mood. Weirded out, Finn arches an eyebrow as he tries to compute my kindness.

Processing, I read in his eyes.

Then, "*System failure, try again.*"

"Don't do that," he says, cold as ice.

"Do what?" I play dumb.

"Whatever the fuck *this* is, it's nauseating." Finn moves around me, picks up the shot of espresso I made for myself, and drags a long sip. "Shit, were you going to drink that?"

I know from the way he stares that he craves a reaction. He wants to see me get mad, if only to feed his ego.

"I was, actually."

"My bad. You don't mind if I finish it, though?" He finishes the whole thing before I can answer.

Annoyance mixes with the blood in my veins.

Don't give him what he wants.

"No, of course not. Enjoy."

He looks at me like I just grew a third tit, and I chew on the inside of my cheek to bury my smile as I check my phone. My best friend should be here any minute to pick me up. We're supposed to be having lunch with my family.

Aveena's text message comes through the next second.

Aveena: I'm outside.

Shoving my phone in my jeans back pocket, I saunter toward the front door with my bag dangling down my shoulder. Finn's gaze shadows me across the room.

"Have a nice weekend," I tell him and pry the door open. I've barely taken a step before his voice cuts through the air.

"Wait."

I glance back at him.

He's put down the espresso shot and is now spinning his basketball on his index finger without breaking a sweat.

Show-off.

"You coming back next week?" he asks.

I'm stunned, fairly certain that I hallucinated the question. Why would he ask me that? Does he *want* me to come back? Is he finally putting down the weapons and allowing us to be civil?

"Yes?"

Then he shoots my foolish hopes dead with one sentence. "Then I won't have a nice weekend."

Fucker.

***

"A whole week? I didn't think you'd last this long. Damn, sis," my brother, Jesse, comments as he rests the potato salad dish on the kitchen table. *Silly me*, thinking I could get through one meal without being hounded with questions.

"Damn?" Charlie, my three-year-old brother, repeats, tasting the word on his tongue for a bit before deciding that he likes it. "Damn, damn, damn."

"Don't say that, sweetie. It's a bad word," Gaten, my dad,

scolds, throwing Jesse a murderous glare. Aveena snickers in her chair, tilting her head forward and hiding behind her caramel-brown hair.

"Honey, give Charles some milk, will you?" Gaten asks my other dad, Dave—it gets confusing, so I call them by their names to differentiate them. Dave nods, rises off his chair, and threads his way to the fridge.

"Not milk, *juice*," Charlie protests.

Dave casts a glance over his shoulder at his husband for confirmation. This is how these two make parenting decisions nowadays.

I couldn't have been older than five when I realized that Dave was my "*Yes*" dad, while Gaten was my "*Hell to the no*" dad. My older siblings, Jesse and Catalina, figured that out right off the bat. These assholes spent most of high school tricking my dads into disagreeing with each other.

By the time *Yes Dad* had agreed to something, they were out the door, and it was too late for *No Dad* to hit the brakes—oldest trick in the book, you know the drill.

"Any more sugar and he'll be impossible to put down for a nap." Gaten shakes his head, and Dave nods in approval, pulling the milk out and filling up Charlie's spillproof cup.

"Juice," Charlie insists.

"I said no, Charles," Gaten declares.

"*Damn*," Charlie blurts, recycling his new favorite word, and Jesse chews down on his bottom lip to keep from laughing.

"Jesse, don't encourage him," Gaten reprimands.

"He's right. This isn't funny," Dave chimes in.

Jesse laughs into his fist. "It's a little funny."

I'm next in line, my loud snort rippling through the room.

"Diamond!" Gaten scolds.

My weakness is the final domino to a long line of muffled chuckles, sending a chain of laughter around the kitchen. There isn't a single serious face to be seen as my parents try to scold my little brother for his potty mouth.

"Wasn't Catalina coming home?" I change the subject once order has been restored. I'd be lying if I said I'm not relieved to see my older sister is MIA today.

Most of the makeup Finn ruined was hers, and there's no doubt she's going to skin me alive when she finds out. Finn wired me the money to replace it, but I haven't had a chance to hit the mall yet.

"She couldn't make it. Something to do with her boyfriend," Dave explains.

"Which one?" Jesse mocks in a whisper that only Aveena and I catch.

My best friend and I trade glances.

He's not lying.

Catalina's been all over the place since breaking up with her long-term boyfriend, Mal. They'd been together for years. Malek was her first *everything*. Until he vanished overnight, leaving the country without a trace just weeks after he proposed to her.

The dude took ghosting to a whole new level. He deactivated all his social media, quit his job, cleared out his apartment, and fell off the face of the earth.

The worst part is, Cat and Mal were the couple you're jealous of. The couple that irritates the shit out of you because they're *that* perfect.

It was just something about the way he looked at her. Like Cat was the only woman whose language Mal understood and her eyes the only place where he felt at home.

Every lead Catalina came up with turned out to be a dead end. The police told her he'd most likely done a one-eighty and started a new life. She was in therapy for months afterward. In time, she found comfort in the only person who was also left behind after Mal disappeared.

His best friend, River.

She's been on and off with him for months now. The truth is, she's still not over Mal, and I have a feeling no rebound could make her forget the guy she was supposed to grow old with.

"How was your first week of work, sweetheart?" Dave follows up.

It's fine, you've got this.

Just don't tell them you live with a boy.

"It was…"

Awful.

Hell.

Definitely wouldn't recommend.

"*Different.*" I skim around the truth. "A lot more work than just dog-sitting on the weekends. At least, the dog I'm watching is great." I take a large bite of my food, praying for the interview to end there.

"Isn't it strange living all by yourself?" Gaten questions, and I drag out my bite.

"You were terrified of the dark when you were a kid. No way you live alone in a mansion," Jesse scoffs.

That's the thing. I *don't* live alone, inner Dia says. I live with a cocky basketball player with stupid good looks and a bad attitude.

"I manage." I shrug.

"The crib is so big some sicko could break into the house in the middle of the night without you knowing. Doesn't that freak you out?" Jesse says for the sole purpose of scaring me.

Been there, done that.

Except the sicko is my boss's son, and I'm nowhere near as freaked-out by the thought of a random person breaking into the house as I am by those cruel eyes.

"Nope." I jump at the chance to take another bite and notice Gaten eyeing me suspiciously. Luckily, Aveena takes notice of the panic blooming in my eyes.

"So, Gaten," Aveena swoops in. "I noticed the two-for-one promotion is back at the restaurant. How are things going? Looks like business is good." Vee knocks her knee against mine under the table as a sign of support.

Aveena knows Dad's restaurant is his sweet spot. He can't resist talking about his fifth child and proudest accomplishment. As expected, Dad doesn't waste a second sharing the latest with her, and my body relaxes as the conversation shifts to safer topics.

If you were ever wondering if Aveena Harper is a good friend, there's your answer. Vee and I are worlds apart sometimes, and yes, lately, I feel like we differ in opinions—she has absolutely no interest in the male population, for starters—but her loyalty?

That will never change.

The girl's practically a professional fixer, both at home and in her social life. She's been acting as an assistant to Ashley, her music prodigy sister, for years now. I'm surprised her mom even allowed her to have lunch with us.

Ashley's schedule is just as packed on the weekends as it is on weekdays, and Aveena rarely gets a break. Just one of the downsides of having a talent show winner for a sister.

Gaten goes on about how the promotion is bringing in more customers than ever for ten minutes, and Aveena listens with a smile on her face, nodding along to his story.

"Oh, I almost forgot," Gaten remembers just as he starts clearing the table. "Diamond, Jesse will be driving you back to work tomorrow."

My mouth parts.

"*He what?*" I blurt.

"*I'm what?*" my brother says at the same time.

Jesse and I exchange looks from across the table.

"In fact, he'll be driving you every Sunday until you get a car," Dave chimes in.

"But Sunday's my only day off work. Can't she just walk?" Jesse counters.

"She could, but she wouldn't have to if you hadn't totaled her car," Dave cuts in. "It's about time you learn your actions have consequences, don't you think?"

Heavy silence wraps us up.

It's no secret that my dads have had enough of Jesse's shit.

My big brother's always been on the reckless side—losing his license, ditching school, sleeping with girls he has no intention of calling—but his plowing into the back of my car at the end of my junior year was the last straw.

Jesse likes to say that, if they could, our dads would travel back in time and leave him in foster care, in the dirt-cheap home where Jess and I had wound up when they found us.

Get a refund on his rebellious ass—*his words.*

I don't remember my life pre-adoption, but I think my being an infant at the time gives me a pass. Everything I know, my dads told me. Story has it, Jesse and I lived in a shitty foster home, with an even shittier foster family.

How did I end up there in the first place, you ask?

Cue the tragic backstory.

My biological mother died giving birth to me, she didn't have any relatives to take care of a baby, and my father was a no-show. The end.

I don't know how old she was when she had me, or where she was from, but my parents told me she was a kind soul trapped in a life she didn't deserve. Someone chasing a second chance she could never catch.

I only have one thing of hers.

A Radiohead T-shirt.

And a letter, scribbled on the tag inside the collar.

B.

"It's fine, I swear. I don't mind walking," I assure them.

What I *do* mind is the possibility of Jesse seeing Finn when he drops me off and telling my dads I live with a boy.

"See? She doesn't mind," Jesse pleads.

"Doesn't matter." Dave won't budge.

"Seriously? You can't make me drive her on my *one* day of freedom."

"You will if you want to live under my roof rent-free until you find a new place." Dave dangles my brother's messed-up living situation in his face.

Jesse got kicked out of his old apartment by his landlord for failure to pay the rent a month back. Suffice to say, my dads weren't too happy about their twenty-nine-year-old son moving back home.

Granted, they were always harder on him than they were on Cat and me. Probably because Jesse's the oldest. Every decision my brother makes, my dads dissect carefully. They have an opinion on *everything* he does, including the people Jess chooses to surround himself with.

He and Finn's older brother, Brody Richards, were buddies for a while when Brody was still in high school and Jesse was in college. My dads thought Jesse having younger friends meant he wasn't ready for adulthood.

In his defense, Jesse never really got to be a kid.

He had to look out for himself for almost *thirteen years*, constantly bouncing from foster home to foster home before we ended up in the same place and found our forever family.

"Sorry, kid, it's not up for discussion. You trashed your sister's car, you drive her," Dave asserts.

Jesse sags into his chair, defeat written all over his face.

It's official…

I'm *screwed.*

* * *

"Must be nice being Daddy's favorite," Jesse grumbles under his breath as we turn onto Paxton Ave., the main road separating Silver Springs' wealthy and the rest of us peasants.

Normally, I'd be over the moon about my brother sparing me a long walk, so I've been pretending like I'm not terrified of him telling my dads their daughter is a big, fat liar.

"*I'm* the favorite?" I scoff. "Please. Dad sold part of the restaurant so you could go to college. If anyone's Dad's favorite, it's you."

"Favorite bad decision, maybe," Jesse mutters, his voice so weak I almost don't hear him.

His words take a moment to sink in.

"You're not kidding, are you?"

Jesse flicks his head to look at me at a red light.

"When you say they should've never adopted you," I elaborate, "you really believe that."

Silence sits between us like a wall we can't knock down. Jesse holds my gaze for a second as though he wants to say something but doesn't know how.

"I'm just saying they might've thought twice if they'd known the shit they were getting into."

There it is.

For as long as I can remember, Jesse's felt unworthy.

When he was a kid, he'd look at my dads like they'd moved heaven and earth the day they took him home. Like he didn't understand how they could possibly choose *him.*

People said he was too old, that families wanted babies. Not teenagers with trauma coursing through their veins. But my parents disagreed. And Jesse's spent every day since then trying to prove them wrong.

Jesse pumps the gas as soon as the light turns green. He's pulling up to Finn's driveway less than a minute later. I squeeze my phone into a firm grip to calm my nerves.

If he sees Finn, it's over.

Please don't be home.

Please don't be home.

Please don't be…

Fuck. My. Life.

"What the hell?" I hear my brother whisper to himself as he comes to a full stop in the driveway. Two cars—one black, one red—are parked by the stone water fountain.

I'm guessing Finn has a friend over?

"Thanks for the ride." I grab the door handle, prepared to make a run for it, but Jesse locks me in from the inside with one click of a button.

"Whose cars are those?" Jesse squints. "I thought you said you were the only one there?"

Make up a story, Dia. Anything.

"Oh, that. It's just the gardener. And the maid. They come every Sunday."

Jesse's attention drifts between me and the cars.

"But you're alone the rest of the time?" he asks.

"That I am." The lie aches in my throat.

He nods, not completely sold but not nearly as unsure as he was a moment ago. I can almost taste success. Visualize Jesse driving far, far away from here, allowing me to keep this job and continue to save up for a car.

Then it all falls apart.

The glass door to the mansion opens, and my worst

nightmare trails out of the house, shadowed by Theodore Cox, a black-haired basketball player I know from school.

Finn spots my brother's car instantly and stops. He stares for a bit, and then pads to the red car parked out front. They both lean against the hood as Theo lifts a blunt to his lips to drag a hit.

My brother's face decomposes in slow motion.

It's not Jesse's first rodeo with the Richardses.

He spent most of college tight with Finn's older brother, Brody, and while they stopped speaking years ago—he refused to tell us why—he could never wash down the sour taste that family left in his mouth.

"Mind telling me what the fuck he's doing here? I thought he was supposed to be gone all summer?" Jesse asks.

Join the club.

Coming to terms with my fate, I manage a weak "Plans changed."

"Plans changed?" Jess blurts. "*That's it?* That's all you have to say to me? I'm going to need a bit more than that, sis."

I exhale a deep sigh.

"He got kicked out of basketball camp and showed up out of the blue a week ago. What was I supposed to do?"

"Well, you sure as fuck weren't supposed to lie to everyone about it. What the hell, Dia?"

I cringe. "Put yourself in my shoes. I knew if I told our dads, they'd tell me to quit."

"As they should! Do you have any fucking idea what kind of people these guys are?"

"I don't need to know," I snap. "It's two months, Jess. *Two months* and I'm gone. I might even leave earlier if I'm able to afford a car before then."

"Hell no. I have this family down to a fucking science at this point, and Brody's brother—" Jesse glares at Finn, who's still eyeing us from afar. "—he's fucked-up."

Tell me something I don't know.

"What kind of brother would I be if I left my sister alone with some masochist all summer?"

I open my mouth to speak but find myself clinging to the noun he chose.

"Masochist?" I repeat.

"This is for the best. I promise you'll thank me one day."

"What do you mean *masochist*?" I badger. "Like… he wants to hurt people?"

I know he wishes he hadn't said that by the way he clenches his teeth and blows out a low "Doesn't matter. Drop it."

I cock an eyebrow at him.

Do we know each other?

"Jess, is he a danger to others, yes or no?"

"No," my brother reluctantly admits.

A wave of questions submerges me.

"So, he's a danger to himself, then?"

He's about to answer when a loud set of knocks rattles the

driver's-side window. Jesse and I whisk our heads to the left to see Finn standing inches away from the glass.

Fuming, Jesse gives me the side-eye and rolls down the window to face my housemate. I've barely had time to prepare for whatever stupid shit is about to come out of Finn's mouth when he says, "Sorry to interrupt, sir. I just thought I'd come over and introduce myself. I'm Finn. Your daughter works for my dad."

I understand when he holds out his hand to Jesse with a wicked grin that he only came over because he saw we were in a fight and thought to himself, "*Hey, I should go make shit worse.*"

Jesse doesn't even bat an eye at Finn's hand held out to him, staring bullets through his head. A thousand-pound silence weighs me down, and I feel the need to speak before Jesse jumps down Finn's throat.

"He's not my dad," I correct.

"Don't pretend like you don't remember me, punk," Jesse accuses, and Finn pulls back an inch, assessing my brother thoroughly.

His eyes light up a few seconds later.

"Holy shit, Jesse?"

My brother doesn't confirm his identity, but his glare speaks for him.

"Long time, man," Finn adds.

"Not long enough," Jesse says bluntly.

Ignoring my brother's comment, Finn leans forward to brace

his forearms on the window frame. A familiar glimmer of hate streaks through his gaze when he spots me in the passenger seat.

"A little young for you, don't you think?" Finn makes a vomit-inducing assumption.

Jess shares my disgust. "Oh, fuck off. She's my sister."

Shock merges with the cockiness in Finn's eyes.

"Your sister, huh?"

"Is that so hard to believe?" Jesse spits.

"Nope, small world, that's all." Finn plays the nice-guy act to a T. "Well, no introductions needed, then. I'll leave you two to finish your… *talk*." He fails to conceal his smile, knowing damn well the appropriate word here is "fight."

Finn gives himself a push and starts to walk away but halts two steps in.

"Oh, and sitter girl?"

Our eyes lock across the driveway.

"Welcome back." He tops it off with a smirk that's full of ulterior motives.

"Yep, you're coming home," Jesse declares the instant Finn is at an acceptable distance.

As though he can feel his master plan working, Finn glances at us over his shoulder, flashes a conniving smile, and gestures for Theo to follow him inside.

"You do realize he did that precisely to piss you off?" I point out once the boys are out of sight.

"Well, it worked. Let's go." Jesse starts the car, and my hand jerks to the ignition.

"Jess, please, I really need this job."

He shrugs. "You can get another one."

"Not one that pays this well," I argue.

"I don't trust him, Dia. He wants to get in your pants."

I'd sooner die.

"So? Even if he did, do you seriously think I'd let anything happen? Come on, Jesse, you know me better than that."

The muscles in his jaw twitching, Jesse sags into the driver's seat and thinks long and hard on his response.

"I just want to get through the summer, buy a car, and forget any of this ever happened. *Please.*"

Dead quiet, my brother runs a hand through his dark, untidy hair before releasing one of his "I'm going to regret this" sighs.

"Fucking hell, *fine*," he gives in.

Did he just… agree?

"Wait, so, you're not going to tell on me?" I cover my bases.

An eternity later, he says, "No."

All I can do in response is extend my arm around my brother for a brief side hug.

"Thanks, Jess. I owe you one."

"But you keep me updated, got it? You call me if he tries anything, and you come back home every weekend, *no exception*."

"Yes, Dad," I joke as I pull away, but Jesse doesn't laugh, the ice walls around him back up in an instant. "I mean, *yes*."

"Now, get out of here before I change my mind."

"Copy that." I nod and hurry out of the vehicle.

Jesse watches me like a hawk as I gather my luggage from his back seat, throw the strap of my bag over my shoulder, and speed walk toward the mansion.

He doesn't drive away until the exact moment the front door closes behind me.

Barking is the first thing I hear when I step inside the house. I spot Lexie in her dog bed and smile. She sits up, her tail wagging, and rushes down the hall to meet me. She's so excited she nearly slips on the hardwood floor in the process.

Dropping my bag, I kneel to give her a proper greeting, and Lexie throws her paws over my shoulder. Her body wiggling from left to right, she alternates between licking my face and barking.

"Did someone miss me?" I chuckle. She's so hyper I can barely pet her, and my heart swells.

It isn't long before Lexie gets tired of our reunion and retreats to the living room to nap. She circles multiple times before dropping down on her dog bed.

Milking every drop of courage in my body, I kick off my shoes on the welcome mat, pick up my bag, and trail toward the kitchen.

I can hear the boys laughing in there, but I haven't had lunch today, and *nothing*—not even Assface Richards—will stand in the way of me and the tuna casserole I left in the fridge last week.

The conversation gets dry the moment I enter the room, and

I glance at Finn just in time to see his dimpled smile slip off his face. He proceeds to glare at me as though he's hoping he'll *stare* me out the door.

We're about two seconds away from ranking a solid ten on the *Awkward* scale when Theodore Cox, nicknamed Theo by everyone at school, cracks a hint of a smile.

"Told you." Theo snorts, unfolding his hand in front of Finn. "Hand it over, fucktard."

Cursing beneath his breath, Finn digs into his pocket and lobs something into his friend's face.

A twenty-dollar bill.

These assholes…

They bet on me quitting, didn't they?

They probably thought Finn's stunt to infuriate Jesse would seal the deal, or maybe they thought I wouldn't show today after everything Finn put me through last week.

To be fair, most girls wouldn't have come back for round two, but most girls don't desperately need a car. I'd take *five* more summers like this over having to ask my dads for rides everywhere until I leave for college.

"Classy," I mumble under my breath and edge my way to the fridge to grab a plate of food.

The beeping of the microwave cuts through the kitchen just as I'm pulling the refrigerator door open. Finn rises off his seat to get whatever unhealthy shit they're eating, but I don't think much of it. Until I rummage through the fridge for my casserole and realize…

It's not their food that's ready.

It's *mine.*

"What the…" I say and swivel around to see the boys inhaling the tuna casserole, going through their plates like they haven't eaten in decades.

I spot the dirty glass container dumped in the sink.

I spent an hour making this before I went home for the weekend so that I wouldn't have to worry about meal-prepping for at least a few days.

And now?

It's all gone.

It was at least six servings. You mean to tell me Finn went through the whole thing in just two days?

How?

Maybe he wasn't alone?

"Who told you you could eat my stuff?" I'm fuming as I watch the basketball players munch their way through my food.

Neither boy answers me—or even looks at me, for that matter—taking their sweet time finishing the food I've been thinking about all weekend.

Riled up, I march to the kitchen island and slam my palms on the counter. Finally, Finn's eyes snap to mine, his face still an unsolvable riddle.

"Who told you to come back here?" He fake gasps. "Oh, that's right, *no one.*"

Swallowing the anger clogging my throat, I inhale a slow breath to keep hungry Dia on a leash—anyone who values their lives does *not* want to see me hungry.

Worst part is, it's not even the fact that he ate my food so much as the *price* of said food.

I had to use the emergency credit card my dad gave me to pay for the ingredients because Mr. Richards hasn't given me grocery money yet. Thank God the job includes "room and board" because I have around ten dollars to my name right now.

Theo's phone rings the next second.

His deep laugh travels through the kitchen. "*Yep*, you're on your own." He lifts off his stool and walks to the sliding glass door in the dining room. "Don't kill each other before I come back."

With that said, Theo steps out onto the patio. Silence envelops the kitchen, and while Finn and I don't say a word for a short moment, our eyes say plenty.

Neither one of us is backing down.

I'm the first to speak up.

"You're going to pay me back or—"

"Or what?" Finn knocks the breath out of me by pushing to his feet. "Fucking *what*, sitter girl? You're going to blackmail me again?"

He's crossing over to my side of the kitchen before I can blink. He's getting closer. And closer. *Okay, that's close enough*, I want to say, but my housemate clearly doesn't give a damn about personal space because he's still charging toward me.

I have the reflex of moving away, but I'm not fast enough. He's got me backed up against the closed pantry the next second, his palms braced on each side of my head.

"Let me tell you what we're *not* going to do." His words hold no trace of a threat. He's not trying to scare me anymore. He's stating *facts*. "We're not going to pretend like you have any fucking leverage over me when it's clear as shit that your brother had no idea I was back from camp."

Fuck.

"I'd also bet a kidney your parents don't know their little girl is living alone with a boy, do they?" His breath tickles my cheek.

My mouth falls open at his assumption, but I clamp it shut, refusing to give him an answer. Only, he doesn't seem to need one because he scoffs.

"*That's what I thought.*"

"It doesn't change anything," I croak.

"You want to know what *I* think?" He twists a strand of my black hair around his index. "I think it changes everything. I think it means I don't have to be nice to you or pretend for one fucking second that I want you here. In fact, I don't even have to worry about your snitch ass ratting me out anymore."

I try to come up with a hundred counterpoints but can't find a single one.

Because he's right. He's got me backed up in a corner—metaphorically and literally. The possibility of me telling Xavier

Emery about Finn hooking up with his girlfriend was my only advantage. Without it, Finn is free to return to his old ways.

"So, why don't we make a deal?" He releases my hair.

I've given up on breathing like a normal person at this point.

"You don't tell my best friend I know what his girl's pussy tastes like, and I don't tell your parents their daughter is a dirty fucking liar, how's that?"

I don't speak for a long moment, attempting and failing to calm my racing heart.

"*Deal?* Or do I need to call your daddy?"

I pretend to think about it, well aware that I have zero ammunition right now.

He grows impatient. "Last chance, Gem."

My heart pulsing in my brain, I break one of Hollywood's biggest rules: *Never negotiate with terrorists.* Granted, Finn isn't a terrorist, but I swear, right now, with the way those merciless eyes observe me, like he has every intention of setting my world on fire and dancing upon the ashes…

He sure as hell feels like one.

"Deal," I choke out and push him away.

He barely stumbles back a step, and I squeeze my way past him to reach the stairs, growling stomach be damned.

"Oh, and Gem?" he calls a second later.

He's never going to remember *which* gemstone I'm named after, is he?

I stop in my tracks but don't look at him.

"My friend Theo will be staying with us for a while."

I don't make a sound.

"Unless... you got a problem with that?" he baits.

He's testing me.

Making sure I know where my place is.

I want to rain hell down on him, but I know I can't refuse. Well, *I could*, but it wouldn't do squat. I have the short end of the stick now. If I snitch on him, he could lose his best friend—it'd piss him off, but the guy clearly doesn't love anyone, so he'd get over it—but if he tells on *me*?

I could lose my parents' trust, and after everything my dads did for me, from plucking me out of a terrible home as a baby to giving me a great life, I couldn't stomach it.

"Fine," I grumble.

That's when he gives me a *look*. One that swaps the blood in my veins for ice. His eyes are still packed with hate, disdain, and resentment, but this time...

This time, there's also a glimmer of *interest.*

A drop of curiosity that wasn't there before. He looks at me like I'm a ticking time bomb he finally knows how to detonate. And as I glide up the stairs with my luggage, I know...

I'm in for the worst summer of my life.

Four

Diamond

Cold.

I'm cold.

No, not cold—*freezing.*

Half-asleep, I tug on the blanket to try and cover my shoulders. It doesn't help warm me up, and I groan in annoyance, driving the blanket over my head.

"What the hell?" My teeth chatter, and I pry my eyes open, analyzing my surroundings to make sure I didn't magically teleport to Antarctica.

I'm in the exact same place I was when I fell asleep, curled up in the queen-sized bed of the guest bedroom, but there is one major difference.

The temperature.

I reach for my phone on the nightstand. It's 8:05. I set my alarm for 8:15 to take Lexie on her morning walk, but there's no way I can sleep ten more minutes in this ice age.

I check the weather app on my phone and frown at the digits on my screen. It's eighty degrees outside. A warm, gorgeous day

I have every intention of spending by the pool with Lexie. So, then *why* is it so cold in here?

I climb out of bed and wince when my big toe meets the chilly wooden floors. The thermostat in my room reads sixty degrees when I know for a *fact* that I set it to sixty-eight last night. Maybe it's a glitch?

It would make sense, seeing as the house is filled with smart devices—thermostat, blinds, lights, even door locks.

"Weird," I say under my breath before pressing the touch screen to raise the temperature.

A loud beeping sound startles me, and a message appears on the fancy thermostat.

LOCKED. PLEASE ENTER PASSCODE TO ADJUST TEMPERATURE.

I know that I was wrong instantly.

It's not a glitch.

It's *him.*

"You've got to be fucking kidding me." I dial a handful of number combinations, all of them followed by the same message.

Locked.

Locked.

Locked.

"I swear this boy has a death wish," I say through clenched teeth. I throw on an oversized hoodie that stops just above my knees and storm out of my bedroom.

I rush down the stairs, ready to rip Finn a new one. I thought maybe he'd only changed the temperature upstairs since he has access to every room from the controller in the kitchen, but the rest of the house is just as cold.

The fucker is trying to force me out the door by making me *freeze to death.*

I'm surprised to see Lexie isn't downstairs waiting for me when I reach the living room. Poor baby, she must be freezing, too. I get that he'd want *me* to freeze, but his dog? What kind of monster does this to his own pet?

Turning the corner in a hurry, I search for Lexie but can't find her. Worry creeps under my skin as I wander into the kitchen and call her name a few times, with no result.

I stop short at the sound of her familiar barking.

It's coming from the backyard.

Rubbing the goose bumps on my arms away, I dash toward the large windows and release the biggest sigh of relief when I see Lexie running around the lawn. She's chasing after Finn, playing fetch and living her best life.

At least he had the decency not to let her freeze.

I glance at the rope hammock near the pool house and spot Theo napping in it. He's bathing in sunrays with his forearm and dark hair covering his eyes.

Right, I forgot.

He lives here now.

Chills skitter down my back, a reminder that I'm still freezing my tits off, and I swing the glass door open to walk outside. I know he heard the door close, but Finn doesn't glance my way, throwing Lexie a dog bone.

Aw, he thinks he can ignore me.

Cute.

"Change it back." I cross the yard in a few strides.

The silver chain he always wears is clasped around his neck, and he's shirtless, sporting black sweats with a backward baseball cap that makes him look so damn good it's infuriating. His stupid, glorious body basks in the sun, his veiny forearms and tattoos holding my eyes captive.

His eyes are small, too.

Like he just rolled out of bed.

He's *never* up this early.

This was all part of his plan, wasn't it? To get up before me, mess with the temperature, and head out so that *he* wouldn't have to freeze? He pays me no mind, to no one's surprise.

"*Hey, Satan,*" I shout. "I'm talking to you."

I reach his side a moment later and peek at Lexie chewing on her dog bone a few steps away.

"You're a fucking child, you know that?" I erupt.

"And you're a ball-busting pain in the ass. Anything else?" Finn drawls like he's eager for this interaction to be over.

"A password? Seriously?" I scold, but he denies me eye contact. Irritated, I leap in front of him, giving him no choice but to look at me. "It's as cold as fucking ice inside."

"Really?" He tilts his head to the side, the corners of his lips curling up into a vicious smile. "Didn't notice."

I'm fuming.

"Change it back."

Finn doesn't reply for long seconds, just staring at me without flinching. I swallow hard when he notices my attire. His eyes roam down my body, lingering on my bare thighs for a beat too long, and my cheeks heat up.

This hoodie does little to cover my legs. Just one inch shorter, and you could see my ass cheeks hanging out of my mini shorts. I was so pissed I didn't even think to change out of my pj's.

"Hate to break it to you, sunshine, but you don't get to tell me what to fucking do." His eyes dart back to mine.

Our conversation from the night before pops into my mind.

He keeps my secret, and I keep his.

That was the deal.

Was I crazy to think this could be the start of a truce?

"Then do it for Lexie," I snap. "You know damn well she's going to freeze in there."

"Sorry, I don't know what you're talking about." He keeps up the charade, and I fight the urge to shove Lexie's dog bone down his throat.

"Not buying it," I grit out and step closer to him in the midst of my fury.

Standing this close to Finn, the height difference is highly noticeable, and I have to stretch out my neck to meet his eyes. I want to move away as soon as I realize my confidence disappeared when the gap between us did, but I also don't want him to think he affects me.

Because he *doesn't.*

He's just a rude boy rotting on the inside.

Doesn't matter that the outside is the most beautiful thing I've ever seen…

"You can't keep it like that forever," I point out.

I see the muscles in his jaw quiver. We're way too close to each other now, and I try to hold my breath not to smell that delicious, earthy cologne he wears.

Then he drops the act.

"Watch me." His voice is darker, rougher, and my traitorous heart climbs up my throat.

"Eat my ass, Richards." I turn away.

"My pleasure. *Bend over,*" he calls behind me.

Unbelievable.

I don't bother replying and flip him off over my shoulder. I hear him laugh at my parting gift just before I head back inside the freezer he calls a house.

There's a pit in my stomach.

A big one.

He didn't tell me anything I didn't already know, but I'm more worried than ever before. Because now, I know our deal didn't change a thing…

He still wants me gone.

And he's not going to stop until I break.

* * *

Finn

"Was the tape really necessary?" Theo sneers from the kitchen, his head inside my fridge as he sifts through it. Tossing the video game controller in my hand onto the living room table, I sag into the couch we haven't left all morning.

"Considering the girl can't take a fucking hint? *Yes, it is.*"

I spent most of last night labeling nearly everything in the house, including the food in the fridge, as mine. I couldn't find sticky notes, so I settled for masking tape instead.

The house sitter was getting too comfortable for my taste, and if my name in black Sharpie everywhere doesn't remind her that she's in *my* fucking house, I don't know what will.

I was hoping yesterday's thermostat ploy would do the trick, but the girl was right about one thing. I couldn't keep it like that forever. It was cold as fuck in the house, and when it started hailing in the afternoon, we were forced back inside.

I must've lasted two hours before wussing out and removing the passcode. I could handle being cold, and I couldn't have cared less about Theo bitching that his balls were turning into icicles, but then I saw Lexie shivering in her dog bed, and I knew it was over.

No prank is worth Lexie feeling this way.

Ever.

"You don't have shit in there, Richards. I'm starving," Theo complains for the third time today.

"You're crashing at my place rent-free, asshole. Now, I have to feed you, too?" I scoff, but deep down, I'm right there with him.

The last time I had an acceptable meal was when the house sitter cooked that casserole—best food I've had in a hot minute, but I'll die before telling her that.

I blew through all the money I had for this month a few days ago. I could hardly see myself telling my dad I wasted my allowance in a single night. Thank fuck I had enough left to buy Lexie's food.

I know Theo thinks because my dad owns tons of shopping malls on top of his company, I'm swimming in cash, but my old man is a firm believer in his boys learning the value of money.

Brody, my big brother, had to start working when he was thirteen to pay for his shit. It was different for me, though. Dad wouldn't let me get a job.

He said he wanted me to direct all of my focus into basketball. He probably thought his delinquent son couldn't focus on sports, get a job, *and* keep it together.

Theo and I have been eating ramen noodles and whatever snacks we could find in the pantry since he got here. Not that Theo minds. As long as there was something even *remotely* edible in the house, he didn't say shit—anything is better than living with his parents—but we're out of even the most basic stuff now.

Hopefully, Gem girl buys more food before we starve.

Theo comes back from the fridge empty-handed, plopping down on the leather couch. "What's next?"

I arch an eyebrow at him.

"I assume you're working on your next move to get rid of the house sitter?" he sneers.

He thinks I'm wasting my time.

He says she doesn't seem like the type to quit, and chances are, if she hasn't thrown in the towel yet, she never will. According to him, the girl isn't going anywhere.

I'm going to have the time of my life proving him wrong.

"Jesus, it's hot in here." Theo, who's wearing a gym tank top, peels his bicep off the couch, his skin sticking to the leather.

He's right.

I convince myself it has something to do with my messing with the thermostat yesterday and shrug. I lob his video game controller at him to unpause the game we abandoned. We barely play for ten minutes before it becomes unbearable.

"Okay, I'm fucking melting. Do something," Theo urges.

"News flash, Cox, you have legs."

"I don't know how your rich-people thermostat works, dipshit," Theo argues.

Annoyed, I rise off the couch and edge my way to the kitchen to adjust the temperature.

90 degrees.

Did I break something yesterday?

Why is it so fucking hot?

It's hot as hell outside, sure, but the AC should be kicking in. I press the button to lower it back to normal levels, but an alert message pops up on the touch screen.

LOCKED. PLEASE ENTER PASSCODE TO ADJUST TEMPERATURE.

My mouth drops.

She didn't.

I hear footsteps and Lexie's paws rattling the floor.

"Morning, boys." Gem's chirpy voice tips me off instantly.

Looks like she just turned the tables on me.

I spin on my axis and hate how quickly the hate stirring in my gut dies down.

Fuck. Me.

The house sitter is standing in the doorway to the living room with Lexie, wearing white shorts and a neon green bikini top that makes her tits look…

I can't lie, she's a fucking ten.

I knew she was my type from the second I caught her in my bed in her underwear that night, but I was too pissed at my dad to care. She's curvy in all the right places, with full, pouty lips I want to fuck and a noticeable birthmark above one of her breasts.

Her long, curly black hair is thrown over her shoulder,

cascading down her tan stomach. My dick jerks in my pants as I imagine myself gripping that waist and ramming myself inside her from behind.

Fuck, Finn, stop.

I hate her.

I really do.

I just wish my cock hated her, too.

"Beautiful day, isn't it?" Gem saunters to the living room table to grab the few beer cans we didn't get around to throwing away. I can't take my eyes off her as she huddles up the empty cans into her arms.

Still in the kitchen, I peek at Theo on the couch, and I know he's having the exact same thoughts from the way his eyes flare. Gem glances at Theo sweating like a pig, and her plump mouth curls into a smile.

She's enjoying this way too much.

Her gaze shifts to me, but she immediately tears her eyes away when she realizes I was already staring. Avoiding my glare, she ambles to the dining room table.

"I was thinking of going for a swim, then running to the grocery store this afternoon. You guys want anything?" She pulls a grocery list out of her pocket.

"Hell yeah." Theo pushes off the couch and grabs a seat at the dining room table with her. He starts walking her through all the items he wants, and I can't even blame him.

Theo is broke.

"Not a dollar to his name" broke.

He's worked for his parents his whole life but decided to quit shortly before summer started. He said he needed a break. And not just from his job. From his whole family.

It's no secret that the Cox family dynamic sucks ass. Theo gets kicked out of his house by his parents on the regular for failing to be the academic success story they'd hoped for.

And while everybody else in Silver Springs is *obsessed* with basketball, Theo's folks think basketball is garbage and a complete waste of time. In their eyes, their son is setting himself up for failure by thinking "*throwing a ball into a hoop*" is more important than his grades.

It also doesn't help that Theo's parents have been at each other's throats for as long as he can remember. At this point, he's just waiting for one of them to grow some balls and pull the plug on the marriage.

Propping my elbows on the kitchen island, I scroll on my phone, listening to Theo flirt with the house sitter so shamelessly I roll my eyes to the point of eye strain.

I'm going to vomit.

"Great. All set, then." Gem rises to her feet and walks to the sliding glass door that leads outside, giving us a shot of her perfect fucking ass in the process.

She jerks the door open, Lexie not far behind. Just as she's about to step onto the patio, I remember something.

"Hey, sitter girl?"

She stops.

"Give me the code first." I don't need to explain for her to know I'm talking about the thermostat. In response, she looks me dead in the eyes, nudges a strand of her curly hair away from her face, and flashes an innocent smile.

"Sorry, I don't know what you're talking about."

Then she's out the door.

Floored, I watch her stroll to the pool with Lexie and realize there's a hint of a smile on my lips. She just used my own words against me, and what's worse? I can't even be mad.

She might've just beat me at my own game…

But I taught her how to play.

Five

Diamond

Whoever came up with the "kill them with kindness" approach is a genius.

Granted, being nice didn't work for shit on my kindergarten bullies, but it works on narcissistic, sinfully hot rich kids, and that's good enough for me.

Three whole days have gone by since I switched up the narrative on Finn and became Little Mary Sunshine. As much as I loved watching the boys sweat their asses off, I couldn't take another second of this heat and eventually removed the code.

The result?

No more pranks.

Not even one snarky comment.

Well, Finn did brand everything in the house with his name on masking tape—because everybody knows Finn Richards is the *picture* of sanity—and the nasty looks are still an everyday thing, but I can handle a few looks if it means he's going to let me do my job in peace.

I'm surprisingly grateful for Theo living with us. I can't

imagine being alone with Finn full-time, and Theo says actual words to me, rather than rolling his eyes and leaving every time I walk into the room.

I'm aware there's a good chance Theo's only nice to me because I feed him, but I have to admit our little routine is growing on me.

It's a rinse-and-repeat process: I cook for myself while making sure to have tons of leftovers, throw them in the fridge, and when I come back, the food is gone.

Theo is decent enough to thank me every once in a while, but Finn? I'll be on my death bed before he manages to say the words *thank you.*

It's past 9:00 a.m. when Lexie and I stride down the stairs together. It was pretty hard to ignore her crying at my door every night, so I caved and let her in. She sleeps in my bed now, only leaving my side when I open the door in the morning.

I hear what sounds like shuffling in the fridge as soon as my feet connect with the main floor. Must be Theo eating last night's leftovers.

"Damn it, Richards. You ate the last slice of pizza." I recognize Theo's voice and stop to think.

I didn't feel like cooking yesterday, and Mr. Richards finally wired me the money for food, so I ordered a large pizza for dinner with extra olives to piss off Finn.

He told me he hated olives as I was ordering because he knew he and Theo would end up finishing it. He even went as far as to say if there was even *one* olive on the pizza, he wouldn't touch that shit with a stick, but apparently, he ate it?

In what world does that make sense?

Pushing the thought to the back corner of my mind, I make my way to the kitchen with an excited Lexie on my tail. The first thing I see when I walk in is Theo digging through the fridge, then Finn in a black tee and jeans, leaning against the kitchen counter with his arms crossed.

He looks ridiculously hot, *when does he not*, but I don't spare him another glance, focusing on the only guy in this room who treats me like an actual person.

"Morning," I tell Theo and watch Lexie charge toward Finn, seeking a good petting, which Finn gives her without a second thought.

She might like me now because I take her on multiple walks a day, but I know for a fact that I could never top Finn in her eyes. She only came crying at my door a few nights ago because Finn didn't let her into his own room.

It's the way his face lights up when he sees her, how hyperfocused he is on her needs.

There's no denying that he loves her.

Theo greets me with a flick of his chin, and Lexie parts from Finn to find her food bowl by the entryway. I trail to the espresso machine. Problem is, Finn slid back into his previous position—arms crossed, leaning against the counter—and is blocking access like a fucking brick wall.

"Move," I say bluntly but feel my confidence shrink when his cold eyes snap to mine.

"Oh, am I in your way?" he taunts with a small, devious smirk I want to punch off his face.

"Yes." I swallow my nerves and expect him to step aside.

Instead, he stares down my face, positions his lips next to my ear, and rasps a satisfied "*Good*."

I should be annoyed, mad even, but all I can think about is how close he is to me right now. His breath crashing against my earlobe and the shivers crawling up my spine. I wonder what his mouth would feel like sucking on my neck, marking me all ove—

What the hell was that?

I snap out of it and pull back an inch to regain my composure. He's batshit crazy if he thinks he can stand in the way of me and my morning coffee.

"Move. I'm not going to ask again."

He ignores me, wetting his mouth by running his tongue across his bottom lip, and my eyes follow the motion.

"Fine." I huff, deciding it's too early to plan a murder.

An alarm rips me from my thoughts.

Theo jerks his phone out of his pocket.

"Fuck, I have a job interview in ten minutes. *Later*."

He's out the door before I know it. We hear his red car speed out of the driveway a few seconds later. That's when a text comes through on Finn's phone, and he pulls it out of his pocket. I catch his smirk when he sees the sender.

Booty call alert.

Is it Brie again?

None of your business, Dia.

He's quick to snatch his keys out of his pocket and walk to the door.

"Hey?" I shadow him to the entryway.

Opening the door, he glances back at me.

"Why'd you eat it?" I ask.

He frowns. "Eat what?"

"The pizza. You said you hated olives."

He bites back a smile from the moment the words slip out of my mouth.

"I lied. I knew if I told you I hated olives, that's exactly what you'd order."

My mouth goes slack, but he exits the house before I get a chance to react. The boy played me like a fucking marionette.

Clever bastard.

Lexie's tongue sweeping across my palm brings me back to reality, and I pet the top of her head while she presses her cheek to my leg.

"I'm going to shower. Then we're going for a walk, okay?" I ask as though she understands me. I'm halfway to the upstairs bathroom linked to my bedroom when my own phone chimes with a text.

From an unknown number.

Unknown Number: I rearranged your bathroom a bit. Thought you could use more counter space. You're welcome.

It's Finn.

Has to be.

And according to the blaring sirens in my head? He did a hell of a lot more than just "rearrange" my bathroom. My pulse accelerating, I bolt up the stairs and swing the door to my bathroom open.

I find the counter where my stuff was yesterday completely cleared out. How could I miss this? Wait, I used the downstairs bathroom this morning, didn't I? I cringe when I notice the toilet seat is up and run to it.

It's all there.

Sitting at the bottom of the toilet.

My makeup bag, my hair straightener, hair ties, expensive face cream, even my fucking toothbrush. Anger stirs in my stomach as I roll up my sleeves to fish my stuff out.

Oh, it's on.

* * *

There are nine bedrooms in the Richardses' house.

Nine bedrooms, and I've been inside all of them.

All of them except *one.*

"What's wrong?" I ask Lexie, who's been crying in front of

the frosted French doors on the second floor for the past ten minutes. I've found her here *twice* in the past three days, whining at the door for hours on end.

This is the only room I didn't go into when I gave myself a tour of the house. Finn had plastered a less than welcoming sign on the door, and I wasn't trying to incur his wrath after he'd *just* used my clothes as lawn fertilizer.

Curiosity grabbing a hold of me, I rip off the sheet of paper my lovely housemate stuck to the door.

How to enter this room in one easy step.

Step one: Don't.

On any other day, I would heed his warning, but I just spent an hour sanitizing my things after pulling them out of the toilet, and I'm feeling vindictive.

Hesitantly, I pull on the black knobs, sucking in a breath when the doors creak open. Lexie charges inside the room, and the million scenarios I cooked up come to a screeching halt.

I was wrong.

It's *not* a bedroom.

An impressive oak desk sits in the center of the room, a sewing machine and a handful of stackable storage bins on top of it. The wall facing the entrance is painted a gorgeous cream color, and a rustic jewelry organizer is mounted to it.

Colorful necklaces, bracelets, and rings hang from the

organizer's hooks, and a fabric roll rack is fixed to the wall on my right.

The jewelry slash sewing room is illuminated by end-of-day sunrays peeking through the window, the dust particles in the air visible to the naked eye. I can tell from the look of things that the room has been kept clean over the years, but I wouldn't be surprised if the maid was the last person in here.

I venture deeper into the room, soaking up a memory I know doesn't belong to me, and skim the pad of my fingers over the fabric rolls on the wall.

A small letter is engraved into each roll.

N.

N as in…

Nora Richards?

I know I shouldn't be in here. Odds are, if Finn finds me in his mother's office, I'm as good as dead, but there's something fascinating about a moment frozen in time.

A story you can still read long after it ended.

I wonder what kind of mother she was, if this was her job or just a hobby, if she's the one who made the silver chain her son never takes off.

The storage bins on her desk contain wire cutters, precious and semiprecious stones, clasps. All the tools you need to make jewelry.

I glance over to see Lexie huddled up in a velvet dog bed by the window. It looks natural to her, like a habit she never grew out of. The thought of her lying there while Finn's mom worked all those years ago makes my chest tighten. I feel like an imposter when I sit down on her leather office chair. Like I'm trapped in a dream *she* never got to wake up from.

But my dads always told me you can create something beautiful from even the most devastating stories. So, with my heart in my throat, I reach for the storage bins on Mrs. Richards's desk, remove the lids one by one…

And *create.*

* * *

The clock reads 11:20 p.m. when I step out of Finn's shower.

I've been home alone since the boys left this morning, and I wasn't about to miss the opportunity to shower in the biggest, nicest shower in the house. Who cares that said shower is connected to Finn's bedroom?

In a hurry, I dry my body and hair with a towel, then throw on a pair of silk shorts and a loose T-shirt. I'm about to head out of the bathroom when I spot the black onyx bracelet I spent *hours* making on the bathroom counter.

I've been carrying it around since I finished it earlier.

I wasn't too sure what to do with it at first. I could hardly see myself wearing it knowing none of the materials were mine. Then I realized it only made sense for Finn to have it.

He's the one who lost his mom.

Maybe this way, he can carry a piece of her with him?

I'm not even sure why I made that bracelet.

I went into Nora Richards's office with the intention of hurting Finn and walked out with this overwhelming sadness for him. Plus, it wouldn't be *that* far-fetched for me to give him a gift considering my new "kill them with kindness" mantra.

I slide the bracelet over my wrist to remind myself to give it to Finn the next time I see him and start to turn arou—

"What the fuck do you think you're doing?"

I shriek in surprise, dropping the wet towel in my hand on the bathroom tiles. A grumpy Finn stands in the doorway to the bathroom, his hard stare filled with daggers and poison-laced bullets.

"I..." The words won't cooperate.

"You what?" he says dryly.

Get a grip.

"What's it look like, smart-ass? I was showering," I fire back. Familiar with our bickering, Finn cocks an eyebrow at me and flashes a small *here we go again* grin.

"I know what you were doing, Gem. What I want to know is why."

Gem...

I wish he'd stop calling me that.

Sometimes, like right now, it sounds nice.

Affectionate, even. Like it could be "our thing" instead of what it truly is. A reminder that he couldn't be bothered to remember my name.

I stick my hands up. "You've got the best shower in the house. Sue me."

Bracing his shoulder against the doorway, Finn gives me a once-over, and my arms erupt in goose bumps. I assume he's looking for the perfect insult to throw in my face until he shrugs.

"Whatever."

Whatever?

I don't let myself overthink it and squeeze past his broad frame to exit the bathroom. I've barely taken two steps before I remember that I left the towel on the ground and swivel around.

Finn seems to have had the same reflex because we both reach for the towel at the same time, our fingers touching for a split second. My pulse quickening, I withdraw my hand, taking the used towel with me and blinking up at him.

He's staring at me, too.

Hard.

Only...

It's not my face he's looking at.

But the black bracelet around my wrist.

***

Finn

I've always known the house sitter lacked common sense.

I mean, *come on*, anyone with half a brain would have run for the hills the day I dumped her luggage into the water fountain. But when I see the black stones clasped around her wrist, the innocent look in her deep brown eyes…

I realize it's worse than I thought.

She doesn't just lack common sense.

She also lacks basic human decency.

"What the fuck?" My voice cracks on a mix of anger and disgust, but there's also a pinch of pain I want to smother to death.

Gem staggers back a step at my words and I watch it sink in. The realization that she broke all of my rules and boundaries.

And there's no going back.

"Right, I… I stumbled upon your mom's office today, and I… I made this for you." Her voice trembling, she glides the bracelet off her wrist and hands it to me.

I see red instantly.

"You touched her stuff?" I spit, but it comes out as a question. I'm shocked, in disbelief. I feel like she just dropped a massive fucking bombshell on me.

She. Touched. Her. Stuff.

I shift to autopilot, my fingers clutching the bracelet and ripping it out of her hand violently. I throw it across the hall so hard the house sitter shrieks.

Her chest heaving up and down, she struggles to speak. "I just… I thought it'd be nice for you to have something of hers."

I almost laugh.

My mom left me plenty of things when she died.

PTSD, nightmares, never-ending guilt.

But I sure as hell don't need a bracelet made by a stranger.

She starts to move away, but I stop her, reaching for her wrist and yanking her body to mine. The worst part is, I know she meant well. She's so full of light, kindness, good intentions. But right now, with her chest pressed against mine, I want to suck her dry.

So, so fucking bad.

I want to bend her over and plunge inside her until she tells me how sorry she is, make her beg, cry in pleasure as she comes and hates herself for it.

I shift my hips a bit so that she doesn't feel how rock-hard I am, but I'm pretty sure she feels it anyway because she stops breathing for a second.

Fuck.

This girl is my worst nightmare.

Something I hate just as much as I crave.

"Do you think I've been mean to you?" I shock her by saying.

She swallows hard.

"Do you?" I insist.

Her exhales uneven, she nods.

"Then mark my words, if you ever step foot in that office again, I'll make everything I've done to you since you got here look like fucking child's play."

She's not looking at me anymore, and I need those eyes.

I *need* to know what's going on in her head.

"Got it?" I clench my teeth and lift her chin with my index. A few tears are beginning to form in the corners of her eyes, and it makes me even harder.

Fuck, there's no way she doesn't feel that.

We stay this way for long seconds, staring into each other's souls. Until finally, she chokes out a weak, barely audible "*Got it*."

Next thing I know, she's pushed me off her.

I hear her scamper down the hallway, then her bedroom door slams in the distance. For a moment today, I thought maybe, in time, I could grow to tolerate having this girl in my house, after all…

Spoiler alert?

I was wrong.

Six

Diamond

Since the day I moved into this house, I've heard Lexie cry three times. The first was when she cried at Finn's bedroom door, then mine at night to be let in.

The second was when she parked herself in front of Nora Richards's office for hours, and the third…

The third is *now*.

Drowsiness weighing me down, I groan and pat the mattress beneath me in search of Lexie.

She's not here.

Weird?

She *always* sleeps in my bed.

My eyes are screwed shut, and it takes superhuman strength for me to pry my lids apart. The room is dark, and I check my phone to see it's 3:00 a.m. The house is quiet with the exception of Lexie wailing in the distance.

Rubbing my eyes, I sit up in bed and listen.

I've never heard Lexie cry like this.

There's despair, *distress*, in the way she howls, and I know something is wrong when I spot the small gap in my bedroom door. She snuck out on her own.

But why?

Worried, I drag my ass out of bed, slide my feet into my slippers, and venture into the hallway. Am I supposed to believe that *no one else* heard that?

Theo, I can believe.

He sleeps in one of the first-floor guest bedrooms, far enough not to be woken up, but Finn should be up looking for her. Where the hell is he?

My sight still blurry, I follow the noise. I sigh in relief when I turn the corner and spot Lexie by the double wooden doors at the end of the hallway.

I know where these doors lead, and I can't make sense of her crying in front of an empty library.

"Lexie, what's wrong?" I say softly and approach her.

She runs to me the moment she sees me. I pet the top of her head, which she barely lets me do, and her cries grow louder as she leads me back to the door and barks again.

She's trying to tell me something.

The question is what?

"It's okay, baby. You're okay," I tell her, hoping it isn't a lie, and reach for the doorknob.

I think I'm going to have a heart attack when I open the door…

My first instinct is to scream when I see him, but a voice in my head instructs me not to make a sound. He's standing in the opened window with a booze bottle in his hand, looking down at the void below him in utter silence.

We're on the highest floor.

What if he falls?

Or worse, what if he *jumps*?

Lexie runs to her owner to check on him. How she knew he was in trouble, I'll never understand. He doesn't spare Lexie a glance, ignoring her barking as he stares blankly into the night.

Dia, say something!

"Finn?" My voice breaks around his name. "What… What are you doing?"

These are the first words I've spoken to him since the night he threw away my bracelet.

Two days went by after he went apeshit on me, and we've made a profession out of ignoring each other. I haven't been able to stop thinking about his hand gripping my wrist, those deep, soulless eyes plunged into mine.

And how hard he felt against my thigh.

God…

"Finn?" I repeat when he doesn't respond. "Answer me, or I'm calling the police."

Then, he laughs.

He fucking laughs.

It sounded real, too, and I don't know what to make of it

until he whisks his head back and looks at me over his shoulder. There's a barely-there smile on that wicked mouth.

"Relax, I'm not going to jump," is all he says before returning to his stargazing.

"Great, then you won't mind getting off the window." I cut to the chase, but he doesn't react.

I try again a few seconds later.

"Get off the window, Finn."

This time, he glances back at me, and our eyes lock across the room.

"*Please*," I beg, my throat aching terribly.

He thinks about it for a moment and shrugs. "Fine."

I can't breathe, think, or speak as I watch him take a seat where he first stood, his feet hanging in the emptiness.

"I'm telling you, you don't know what getting a breath of fresh air feels like until you try this," he says like me finding him standing in an open window at 3:00 a.m. is *normal*.

Lexie, who's still watching her owner like a hawk, seems to decide the situation is under control because she lies down on the floor next to him.

As for me, I'm speechless.

"Are you going to say something or creep on me all night?" he taunts when my silence becomes too loud for his liking.

"You could fall." I state the obvious.

In response, he scoffs.

"And that would be tragic, right?"

"Will you just get off the fucking window?" I nag.

Annoyed, Finn huffs. "Come here."

My heart starts racing, but I'd rather get a fucking cardiogram than admit he's the reason why.

"W-What?"

"Come here." He gestures to come closer.

So, I do, my footsteps hesitant and my legs wobbly. I shiver once I reach his side, a frisky gust of wind rippling on the inside of my clothes.

"Look," he commands. "It's not nearly as high as you think it is." He points at the void beneath his feet. His inebriating cologne fills my nostrils as I inch closer to him to peek over his shoulder.

A wave of nausea immediately washes over me. I don't know what the hell he's on, but we have *very* different definitions of "not that high."

"You do realize I'm not leaving until you get off that window?"

He flashes a lazy smirk.

"Then pull up a chair because you're not going to bed anytime soon."

With that said, he motions to the leather sofa by one of the tall bookcases in the library. The taste of defeat fresh on my tongue, I make my way over to the sofa and plop down onto the cushion.

I don't know how he can just sit there in a T-shirt, with the night breeze blowing all over him. I'm wearing sweatpants and a long-sleeve Duke University sweater I stole from my brother, and I'm *freezing*.

A thousand questions flood my mind when I see him tip back the bottle of booze he placed on the window frame.

"Are you drunk?" I ask.

"No."

"Are you stupid?"

He laughs. "*Probably*."

Silence descends over us.

"I wanted to apologize." His deep voice cuts through the air.

Did I hear that right?

My gaze lifts to him, but he's not looking at me, his focus drilled into the night.

"Can you say that again? I didn't record it," I tease.

"I wanted to apologize." He deadpans and looks at me. "*Did you get it?*"

A laugh climbs up my throat, but I keep quiet out of self-respect. I shouldn't be laughing at his jokes. I haven't forgotten what he did to me after I gave him the bracelet.

"I shouldn't have lost my shit two days ago. I'm sorry." He breathes out.

"By all means, keep going," I prompt.

He bites back a smile. "Afraid that's all you get."

I know we're joking, but in that moment, I almost wish I *had* recorded him. No one will ever believe Finn Richards apologized to me, the house sitter he's been trying to get rid of since day one.

"I'm sorry, too," I confess. "My birth mother died when I was a baby and I only have one thing left of hers. If someone touched it, I'd lose my mind…"

I watch as he flings his legs inside.

He leans back against the window frame, one of his arms braced on his knee and his right leg huddled up to his chest while the other hangs down on his side.

Fuck, he's gorgeous.

With the moonlight hitting the right side of his face, outlining his tattooed biceps and flawless features. His dark brown hair is an eternal mess, strands cascading down in front of his eyes.

"What is it?" he asks. "The thing you have of your mom's?"

"An old Radiohead T-shirt with the lyrics of "Creep" on it."

Finn gives a small nod.

"It never goes away, does it?" He's back to staring at nothing in particular.

"What?"

His hazel eyes cut back to mine. "This fucking void."

I catch on instantly.

"It does," I disagree. "But only when you're ready to let go."

He says nothing.

"Are you?" I ask and instantly wish I could take it back. It's like my words just gutted him in the stomach. I see a twinge of rage stirring in his gaze, and he looks down.

"Is anyone?" he mutters.

His phone pings with a text before I can reply, and he pulls it out of his pocket. It's past 3:00 a.m. Who could be texting him at 3:00 a.m.?

It comes to me.

A girl, who else?

Maybe the same girl as last time? His gaze skims over the screen briefly, and he shoves the phone back into his pocket without answering.

"Booty call?" I question.

He shrugs. "Not sure she counts as a booty call."

What is she, then?

His special friend?

"I assume you're talking about Brie?"

"Nosey much?" he taunts.

"*Very* much." I own up to it.

He cracks a small grin, seemingly surprised by my honesty.

"Don't stay here on my account. By all means, go see her."

He pauses.

"What makes you think I want to fuck Brie again?"

Apart from the fact that she's a stick-thin, drop-dead gorgeous red-haired goddess? Gee, Finn, I don't know.

"Hey, I'm not judging." I snort, my stomach churning. "It's just… Last I checked, making good decisions isn't exactly your strong suit."

I wait for him to put me in my place, the way he did two days ago, but instead, he grabs the bottle of whiskey he probably found in his dad's stash and takes a long sip.

He confronts me as soon as he's put the bottle down.

"Why don't you say what you really mean?"

I force a laugh. "Which is what exactly?"

"You want to know why I did it."

And the cherry on top?

He's right.

"Go ahead, ask me," he challenges, never tearing his eyes away from me. My thoughts completely out of whack, I clear my throat and give in to his request.

"Okay. Why'd you sleep with Brie?"

He doesn't speak for a few seconds.

"Because I could."

My breath catches in my throat.

"I did it because if I can't have my own father's respect and *he* can, you best fucking believe I'll take everything else."

He's talking about Xavier Emery, isn't he?

Something breaks in his eyes right then.

Something he never wanted me to see.

I'm at a loss for words, desperately trying to process his admission. Thankfully, he doesn't seem to be waiting for a reply because he chugs another sip of whiskey and dries his mouth with the back of his hand.

"I slept with my best friend's girl to get revenge on

something he didn't even *mean* to do," he adds. "Now, tell me that isn't the most fucked-up thing you've ever heard…"

It *is* one of the most fucked-up things I've ever heard.

It's vile.

And awful.

And unforgivable.

So, why am I not repelled?

Why am I not *horrified*?

If anything, his coldhearted betrayal makes him all the more intriguing to me. I want to know how his brain works, what happened to him that day on the lake. Why he feels the need to convince himself that he's a lost cause.

But mostly, I want to see how far he can go…

Before the whole world believes it, too.

"The worst part is, I'd take a fucking bullet for this guy." Finn huffs out a bitter laugh. "I'd die for him. He's like my brother. And yet… there's a part of me that hates him."

The urge to ask him a question consumes me.

But I'm scared of his answer.

I keep my eyes on the ceiling, aiming to fill up on courage until I realize I might not have a choice but to get it in liquid form.

"Fuck it," I whisper to myself and rise to my feet.

I head straight for Finn sitting on the window and rip the bottle of whiskey out of his hands. His eyes grow at my initiative, but he doesn't speak, watching me trail back to the leather sofa.

I've never had strong liquor before. I had fruity wine at my aunt's wedding once, but that's as far as it's ever gone.

It's not that I *don't* want to drink.

The opportunity just never presented itself.

Aveena isn't exactly big on drinking because of trauma she experienced as a child, and I could hardly see myself rubbing salt into her wound.

The whiskey feels like lava coursing down my throat, and my gag reflex kicks in. A drop of liquor slips free from the bottle and rolls down my mouth. Finn watches it happen, his eyes following my thumb as I wipe the excess alcohol off my bottom lip. Then he traps his own lip between his teeth.

And I stop breathing.

Nah, I'm probably crazy.

"And me?" I gather the courage to say.

He arches an eyebrow, willing me to carry on.

"Why do you hate me? Scratch that, why do you hate everything?"

His answer is immediate. "I don't hate everything."

I snort. "Name me *one* thing you don't hate."

He doesn't answer right away, pushing off the windowsill and stealing the glass bottle back from me. He only speaks once he's regained his seat on the window.

"I'll have to get back to you on that."

I gasp. "*Shocker.*"

I assume our conversation has reached its natural decline

until he adds, "And I don't, by the way."

"Don't what?"

"Hate you. I don't," he clears up.

His pranks, harsh words, and nasty looks beg to differ.

"Then why are you so awful to me?"

The silence that ensues is thicker, heavier than any silence I've ever suffered through. Finn flips his head to look out the open window, losing himself in the night sky before whispering a truth I thought would never come.

"Because you're everything she would've wanted me to be."

I'm confused for a moment.

But it quickly becomes clear.

He's talking about his mom, isn't he?

"Hell, you're everything she was…" Finn scoffs and tips the bottle back for another sip. "Trustworthy, understanding, kind. God, you're so fucking kind it makes me *sick*."

To my own disbelief, I laugh. It's not particularly nice, but I still find humor in the backhanded compliment.

"Thanks?" I'm not sure what to say.

Against all expectations, Finn laughs, too.

This has to be the first time we've ever *truly* laughed together. This is definitely our first genuine conversation, too. I could get used to this, but I know better than to think "decent Finn" will ever be the norm.

We don't speak again after that.

Finn resumes his staring into the night, and I return to

waiting for him to get off the window.

I don't mind the silence.

I want to remember this moment.

I want to remember, once the sun comes up and he inevitably reverts back into his cruel self, that for that one fleeting moment, the walls he built around himself were no more. For that one fleeting moment, he was *real.*

And maybe…

Just maybe…

Finn Richards isn't the monster I made him out to be.

Seven

Diamond

"Gem?"

The masculine voice is but an echo in my head.

"*Gem?*" Someone is shaking me.

My eyes are heavy, feeling almost screwed shut, and I can't scrape up the energy to open them.

"Gem, wake up." His voice has a certain urgency to it.

My brain trapped in a thick fog, I open my eyes a crack to see Finn leaning over me in the darkness of the library, his hand planted on my shoulder.

Shit, I passed out, didn't I?

How long have I been asleep?

"What time is it?" I sit up straight and realize a blanket is covering me.

Did I fall asleep with a blanket?

I can't remember.

"Almost five," Finn answers.

I don't think I had a blanket before.

Does that mean… Finn put it on me?

"It's been fun having you play bodyguard and all, but I'm going to hit the sack. Thought you'd like to spend the rest of the night in your bed," Finn adds.

His kindness is nothing short of a miracle. You mean to tell me he's been nice to me for *two* consecutive hours? I should buy a lottery ticket.

"I… Thanks," I say, still out of it, and start to rise off the sofa. My blood pressure drops from the moment my feet touch the ground, and a sudden tide of dizziness scolds me for getting up too fast.

Thankfully, Finn catches me at the last minute, his hands flanking my waist with a grip so tight my knees buckle for an entirely different reason.

We stand there for long seconds, his hands on my hips, our gazes fused together, and our bodies too close for my brain to comprehend. We're both breathing harder than we were a second prior, and I catch myself zeroing in on his mouth.

He's usually despicable, but right now, he's nice, and I hate that it's making me blind to all the times he wasn't.

"You can let go now," I say, even though my body is dying for him to hold me like this for two more minutes. I expect him to listen and back away, but he only holds on tighter, directing his focus onto my lips.

"I could." He shrugs without a fuck given, and I'm pretty sure my heart skips a beat for every extra second he keeps my chest flush with his.

It's the darkness of the night.

The quiet of a town that's sleeping while we're awake. It's dangerous. Alone in this library, it's easy to forget that we have to get up tomorrow and go back to hating each other.

"Why don't you?" The answer terrifies me.

He usually has an answer for everything, but this time, he seems hesitant to share. I wait and I wait for him to drop it on me, but he never does. Instead, he releases his grip on my waist and starts to leave.

"Don't ask questions you can't handle the answers to." He's back to his cold self in the blink of an eye.

Every fiber of my being screams at me to do something as he approaches the door.

"Who says I can't handle it?" I call behind him.

Fuck, what am I doing?

I should let him leave.

I should let us forget that for one night, we weren't completely miserable in each other's presence. But if he leaves, the truce will officially be over, and it scares me shitless.

Finn stops dead but doesn't look at me right away. He's standing in the doorway when he heaves an "I can't believe this girl" scoff and swivels around.

"You really want to know?"

I consider retracting my question, but it's too late.

He's already charging toward me.

I'm backed up against the large bookcase behind me in a matter of seconds. The space between us is but a few inches now, and my focus dips to his mouth. His tongue glosses over his bottom lip as he glares through my soul. His lips are sultry, and *shit*, they look soft. I just wish the words coming out of them weren't so brutal all the time.

"You really want to know what I'm thinking about right now?" Finn warns like he's trying to prepare me for impending doom. I swallow hard and manage a small nod.

My silent answer causes him to move even closer, our mouths nearly touching as he destroys the wall of hatred I'd carefully built between us.

"I'm thinking about the thousand ways I could make you come right there on that rug."

Just like that, there's no more air in the room. There's no more truce, or peace offering, or waving of a white flag. He's ready for battle, and I'm scared I'll have to surrender.

"I'm thinking about the thousand times I've wanted to back you into a corner and eat that pussy until you were soaking my whole fucking face." He doesn't even flinch.

Oh.

My.

God.

My mouth falls open at his admission, and he smirks, running his thumb over my bottom lip and driving any resistance I had left to this attraction into the ground.

"I think about you *begging* me not to tell your boss you like what his fucked-up son does to you with his tongue."

The silence that follows makes me reconsider everything I thought I knew. He's still looking at my mouth—scratch that, he's downright devouring my mouth with his eyes—and I hate myself for it, but…

If he wanted my first kiss right now?

I'd give it to him.

I fear my heart might pop like an overinflated balloon when Finn grabs my cheeks with one hand, squeezing my face and bringing me closer until his mouth is hovering near mine.

"And that, Gem…" He pauses. "*That's* the reason you can't handle it."

Then he walks off.

No further explanation, no apology for his bluntness.

Nothing.

He just leaves me there. In the middle of four walls that heard a confession I'll never be able to forget.

* * *

I spent the following weekend trying to reprogram my brain.

Wasn't easy, but the articles online did warn me it would take a fair share of discipline. The main goal? Stop thinking about Finn. I'm not quite there yet, but his words are no longer playing on a loop in my head, so… *baby steps*?

I was strangely relieved to find the main floor empty after Jesse dropped me back at the house yesterday.

Finn wasn't home.

Neither was Theo.

It was just Lexie and me.

I jumped at the chance to watch a cheesy movie on the living room flat-screen while the boys weren't around to roast me. Then I crashed and didn't leave my room again until this morning when I pulled myself out of bed to make breakfast.

"*Please* say there's some for me." Theo's voice carries through the first floor, and I spin my head to see the tall basketball player dragging his feet to the kitchen.

He looks like shit.

His black hair is a tangled mess, his green eyes are rimmed with circles so dark I can see them from here, and his skin is pale, bordering on ghostly.

Someone had too much to drink last night.

I swallow a laugh, turning away from the omelet I'm cooking on the stove. "Damn, Theo, you look…"

"Good for a dead guy?" he finishes and plops down on one of the stools around the kitchen island.

I snicker and focus on flipping my omelet. "I was going to say under the weather."

In response, he braces his elbows on the marble counter, links his fingers on top of his head, and lets out an irritated groan at what seems to be a killer headache.

"When did you end up rolling in last night?"

"Late." He scoffs. "News flash: two hours of sleep? Definitely not enough."

I laugh. "Must've been quite the rager, huh?"

"First party of the summer, you know how it is. If everyone's not throwing up by the end of the night, what was the fucking point?" Theo pokes fun at the popular kids' mentality, and I abstain from hounding him with questions.

The truth is, I *don't* know how it is, and believe me, it's not for lack of trying. I could never score an invite to one of these things.

Theo rubs his temples. "Finn was so fucked-up, he's going to need a whole-ass *liver* transplant."

Finn was at the party, too?

That would explain why he wasn't home last night.

"Did he come home with you? I'd rather not have to tell my boss his son might be lying in a ditch somewhere." I choke on my excuse. I'll never admit it, but I'm curious. Hell, I'm even a little bit worried about his reckless ass.

Why. Do. I. Even. Care.

"Nah, he left with some girl in the middle of the party."

Oh.

I don't reply, grabbing a plate out of the kitchen cabinet and sliding my omelet onto it. I've barely settled down at the kitchen island with Theo before I catch him eyeing my food.

Next thing I know, I'm leaping off my stool and pulling out

another plate and fork. Feeding these boys is becoming a ritual at this point.

"You can have half. That's it," I scold.

Theo's eyes light up.

"Have I ever told you you're my favorite house sitter?" He smirks, watching as I split the omelet with a fork and transfer it onto his plate.

"Eat before I change my mind."

With that said, I put on coffee and find my seat around the kitchen island. Theo doesn't think twice, taking a big bite and offering me a thumbs-up. I'm about to have a taste when Finn pads into the room in joggers.

He's not wearing a shirt, like the compulsive show-off that he is, and while he *does* look like last night's party kicked his ass, he doesn't seem as hungover as Theo.

"What's for breakfast?" Finn says, his voice husky, probably from drinking himself into the grave, and shoves a hand through his morning hair. He's hungover and he *still* looks flawless. I'm starting to think the only way I'll survive this summer is if I throw a paper bag over this boy's head.

"Too late, bro. I got half her omelet," Theo brags, and I suppress a smile.

Finn stares me dead in the eyes. "Damn... Guess I'll have to find something else to eat."

I feel my throat tighten, memories of the night in the library flashing in my mind.

"You want to know what I'm thinking about? I'm thinking about the thousand times I've wanted to back you into a corner and eat that pussy until you were soaking my whole fucking face."

Every nerve ending in my body spurring to life, I break the eye contact and drive the fork into my mouth.

Did he do that on purpose?

Is he even aware of the reference?

Dia, you're overthinking it.

"Man, you look like a bag of dicks," Finn comments on Theo's appearance, and I stop paying attention, minding my business.

Until…

Finn makes his way over to us and leans against the kitchen island as he talks to his buddy. That's when I see the black stones around his wrist.

Is he wearing my bracelet?

He is.

He's wearing my fucking bracelet.

I don't have the guts to interrupt their conversation, so I keep the gazillion questions in my head on a leash and go rinse off my plate when I'm done. Theo follows suit, putting his dish away.

"Where are you going?" Finn asks when Theo ambles to the back door.

"To try and catch up on twenty hours of sleep. *Cheerio.*" Theo lifts his hand to his forehead in a salute and steps outside.

I see him make a beeline for the hammock. The words slip out of my mouth the second Theo's out of range.

"You're wearing my bracelet."

Finn whisks his head to look at me.

"Good eye," he mocks and makes his way to the fridge.

"Why?" I confront him.

He went apeshit on me for making the stupid thing, and now he's wearing it?

"Why not?" He dodges my question, grabbing a water bottle from the fridge door and uncapping it.

"I thought that was gone?"

I distinctively remember not being able to find the bracelet when I attempted to look for it in the hallway after he threw it away. I assumed the maid had tossed it.

He shrugs. "Yeah, well, you also thought taking this job was a good idea, didn't you?"

Wow.

I thought maybe we could put the rivalry behind us after our therapy session in the library, but clearly, that was wishful thinking. My face must give away how weird I find his change of heart about the bracelet because he lets out a quiet laugh.

"What?" He sticks his hands up. "It brings out my eyes!"

I have to force myself not to laugh.

A text pops up on my phone on the kitchen counter, and I reach for it.

Aveena: What time are we meeting tonight? My sister has a music thing, so I can't make it before six.

Vee and I have this habit of eating at my dad's restaurant every year for her birthday. That's right, today is her *birthday*, and she's still stuck driving her superstar sister around like a modern-world Cinderella.

"By the way, I'm going out tonight." I change the subject. "I already asked your dad, and he said it was fine, but I thought I'd let you know."

Finn steers the water bottle to his mouth for a sip and pauses, looking at me in utter silence.

"Why?" He couldn't be *more* blunt if he tried.

"Why what?"

"Why are you going out?" he interrogates me.

"Why not?" I give him the same answer he gave me a moment ago, and he flashes a heart-melting smirk at the irony.

"Can I trust you not to burn the house down while I'm gone?" I'm only half-joking.

"No promises." He shrugs. "I kind of like the thought of my dad being forced back into town."

"And why is that?"

His smirk expands in size. "Because then we wouldn't need you anymore. *Duh.*"

"That shower was amazing. You're all out of towels in the upstairs bathroom, by the way." A female giggles down the hallway.

It only takes a second…

But it's enough for every foolish hope of a "changed Finn" to be drained out of my system.

He brought the girl from the party home.

Typical.

"Shit, hide me," Finn mouths.

Even if I wanted to—which I don't—I couldn't.

Mystery Girl is bursting through the door a heartbeat later, her manicured hand clutching a towel as she pats her bleach-blonde hair dry. I instantly place her as Louise "Lou" Bennett, base in the cheer squad and *exactly* the kind of girl I'd picture Finn Richards ending up with.

These two together would just make sense—basketball jock meets cheerleader princess, *you know how it goes*—but it doesn't stop the turmoil in my stomach when I drink in every inch of her.

She's gorgeous and slim, standing at around five-foot-seven. She's wearing ripped denim shorts and a tie-dye crop top that accentuates her lean abdomen muscles and belly button piercing.

I must've said *one* word to this girl since moving to Silver Springs my freshman year, and I'm pretty sure it was "sorry" when we made eye contact on orientation day. Yes, as in I *apologized* for accidentally making eye contact with her.

It's the look she gave me.

Like I should pay a fine for daring to be in her line of vision.

Finn doesn't seem particularly pleased by her presence. Completely clueless, Louise drops her towel on the kitchen table and hurries over to Finn, a pearly white smile on her face.

"Hey, good-looking."

Cringe.

Finn doesn't say a word, but it doesn't seem to throw her off one bit because she laces her arms around his neck, mashes her breasts with his pecs, and slams her mouth over his.

He doesn't kiss her back at first, but then…

He does.

I watch as his lips move slowly with hers, the way she moans against the filthy, tempting mouth that whispered dirty things to me in the library just three days ago. For a second, I wonder if he said the same things to her last night. What they did, how they did it, where they did it.

"I thought you left." Finn pushes her off a moment later.

"Well, I obviously didn't." She goes from horny to offended in a split second. "Why? Did you want me to?"

Finn starts to answer, only stopping himself to shoot me a glance that clearly means *why are you still here?*

I rise off the stool. "Let me grab my coffee, then I'll be out of your hair."

My intervention earns me one of Louise's extra-nasty looks, as if she *just* noticed that I was here. I'm picking up my filled mug from under the coffee machine when her voice reaches my ears.

"And you are?" she asks.

I pivot slowly, wondering why she even cares.

"Dia?" It comes out as a question, as though I'm not sure of my own name.

Then her face drops.

I glance at my housemate, whose fists are clenched so tight his knuckles are white.

"Is something wrong?" I question.

"I thought I'd imagined it," Louise whispers to herself.

"What do you mean?" I ask.

"Get the fuck out," Finn growls at me before Louise can clear things up, and I look at him like he's on some serious crack but comply nonetheless.

I slide the patio door open, and Lexie leaps off her dog bed to follow me. We step out onto the patio, but seconds before I close the door, I hear Louise say, "*Does she know?*"

What is that all about?

Do I know *what*?

Questions spinning in my head, I pad to the patio set with Lexie, never taking my eyes off Finn and his conquest through the kitchen's large windows.

I can't hear what they're saying anymore, and *damn* do I wish I had super hearing right now. I plop down on the L-shaped patio sectional, Lex hopping next to me, and watch as Louise flings her arms around and yells at Finn.

"Five bucks says she slaps him." Theo's voice startles me, and I yelp, twisting my neck to see him lying in the hammock behind me—I forgot he was napping out here.

"Jesus, Theo." I bring my hand to my racing heart.

"I'm sorry, did I interrupt your creeping?" Theo snorts, and embarrassment taints my skin.

Busted.

"What do you think they're saying?" I ask, and Theo sits up in the hammock for a better view.

"Ew, Finn, I can't believe you used a dirty sock when we ran out of condoms," Theo says in a high-pitched voice to imitate Louise's, and a laugh rips from my throat.

"Would you prefer I use aluminum foil next time?" I reply in a strained, deep voice to imitate Finn. Ironically, our timing is spot on, and we snicker like kindergarteners.

It occurs to me, as I watch the scene unfold, that just a few days ago, Finn was playing with Lexie in this very yard, lying with her in the sun, treating her like his whole damn universe.

And now?

He's stamping on a cheerleader's heart.

"How in the fuck do you go from rolling in the grass with your dog to kicking a girl to the curb?" I wonder aloud, and Theo sags back into the hammock with a breathy laugh.

"Yeah, well, that's Finn Richards for you. Only fucking thing he loves in this world is his dog. Oh, and Remy."

My breath gets trapped in my lungs.

"R-Remy?" My voice cracks, and I clear my throat. "Who's that?"

A girl?

A boy?

Theo snorts. "What do you think? *His car*, of course."

Ah.

"Why'd he name his car Remy?"

"I think Remy is a friend of his. Not sure who. Whoever it is must be important, though." Theo shrugs, lifting his hand to his forehead to block the sun.

"And Lexie? What's the story there?"

"His mom gave her to him as a gift when he was a kid. Around the same time she gave him that chain he always wears...You know, before she..." Theo pauses, the term making him uneasy.

"Drowned?" I complete.

"Yeah, that."

So, Lexie's the only living reminder he has of his mother?

Not to mention she made the matching chains he and Xavier Emery have worn as far as I can remember?

"Does he... ever talk about it?" I question.

"Nah, but who would? His mom's body is rotting at the bottom of a lake, and he thinks it's his fault. Not exactly small-talk material."

"Why would it be his fault?" I push my luck.

Theo opens his mouth to reply but closes it again almost

immediately, staring at the fight that's gotten *way* worse since we last checked. Louise is in tears now, smacking her palms onto Finn's hard chest to push him.

Theo and I exchange glances.

"Oh, it's bad," I state. "Really bad."

"Here comes the slap." Theo guides his fist to his mouth as if to brace himself. "Three, two, one—"

As though she was waiting for Theo's cue, Louise takes a swing and strikes Finn across the face. Finn takes it like a champ, keeping whatever pain he's feeling locked up tight and staring at her until she storms off.

"*Ouch*," Theo comments.

"Meh. He had it coming."

Part of me feels bad for poor Louise. The girl might not be a ray of sunshine, but no one deserves to have their feelings smashed into a thousand pieces. Finn marches out onto the patio the next minute, halting our gossiping in its tracks.

"Damn, dude, what'd you say to her?" Theo calls him out.

Finn pads all the way to the hammock and gestures for Theo to move with his chin. Theo arches an eyebrow but doesn't budge, which results in Finn sitting on top of his buddy without a care.

Theo groans as Finn's elbow plows straight into his abdomen. "Not sure you're aware, Richards, but you're no fucking lightweight."

"No shit." Finn makes it clear he's here to stay, and Theo

starts trying to push him off. They're wrestling like kids before I know it, and I can't help the smile forming on my lips.

Out of breath from laughing, Theo caves, hoisting himself off the hammock and flipping Finn off. Theo plops down on the sectional with me, and Finn lies back into the hammock, propping one of his arms under his head.

"I asked you a question, fuckface," Theo reminds him. "What'd you say to her?"

"I told her what she already knows." Finn shrugs, eyes fixated on the clear sky above his head. "That breakfast is a no-no, and I don't want her ass around unless it's sitting on my face."

My stomach drops.

I sip on my coffee that's growing colder by the second and cast a glance in his direction. I realize, when I see how unapologetic he is about what he just put Louise through, that I needed this reminder.

I needed him to bang some cheerleader after making me believe he had a heart somewhere in that ice cage…

Finn Richards isn't capable of change.

And he never will be.

Eight

Diamond

"What can I get for you ladies?" A masculine but soft voice wedges its way in the middle of our conversation, causing me and Aveena to look up at my dad's employee.

Parker Haynes stands by our table, flaunting his Colgate-commercial smile and the dimples I spent most of freshman year obsessing about.

Aveena shoots me a suggestive side-look before ordering the meal she *always* gets on her birthday. She likes to remind me every chance she gets of my big, fat embarrassing crush on one of my dad's waiters.

I used to think I'd marry this kid.

Swore on my life Parker would eventually notice me and we'd roll off into the sunset together. It was a no-brainer. Parker's sweet, handsome—in a golden-boy type of way—has the shiniest curls I've ever seen, and most importantly, he knew I existed. Granted, I could hardly see him ignoring his boss's daughter and coworker.

If it wasn't for me scoring my first gig as a dog sitter and quitting my job at the restaurant, I'd probably *still* be fantasizing about what our children would look like.

To my surprise, when I give Parker my order and peer into those blue eyes with specks of gold, I feel *nothing*. No butterflies, no heat rushing to my cheeks, not a sliver of attraction.

Parker would never be the kind of guy to back me up against a wall and describe the thousand ways he wants to get me off. He'd never stand in an open window and risk his life just for a "breath of fresh air."

He's not like Finn.

Not that Finn Richards is what I want in a man.

Fuck no.

You hear that, me?

I *don't* want him.

Now, stop giving me dirty thoughts about him grabbing my throat and kissing me until my lips bruise.

"Awesome," Parker says once we're done ordering. "Be back with your drinks." He leaves us with a charming smile I'm sure earns him plenty of tips.

I spot my sister speed walking through the restaurant as soon as he leaves. Dark circles sit under her eyes as she edges her way through the crowd. She's most likely running late for her shift.

Again.

Catalina's been slacking on the job lately. Between her new

relationship with her ex's best friend, her full-time job at my dad's restaurant, and her studies, she's walking, talking proof that you can seem physically fine and be a complete mess inside.

In her defense, we've all been there.

And by we, I mean *all* of my siblings.

We've all worked at my dad's restaurant at least once—well, except for Charlie, but his time will come. We've all turned up late before, broken a bunch of plates, and gotten an earful from my dad, who does *not* give his kids special treatment.

"Shit." Aveena's voice rips me back to reality, and I glance at my best friend from across the booth. She's got her eyes fixed to her phone, a worried scowl slapped on her face.

"Something wrong?" I question, and Vee drops her phone on the table.

"Ashley needs me to get some herbal tea for her voice. She's got a performance tomorrow."

Oh hell no.

"And it couldn't wait until after your birthday?"

"My mom says it's urgent," Aveena explains.

"Nope, not happening. Give me that." I pluck her phone from the table and turn it off.

"Dia…" Vee releases a sigh, but it doesn't sound genuine. She sounds like deep down, she's relieved, damn near *happy* about my intervention.

"They can manage without you for one night," I argue. "Look, your phone is going in my pocket for the rest of the evening, and you can have it back when we leave, deal?"

Vee sinks her teeth into the inside of her cheek, considering her options. I can tell she's so used to playing errand girl for her sister that leaving her on "Read" feels unnatural.

Aveena hit Pause on every aspect of her life after her father passed when she was nine, from going to parties and dating to experiencing even the most *mundane* things in a teenager's life.

I keep clinging to the hope that she'll find someone to put her first one day. Someone to remind her to chase her *own* dreams. Hopefully, before we leave for college and she turns into a sex-deprived cat lady.

"Deal," Aveena has no choice but to say when I squeeze her phone into my back pocket.

I must wish her a happy birthday a hundred times that night.

We talk, eat, gossip, and laugh as the restaurant gradually empties. I'm also careful not to mention Finn wanting to eat me out on the library rug.

We eventually migrate to the bar to keep chatting while the staff cleans up. Gaten's, being the only restaurant in Silver Springs with a bar section, closes at around two every night, and as long as we don't try to drink, my dad doesn't mind if we stick around until closing.

The restaurant is deserted with the exception of the staff and us by the time we take a look around. The clock reads 1:49, and the exhaustion is starting to creep in.

I rub my eyes. "I'm going to call it a night."

My phone chimes in my jeans, reminding me that I still have Aveena's phone in my pocket. I give it back to her before checking my screen.

I have two text messages.

From Theo.

I gave him my number in case of an emergency after I found Finn in the library that night, but I didn't think he'd actually use it. My pulse climbing, I unlock my phone and feel my throat close up.

Theo: You need to come home.

Theo: NOW.

* * *

"Just drop me off here. I'll walk," I assure Aveena when we turn onto the Richardses' street twenty minutes later.

I've *never* seen my best friend this nervous before. She hasn't said a word since we left the restaurant, gnawing on her bottom lip the way she does whenever anxiety takes a toll on her.

And the worst part?

It's my fault.

As soon as Vee turned her phone back on, she realized her mom had been calling her for hours. And from the look on her face as she skimmed through her texts, she's in for quite the welcome when she gets home.

Turns out her daughter celebrating her *birthday* wasn't a good enough reason for Mrs. Harper to give her the night off.

"You sure?" Aveena worries, but she's already slowing down to drop me off a block away from the house. Her mom made it clear she wants her home now.

"I'm sure." I unbuckle my seat belt and open my arms to give her a hug. "Happy birthday, Vee," I tell her again and climb out of her car.

She offers me a weak smile through the window and drives off into the night. Pulling my phone out of my pocket, I relive the absolute dread of reading Theo's texts and set off toward the house.

The closer I get, the bigger the pit in my throat becomes.

I eventually see the metal gate to the mansion wide open for anyone to walk through and know…

Something is wrong.

Very wrong.

Mr. Richards was careful with his words when I landed the job. The gate is to remain closed at *all times*, no exception. It wouldn't be opened unless people needed to come in and out as they please.

My heart lurches up my throat as I pick up the pace.

What if Finn really set the house on fire?

That's when I hear them.

The music.

The bass.

The *voices*.

The apocalyptic scenarios in my head go up in smoke, and I realize that even if Finn didn't set the house on fire, it's still going to be destroyed before the night is over.

Finally, I reach the top of the driveway and curse myself for thinking I could ever trust Finn Richards.

The bastard threw a party.

And I don't mean a small gathering with a few friends.

I mean the *mother* of all parties.

There are cars everywhere on the property. They're damn near piling up in the driveway, and there isn't an inch of available space on the front lawn.

The same goes for drunk people, most of whom are stumbling in and out of the house with a drink in hand, searching for somewhere to barf. Red cups and all sorts of trash litter the yard, and the music is so loud I wouldn't be surprised if I went to bed deaf tonight.

What.

In.

The.

Fuck.

My thoughts spinning out of control, I select Theo's name in my messages and text him back.

Dia: Just got home. What the fuck is going on?

I *know* what is going on, but I still ask him, hoping he can help me make sense of this shitshow. How did Finn get so many people to show up?

Also, who the *hell* are all these people?

I don't recognize most of the guests outside, although I do spot Lacey Mattson, one of Brielle's cheerleader friends, flirting with some guy by the front door.

An older guy.

Much older.

The dude has to be over twenty-two. Why are college students showing up to a high school party? The questions hogging my mind vanish when it hits me.

Lexie.

Oh my God.

She hates loud noises. She must be scared to death somewhere. That's all it takes for me to storm inside the packed house in search of her. If I thought the outside of the house was bad, I wasn't ready for the clusterfuck that's the first floor.

There's glass everywhere in the entryway, probably from some wasted loser dropping his beer, and trash covers every flat surface in the living room.

People are dancing, making out, taking shots on the kitchen island. I can't see Finn anywhere, but I'm pretty sure if I *did* see him, he wouldn't get out alive.

I'm tearing through the crowd toward the staircase in no

time, pushing drunk idiots out of my way. I reach the second floor and make an instant beeline for my room to see if she's in there.

Two guys pass me in the hall as I close in on my bedroom.

They're laughing, both holding trash bags in their hands. We make eye contact for a split second, and the taller one smirks, but I'm so focused on getting to Lexie that I only realize how sketch the whole thing is when the boys disappear down the stairs.

I stop dead in my tracks, replaying what just happened on a loop until it all becomes clear. My room is at the complete end of the hallway. The only way they would've been walking in the opposite direction from me was if…

That's where they were coming from.

I can't see my feet touching the ground as I bolt down the hall and swing the door to my bedroom open.

As I expected, everything is wrecked…

My clothes are scattered over the floor, my luggage emptied out all over my bed, but it's the opened drawers to my bedside table that send me spiraling.

I'm on my knees in front of my nightstand in the blink of an eye, digging through the drawers with a painful throat and tears burning my eyelids.

"No." My voice breaks in a thousand fragments. "*No, no, no.*"

I search and search, but the box I left my electronics in is gone. I figured I'd be stupid to leave my expensive Kindle e-reader and AirPods out in the open after Finn's assault on my belongings my first week here. So, I threw everything in a locked box and hid it in my nightstand.

And in it…

Was my Radiohead T-shirt.

The one thing I truly value.

My birth mother's shirt.

It's… gone.

I want to scream, bulldoze through what is left of my room, burn the house to the ground, but all I can do is just sit there in silence with my mouth open and tears coursing down my face.

In that moment, I'm faced with a choice: scour the house in the hope that I can find the two dickheads that stole my shit before they're never seen again or go find Lexie and get her the hell out of here.

The choice is easy.

My heart aching with every miserable beat, I focus all of my might into delaying my breakdown and dash out of my room. I swing open every door I see and call Lexie's name, not even blinking when I catch Axel Fletcher, a guy I know from school, and some girl fucking doggy-style on Finn's bed.

Good. Finn deserves it.

A sob escapes me when I finally find her.

Lexie's huddled up in a corner of the library, alone in the dark. Her food and water bowls were dumped next to her, along with a toy she doesn't even like.

"Lex?" I croak. "Lexie, baby, it's me."

She doesn't come to me, her whole body trembling as she stares at me in utter terror.

"Oh my God, Lexie, I'm so sorry," I whisper, running to her and dropping by her side.

I instantly feel the puddle beneath me.

The floor is wet.

Shit, did she…

She peed herself.

She was so scared that she fucking peed herself.

Yep, he's dead.

Finn Richards is dying tonight.

My fingers are trembling as I reach out to pet her. I hesitate, but she seems to notice because she fills the gap between us and rubs her cheek against my palm. I must apologize five more times before I make the decision to call my brother.

It's past 2:00 a.m., but he picks up right away.

"Dia?" His voice is rough from being woken up, but he doesn't sound annoyed. He sounds worried. "You okay?"

I didn't know how broken I really was until I try to speak between sobs.

"Can you… Can you come pick me up? *Please*?"

The line goes quiet for a second.

"I'm on my way."

***

Jesse: I'm here.

I read my brother's text and pick up the bag chock-full with Lexie's stuff.

She's coming home with me tonight. My little brother is at my grandparents', and my dads are coming back from a romantic getaway tomorrow, so it's not like they have anything to say on the matter.

And even if they did, I wouldn't care.

I'm not leaving her here. I'll just have to be careful to take Lexie straight to my room to avoid triggering my dad's allergies.

"Come on, baby. We're going home." I have to practically carry her out of the library because she refuses to move. In a hurry, I attach her leash to her collar and brave the shitstorm waiting for us outside.

I keep my hand on the top of her head as we squeeze our way through the crowd and pet her for reassurance. Heads turn as we walk, but I don't give a rat's ass, determined to reach my brother's car.

I feel like I can breathe again when I march out of the house and spot my brother's clunker in the driveway. He's sitting inside, the engine running. He immediately climbs out at the sight of me, and I lead Lexie to the vehicle.

"What did he do?" Jesse's eyes are burning with hatred.

"Not now," I choke out and gesture for him to let Lexie into the back seat. "Open the door."

He looks at me with question marks in his eyes.

"She's coming home with us," I elaborate.

He doesn't argue. Jesse's barely let Lexie hop onto his back seat before Finn's voice cuts through the night.

"Lexie?" He has the *audacity* to sound worried. "What the fuck is happening? Where are you taking her?"

He left his nearly ten-year-old dog alone in the dark without so much as a blanket while he's off getting shitfaced, and he thinks I'm going to leave her behind?

He's an even bigger moron than I thought.

I hear footsteps rushing in our direction and spin on my axis to see Finn departing from a bunch of guys I don't recognize. They're leaning against the hood of a car, smoking blunts and drinking, wrapped up in smoke so thick I don't understand how they're still breathing.

My gaze clings to one of the guys.

I recognize him from the family pictures hung all over the house.

Finn's brother. *Brody, I think?*

I've never met him before—Mr. Richards said he rarely makes it back home from Duke University—but his presence explains why so many older people showed up to a small-town party.

The college guys are staring at us, witnessing the scene from a distance. From the moment I look at Finn, I feel my heart being ripped out of my chest all over again.

He took her from me.

My birth mother.

The only thing I had left.

How could he?

"You're fucking crazy if you think you're taking her," Finn declares as he advances toward me.

Click.

My switch has been flipped.

And there's no going back.

"They took it!" I shout at the top of my lungs, putting my whole chest into it, and Finn stops dead, shock clear in his gaze. I can tell he's confused, but those deep, tortured hazel eyes don't do shit for me.

"My mother's shirt." My anger dies on my tongue, my throat aching like a bitch. "*They stole it.*"

Then I start crying.

Full-on crying in front of him.

And I don't even care.

"Because you couldn't be responsible for one night. It's gone. The only thing I had of hers. Because *you* couldn't be considerate of anyone but your goddamn self for one fucking second." I hammer his shoulder with strong blows, and he stumbles backward.

"And Lexie? I found her terrified in a corner of the library, bathing in her own pee, so yes, I'm taking her. And no, I don't give a shit what you have to say."

His jaw goes slack at my announcement, but I don't spare him another glance, turning on my heels and heading for Jesse's car. I think surely the worst is behind me… until another deep voice slices through the deafening music.

"Damn, bro, you were right. Girl's got spunk."

You have got *to be kidding me.*

I swivel to see Finn's brother, Brody, pushing off the hood of the car to meet us.

"Although I have to disagree with you on her ass. She's kind of flat."

Click. The switch just flipped.

Except this time, it's not mine.

"The fuck did you just say to my sister?" Jesse nudges me behind him.

Brody stops near Finn and laces his arm around his brother's neck. "Jesse, hey. Been a while, man."

Jesse clenches his jaw, staring daggers into Brody's skull. I knew these two didn't part on good terms, but I didn't think it was *that* bad. Eyes as dark as the sky, Finn untangles Brody's arm from his shoulder.

"Don't fucking start, Brody," Finn warns.

"What? Just being honest." Brody pauses. "Shit, Jesse, my bad. I forgot you don't know what *honest* means."

Wait, what?

Struck dumb, I peek at Jesse to find his jaw locked tight and a rage I've never seen on him clouding his features.

"What is that supposed to mean?" I question, waiting for my brother to deny Brody's claims.

"Why don't you ask your brother?" Brody shoots Jesse a cruel glare that reeks of blackmail.

I get the feeling that he knows something Jesse didn't tell anyone. Is that why they stopped being friends?

"Brody, I'm not fucking kidding," Finn repeats, and his brother takes the hint.

"All right, all right. Relax." Brody sticks his hands up and turns away, only to give me a parting glance over his shoulder. "It was nice meeting you, Dia. Maybe do some squats. You know, for your... *problem.*"

I have to hold Jesse back from smashing Brody's face against his windshield. People have started to amass outside, drawn to the chaos. I recognize Theo in the crowd.

"Jesse, let's go. Please." I tug on my brother's clothes. "Get me out of here." Jesse doesn't listen until my third plea, glaring at Brody from afar.

At last, I manage to drag him to the car. I glance into the rearview mirror as we drive off and discern Finn's silhouette standing completely still in the middle of the driveway, watching us leave. Sneaking a peek at Lexie in the back seat, I feel the weight of the world lifting off my shoulders at the thought of waking up in my own bed in the morning. There isn't a doubt in my mind. Tomorrow, I'm quitting.

Nine

Diamond

I've never been afraid of making phone calls.

While most kids my age are embarrassed to make dentist appointments by themselves, it never occurred to me to pawn it off on my dads. I didn't understand how one tiny conversation could possibly make someone *this* nervous.

Until I had to quit my job in a ten-second voicemail…

Sitting on my front porch's squeaky swing with Lexie, I fidget with my phone, trying to drum up the perfect resignation speech. I've been getting Mr. Richards's voicemail all morning, but I couldn't bring myself to leave a message.

Lexie hasn't left my side since we stepped foot inside my house last night. She was nervous—how could she not be in a new environment—but I can tell by the way she clings to me for dear life that she trusts me to protect her.

She knows I'd never do anything to hurt her.

I can't help thinking that if I pull the plug on this job, I'll be betraying that trust.

Abandoning her.

As if she can feel my inner conflict, Lexie rests her chin on my shoulder and gives my cheek a big, wet lick. A small laugh slips from my lips, and I wrap my arm around her for a long side hug.

She braces her chin on my thigh as soon as I let go, and I scratch her behind her ears, my throat painfully tight.

"God, I can't," I whisper. "I can't leave you."

You'd think she understood me by how fast she angles her head to look at me, her adorable brown eyes pulling at my heartstrings.

If last night is anything to go by, Finn can't be trusted to take care of his dog, and I can't imagine myself dropping Lexie back at the house and returning to my life as though nothing ever happened.

My phone lights up with an incoming call.

From Mr. Richards.

I stare at my screen long and hard, petting Lexie with one hand and gripping my phone until my joints ache with the other.

It feels like a test.

One I wish I didn't have to pass.

But my mind is made up.

So, I let it ring.

* * *

"You're making a mistake." My brother *tsks* as he races up Finn's driveway, his accusing voice plaguing me with doubt. He's spent the entire drive here telling me how wrong I am for coming back.

That I should run while I still have the chance.

He also hasn't deigned to answer *one* of my questions about his suspicious altercation with Finn's brother last night. All he said was that Brody is a pro at stirring shit, and none of it was true. I know better than to just take his word for it, but I figured I'd stay out of this one.

"Why would you even *want* to come back here anyw—" Jesse's voice wanders off when we reach the top of the driveway.

Confused, I glance at my brother, then in the direction of the mansion to see what he's looking at.

I connect the dots immediately.

The lot is empty, except for Theo's red car, and the front lawn that was a sea of trash just hours ago is now perfectly clean. Jesse and I scan the property for any sign of the raging party that took place in this very spot but come up empty.

"What the…" Jesse speaks my mind.

"He must've hired a cleaning team," I deduce.

"It's eight in the morning," he counters.

I shrug. "Guess the rich don't care about the rules."

Silence descends over the car as Jesse continues his careful analyzing of Finn's front lawn.

"Anyway, thank you for… you know, *everything*. I should be

all right from here." I reach for the car handle, but before I open the door, Jesse extends his arm to stop me.

"Dia, wait."

I lock gazes with my brother and see worry gleaming in his almond eyes.

He's scared for me.

Genuinely scared.

Or… is he scared for *himself?*

Scared that I'll find out something I shouldn't if I stay?

"You asked me here for a reason last night. Don't forget that."

He's right.

I called him because I was emotional and angry and *heartbroken* about losing my birth mom's shirt, but none of that matters as much as Lexie's safety. I will not abandon her. Even if it means living with a monster for a little while longer.

"I won't, I promise," I reassure him. "Thanks, again."

With that said, I climb out of his car, swing Lexie's door open, and book it to the house to assess the damage inside. I can't see much of the house through the glass door due to the sunrays reflecting off it.

What's waiting on the other side?

Drunk people on the floor?

Broken bottles everywhere?

Ruined furniture?

There's only one way to find out.

"Here goes nothing." I push the door open.

The first thing I notice is the silence.

The house is dead quiet, sounding almost deserted. I step into the entryway that was paved with glass and booze just last night and swallow a gasp.

It's clean.

Just like the driveway.

Just like the front yard.

If I didn't know any better, I'd wonder if there was even a party at all. I unhook Lexie's leash and smile as she takes off running down the hallway.

I trail after her, venturing farther into the house and examining the kitchen. There isn't a single red cup in sight and not even *one* cheerleader passed out in her own vomit.

The hardwood floors look like they were mopped. In fact, the whole house is spotless. Did Finn hire an overnight cleaning crew? Lexie barking in the living room catches my attention.

She stops by the sectional couch, and I hear her lick something. Then that "something" groans, and I realize I'm not the only one here. Ready to kick out the rando on the couch, I rush to the living room and find Theo sleeping.

He's shirtless, lying on his stomach without a blanket, his brawny back and tight muscles on display. His dark hair cascades in front of his green eyes, his cheek mashed against the cushion.

"Lexie, stop," Theo groans, half-asleep.

A few seconds tick by.

Then realization seems to dawn over him because his eyes snap open.

"Wait, Lexie?"

Theo flips on his back, then sits up straight. *Ah*. Finn must've told him I took her back to my place, which explains why he's surprised that she's home.

"Dia, you're… here," he says when he sees me. "I didn't think you were coming back."

I didn't think I was coming back either.

"Why didn't you answer your phone?" I skip the small talk. "You could've told me Lex was alon—"

"No, I couldn't," he cuts in. "I can't answer my phone without a phone."

I purse my lips. "What happened?"

"Fuck if I know. I put it down for a second, then it was gone."

So, he got robbed, too.

I bet it was the same jackasses that stole my mom's shirt.

My anger dwindles. "Still, you could've waited for me to get home. I couldn't find you."

"I was… busy." He drags a hand through his coal-black hair, a small smirk stretching his lips.

"Translation, you were off fucking some girl."

"I warned you about the party, didn't I?" Rubbing his eyes, Theo plants his feet on the floor and sits with his legs parted, elbows braced on his knees. "Doesn't that count for something?"

I'm quick to understand that's the closest thing to an apology I'm going to get from this guy. Releasing a sigh, I sit on the couch's armrest.

"You should've told me about Lexie in your first text," I scold as Theo pets the excited golden retriever next to him.

"I didn't know," he says, seemingly truthful. "No one did."

"Finn had to know," I counter.

"How could he? He's not the one who put her there."

Back up.

"He's not?" I don't buy it.

"Fuck no. Have you met the guy?" Theo snorts. "Brody fed him some BS about having dropped Lexie at the neighbor's house. The lady's a widow who's watched Lexie in the past."

Wait… Finn had nothing to do with it?

Well, technically, the only mistakes he made were trusting his brother and not bothering to check every room in his million-dollar mansion. Still, this might've been a good piece of information to have before I rained hell down on him.

No, Dia, he's still the reason your mom's shirt is gone.

It's his house. He *threw the party.*

"He would've called the cops on the party himself if he'd known about Lexie," Theo assures me. "Hell, he almost did."

"What does that mean?" I question.

"He kicked everyone out. Dude was telling the guests he'd call the cops if they didn't leave."

"I'm supposed to believe he kicked out the guests *he* invited? What kind of idiot do you take me for?"

"Actually, he didn't invite anyone," Theo corrects.

Oh, for fuck's sake, Theo, just let me hate him.

Let me convince myself that there is nothing good or redeemable about this guy.

"Then how did people know to show up?" The answer comes to me as soon as I finish speaking.

Brody.

Of course it's Brody.

I saw enough of him last night to believe he could pull something like this.

"You have Brody to thank for that," Theo confirms. "He and like seven of his college buddies showed up while we were out. Brody told Finn he'd hit up a few people to hang out while he was in town, but a 'few' people turned into thirty, then forty, and well… You get the gist."

I was so certain Finn was to blame. I didn't even consider for one second that he could be the fall guy.

"Thanks for all this." I gesture to the spotless house.

"I didn't clean it." Theo rises off the couch and stretches.

"Then who did?"

Theo's eyes connect with mine. "Who do you think?"

The fury and resentment wreaking havoc in my chest taper off in the snap of a finger.

"Finn started as soon as people cleared out. He didn't stop

until he was done."

This must've taken him all night.

"I don't know what you and your brother told him, but he was furious at Brody."

I recall Theo stumbling out of the house right as the argument was coming to an end.

"How'd you know he was my brother?"

Theo lets out a low scoff as he heads for the kitchen. "Finn told me. Not to mention your brother almost ripped Brody to pieces for talking shit about you. You two seem close."

"We are," I whisper.

I've always felt closer to Jesse than the rest of my siblings. Not surprising considering I knew Jesse before I even knew my dads. My parents claim Jesse was my absolute favorite as a child.

All that changed when puberty hit and Jesse started acting out. He went from protecting me from bullies to bullying me himself. He couldn't stand me for years—to be fair, I was the annoying little sister who followed him around. We may fight and bicker, but at the end of the day, we'd do anything for each other. I'm lucky to have such a great family.

I just wish I didn't wonder about my *other* family…

My parents strictly refuse to tell me anything about my biological parents. They told me my birth mother is dead but kept the talk about my dad to a minimum. Every time I ask about him, they either change the topic or dodge the question.

It isn't lost on me that Finn would set the world on fire for one more minute with his mom while my *own* dad could be living his life somewhere, just waiting to be found, and I'm not doing squat about it.

Is it that my bio dad didn't want to know about me? Or that he didn't know about me *period*? What if he has no idea he has a daughter out there? Granted, this is the only scenario that could justify his absence, but maybe…

It's one that's worth fighting for.

* * *

The time on the stove shows 2:25 a.m. when I drag my feet down to the kitchen for a glass of water. I haven't slept a wink, waiting for the sound of Finn's tires screeching against the driveway.

He's been MIA all day.

Theo says he hasn't heard a peep from him either.

My room faces the front yard, so I cracked a window open to make sure I'd hear him come home, only to end up lying awake, listening to my blinds chattering in the wind with Lexie snoring next to me.

I want to apologize to him.

Finn Richards might be an asshole sometimes—okay, *all the time*—but last night? He was merely collateral damage from his brother's selfishness. He apologized for lashing out at me once. The least I can do is return the favor.

The sounds of keys jingling, then being inserted into the lock startle me a minute later. I stiffen up at the thought of Finn bursting through the front door.

Except… there's no *bursting.*

It happens slowly.

I hear a groan. A low, gravelly "Shit" that's tainted with pain and the door closing with a thud. I don't move a muscle, waiting for him to reach the kitchen and see me, but it takes him a while and a few more groans to even cross the hallway.

Is he… limping?

Every hair on my body stands on end when he turns the corner and we come face-to-face.

Finn spots me leaning against the kitchen counter, gripping my water for dear life. My feet sink into the ground when we make eye contact.

Shock colors Finn's hazel eyes for a fragment of a second, his eyebrows lifting upward like he didn't expect to find me in his kitchen ever again.

And yet, he remains quiet.

I let out a small gasp when I get a better look at him.

He's bloody.

From the crease of his eyebrow to his cheek and bottom lip—*nothing's* been spared. A purplish wound colors the edge of his jaw, and the worst part? None of it even comes close to dimming his beauty.

Even with a ripped shirt that's covered in blood and dirt, he looks like a work of art.

I notice he has a gray duffel bag drooping from his shoulder but don't question it, too horrified by his bruises to think twice about it.

We just stand there, staring at each other across the kitchen. Then, without a word, he turns away, his pain rendered obvious by the strain in his moves, and disappears up the stairs.

I drop on my bed next to a sound-asleep Lexie shortly after. I stare at the ceiling for what feels like an eternity until I hear Finn's door creaking open down the hall.

The wooden floor squeaks as Finn pads down the hallway toward…

My room?

Wait, why is he coming toward my room?

I go from breathing quickly to not breathing at all, his footsteps proving me right when they halt in front of my bedroom. I can see the shadow of his feet through the crack beneath the door. He stays there for long seconds, like he's debating on his next move.

Finally, he knocks.

And walks away.

Okay?

I hear him returning to his bedroom and shutting the door again. I'm not sure what to make of it, but every nerve in my body is telling me to open that door. Creeping out of bed not to wake up Lexie, I slowly open the door.

But there's nothing there.

My gaze dips downward, and I squint to find the gray duffel bag Finn was carrying when he came in on the floor.

My mind racing at a thousand miles per hour, I drop to my knees, unzipping the bag. Right then, it all makes sense—the mysterious bruises on his skin, his disappearing act today, the blood on his clothes.

Inside the bag are three items I thought I'd never see again.

My Kindle e-reader.

My AirPods.

And my Radiohead T-shirt.

Ten

Diamond

"Lexie, *no*!"

I know my yelling was pointless from the moment the pool swallows the golden retriever whole. I should've seen this one coming. *Of course* our spontaneous game of fetch would result in Lexie jumping headfirst into the water.

The wind knocked the Frisbee we've been playing with straight into the pool, and Lexie didn't think twice.

"Lex, what did you do?" I fake-scold, the laughter in my throat drowning out my lecture.

Lex paddles in my direction with the Frisbee in her mouth, quick to jump out of the pool and run to me with a wagging tail. Soaking wet, she drops the Frisbee at my feet, then shakes the water off her fur vigorously.

I shriek in between chuckles, not even flinching at the water flying all over me.

"Look at you." I fall to my knees to pet her. Lexie holds up her paw as if to show me she expects a treat, and I laugh even harder. We spent most of the morning out on the patio. I went for a quick swim, then played with Lexie to tire her out.

"Come here." I peck the top of her head, and she reciprocates the affectionate gesture by planting sloppy kisses all over my mouth.

"Let's get you dry for the vet." I scratch her under the chin and rise to my feet. "I'll be back with some towels."

She's got an appointment at the vet in an hour for a regular checkup, and I'd rather she didn't drag that wet-dog smell in with her.

Lexie barks as I amble to the glass door, following me, and I have to tell her to stay a few times so she doesn't flood the first floor. I don't make a habit of walking around in my bikini—the one time I did it, the guys looked at me like I had two heads—but the house was empty when I woke up, so I thought *screw it.*

The crazy part is, I was slightly bummed that Finn was nowhere to be found this morning. I wanted to talk to him. Thank him for getting back the only thing I have of my mom's.

I've just stepped out of the downstairs bathroom with two towels in my arms when I hear the front door slam. The sound of footsteps travels through the main floor, and anxiety claws at my stomach.

I take it back.

I *don't* want to talk to him.

Please let it be Theo.

I consider sneaking into the bathroom to avoid him, then remember that the clock is ticking, and the vet is in the next town over. I asked Vee to drive us, and she should be here any minute. To make it worse, I haven't even changed yet.

Be brave, Dia.

Clutching the towels in my arms a little tighter, I turn the corner and spot Finn texting in the kitchen. He's wearing a low-cut black gym tank, the curves of his biceps and veined forearms drawing my eye. The gaps under his arms give me a clear shot of his defined oblique muscles, and I swallow hard.

I can tell he just worked out by how sweaty he is.

For fuck's sake, he's *glistening* with sweat, and I still find him insanely attractive. He also has a gym bag strap draping down his shoulder and a water bottle in his other hand.

He notices me the next second, his eyes lifting from his phone and catching mine. We don't speak or acknowledge each other's presence, the same way we did in the kitchen last night.

Giving me uninterested vibes, he starts to look away, only to do a double take almost immediately.

Every inch of my skin tingles when he drinks me in.

I'm still wearing nothing but my bikini but find comfort in the towels in my arms. They're covering part of my body, shielding me from glances I can't translate.

Does he like what he sees?

Does he hate it?

Beats me.

"Hey," I manage to say.

I don't like this silence. I'd take him being an asshole to me over this awkward tension any day.

"Hey," he replies, his voice flat, and steers his focus back to his phone. Either I really pissed him off when I lost it at the party, or he simply couldn't care less about my existence.

I'm not sure why option two bothers me so much.

"Do you know when Theo's coming home tonight? I cooked a shit ton of food." I fish for conversation.

Without even sparing me a look, Finn drawls, "Theo won't be living with us anymore."

I'm stunned.

"Wait, what? Why not?"

It's not that I consider Theo a friend, but he was the closest thing I had to one in this house. Not to mention his absence implies I'm going to be alone with Finn for the rest of the summer, and I'm not even *close* to ready for that.

Finn shrugs. "He moved back home. Something about trying to patch things up with his folks."

"Oh." I give a small nod. "Okay."

No reply.

I turn to leave and go dry Lexie before Vee gets here, but I stop before I walk out onto the patio.

"I… I wanted to thank you," I confess.

It takes me a deep breath and inner pep talk to spin around and face him. My comment seems to have been enough to earn me his full attention because he's staring at me with an arched brow.

"For what?" he asks.

Slowly, I edge my way to the kitchen to meet him. I come to a slow stop in front of him and clear my throat.

"What you did for me, it… it meant a lot."

I'm overwhelmed with the urge to crawl under a rock when he downright laughs in my face.

"What's so funny?" The question comes out as defensive.

"You thinking I did it for you."

Ouch.

I wait for him to elaborate, but he takes his sweet time, guiding his water bottle to his lips and taking a sip. I watch as a drop of water drips down his jaw and throat.

"You're not the only one who got robbed that night." He places his water bottle down on the counter. "A guy from the team saw the losers that did it. He gave me an address, and I showed up to take back what they'd stolen. They kept it all in a bag, so I grabbed that and hauled ass out of there. I was getting my *own* stuff back, Gem." He pauses. "Yours just happened to be in there."

I don't know what I expected, but it wasn't that.

"Did you really think I'd get into a fight for you?"

I chew down on my bottom lip harder than intended, the metallic taste of blood trickling into my mouth.

I'm mad.

Embarrassed.

But mostly, I'm disappointed.

Why am I *so* disappointed to learn he's the heartless bastard everyone told me he was?

"Oh, don't pout." Finn crowds my space, stretching his arm to nudge a loose strand of my hair behind my ear. "You still got your stuff back in the end, didn't you?"

As much as I despise him in this moment, I hate that I *stopped* hating him even more. For a moment there, I thought I'd gotten through to him, but now?

I know without a shadow of a doubt…

The only way I'm going to survive this summer is by hating him as much as he hates me.

* * *

I'm cursed.

No other explanation.

You'd think I'd be used to this by now—being woken up in the middle of the night, only for something to go terribly wrong—but *nope*, I'm just as shocked as I was the night I found Finn standing in the library window.

Lexie barking is my first clue.

The sound of a key being inserted into the front lock is my second. Lying on the couch with widened eyes, I grip the blanket that's wrapped around me. What was I thinking, falling asleep on the couch?

I know it's not Finn.

He came home and went up to his room long before I put on a romantic comedy and passed out. Can't be Theo either. He showed up to gather the rest of his stuff around dinnertime.

Who else could have a key?

Brody, perhaps?

Lexie barks louder when the front door squeaks open, and two unknown voices pervade the entryway. Lexie's barking quickly evolves into growling.

"Fucking hell," a masculine voice huffs. "Get her to shut up."

Another deep voice, this one husky, cuts in. "Lexie, come here, girl."

The growling stops instantly.

I hear Lexie's paws rattling the wooden floors as she runs to the stranger without a second thought, and I understand…

There's no way that's a stranger.

She knows him.

She's licking his face, jumping on him—the whole shebang—as I lie there, stiff as a plank. They can't see me since the couch faces away from the kitchen, but I'm not taking any chances.

"I know, I know. I've been gone for a hot minute, huh?"

"Jesus, Emery, how do you do that? I can't pet her without her trying to bite my dick off," the other guy comments.

My brain short-circuits at the mention of his name.

Emery.

As in… Xavier Emery, Finn's best friend?

That's how Lexie knows him.

I thought he was away at basketball camp?

"And that would be a bad thing *because*?" Xavier heaves a bitter scoff, earning himself a "fuck you" from his companion.

They've barely taken a few steps into the kitchen before Mystery Guy asks, "Where did Finn say he was again?"

"Wine cellar. He's waiting for us," Xavier replies.

That's what this is about? Finn hitting up his friends to raid his dad's wine cellar in the middle of the night?

Why am I even surprised?

"Staircase is down the hall," Xavier instructs, and the footsteps gradually fade. I hear the door leading to the basement opening and shutting in the distance.

Then nothing.

That was a close one.

Lexie is back on the couch in an instant, prepared to doze off, but I can't seem to do the same. I must stare at the ceiling for over five minutes before making the terrible decision of following them.

I eye Lexie, who's snoring already, then lift off the couch. The floor is ice-cold to my bare feet as I tiptoe toward the staircase they just went down.

This is a bad idea.

A *very* bad idea.

But I still find myself at the basement door, my hand

hovering near the knob. My breath trapped in my throat, I slowly open the door, careful not to make a sound. I've only been in the basement once, but I remember how creaky the stairs are.

My heart races faster with every step I take down the staircase, a gust of fresh air engulfing my body as soon as my feet touch the ground.

It's frisky down there, and the crop top and leggings I fell asleep in aren't doing much to warm me up. *Turn around. You shouldn't be here*, a voice in my head warns, but I pay it no mind, sneaking to the wine cellar.

The door is open an inch, but it's more than enough for me to hear the conversation on the other side.

I catch the boys sitting on the floor of the wine cellar through the small gap. They're downing wine, laughing, passing a joint around. Freezing my tits off, I take cover in the corner behind the door to listen.

"Stop hogging the joint, Richards."

"You fucked Lou Bennett on my bed, Fletcher. I'll hog the joint if I want to," Finn retorts.

Only then am I able to identify the guy that came in with Xavier. His name is Axel Fletcher. He's a basketball player, an absolute pig with the ladies, and an overall crappy person. I saw him and some girl going at it on Finn's bed the night of the party.

That was Louise?

She slept with Axel in Finn's bed?

Just a few days after Finn turned her down?

Harsh.

"He's got you there, man." Xavier laughs.

"For fuck's sake, it's not like you were dating the girl," Axel argues. The irony of Finn having slept with his best friend's girl himself isn't lost on me. To think Xavier has no clue. Poor guy doesn't even have an inkling of what happened while he was away.

"I don't give a shit *who* you did it with, asshat. It's the where that's the problem." Finn makes it clear he couldn't care less about Lou.

Lou, who looked at me like I'd taken a dump in her bed the morning I told her my name. I still don't know why it triggered her so much.

"Look at it this way, your stupid-ass dog ambushed us when we came in. Call it even?" Axel snorts.

A long moment of silence ensues.

"Call my dog stupid one more time, Fletcher," Finn warns.

"Dude, relax, I was kidding." Axel blows out a nervous laugh. "It's just a fucking dog. *Jesus.*"

"What was that?" Finn snaps.

"Hey, assholes. I didn't come back from camp to drive your sorry asses to the hospital. Play nice," Xavier intervenes.

Something tells me this isn't the first time Xavier has had to play mediator.

"How long are you back in town for?" Axel changes the topic.

"Two days," Xavier replies. "I'm leaving tomorrow night."

"You met the caretaker of Casa Richards yet?" Axel's question takes me by surprise.

Shit, he's talking about me.

Maybe this was a mistake.

I don't think my ego can take any more hits. It's still recovering from Finn laughing in my face this morning.

"The house sitter, is it?" Xavier sounds like he doesn't care.

"Damn right. Sexy little thing, this one." Axel's throaty laugh sends a wave of disgust down my spine. "I saw her at the party, and you bet if she was living in *my* house, I'd be all over that ass. I can't believe you haven't hit that yet," he tells Finn.

Just walk away, Dia.

You don't need to hear this.

"Well, believe it," Finn drones.

"Seriously, man, are you blind or just playing for the other team?" Axel scorns.

Finn scoffs. "I'm straighter than the pole your mother dances on."

"*Then what*? Is she not your type? Help a brother out. If she's fair game, just say so."

Silence burdens the dark basement.

"So, is she?" Axel won't let it go.

"Is she what?" Finn hisses.

Axel fails to take the hint. "Your type?"

"Of course she's my fucking type. Have you seen the damn

girl? Now, fuck off," Finn snaps.

I tense up.

So… it wasn't all in my head?

The lingering looks, the snarky comments full of innuendo. He might hate me, but he's attracted to me, and the thought makes me feel ten percent less stupid for feeling the same way.

The conversation drifts to random topics until a phone chimes in the gloomy wine cellar.

"It's mine," Xavier informs his friends. I assume he's checking the message as he doesn't speak for a few seconds. Then he blurts, "Seriously, Richards?"

"What?" Finn questions.

"Did you really break into Ben Aster's house and beat him up for stealing a *shirt*?"

That's all it takes for my lungs to fail me.

Finn sneers. "I beat up his brother, too, but go on."

Is he talking about my shirt?

No, he can't be.

Xavier sighs. "You know the Asters shove shit into their pockets at parties. You never gave a damn before."

"Your point?" Finn drawls.

"Theo said he ran into them at Lacey's, and they're thinking of going to the police. This is no fucking joke, Finn. You're eighteen. You can forget about juvie if shit goes wrong. Now, it's straight to jail."

It's obvious that Xavier's the levelheaded guy here. The

golden boy who gives his all to basketball and his dreams while his best friend is off self-destructing and setting shit on fire.

"I have security footage of them leaving my house with three trash bags full of our shit. Let them go to the fucking cops," Finn counters.

"Sure, they stole from you. That doesn't give you the right to break into someone's house and beat them up. Who gives a shit about a *shirt?*"

Finn pauses for long seconds.

"It was an important shirt."

My palm flies to my mouth.

He lied to my face earlier.

All the things he said about getting his own stuff back were bullshit. But why? Why is he so desperate to keep me from seeing the good in him?

"Your dad's going to flip his shit if you get arrested again. What the hell were you thinking?" Xavier scolds.

"Are you my underwear?" Finn deadpans.

Xavier is taken aback by the question.

"Then I don't need you up my fucking ass."

That's when I know I've heard enough.

I rotate, about to walk away, and accidentally knock my knee against the plant behind me.

Fuck.

Fuck.

Fuck.

"What was that?" Xavier questions.

"Do you think the house sitter's up?" Axel guesses.

"Nah, that's probably just Lexie," Finn assures. "Don't worry about it."

Luckily, his friends buy it and resume their conversation. The pressure in my shoulders dissipates, my chest swelling up with relief. I stay there for over ten minutes while the boys talk, terrified to make another move.

"A'ight. I'm beat. You can let yourselves out," Finn says.

"Are you fucking serious right now? You called us all the way out here for ten minutes of smoking?" Axel objects. "I'm high as a fucking giraffe. What am I supposed to do? Go home and stare at the ceiling?"

"Fuck if I know. Go get yourself a hobby or something," Finn suggest.

Xavier scoffs. "Says the jackass who has none."

"I have hobbies," Finn disagrees.

"Jacking off to pictures of your house sitter isn't a hobby," Xavier fires back, and the three of them laugh.

I know he's kidding, but heat explodes in my stomach just thinking about it. Images flood my mind. I see Finn shirtless, lying in bed in the dark, his jaw clenched as he fists his—

"*Out.* Both of you." Finn snaps me out of it, and the boys oblige.

I stiffen up when they exit the wine cellar one by one. The soft creaking of the stairs fills my ears, along with Axel bitching about "not being able to see shit." Then the door at the top of the stairs closes.

There isn't a sound to be heard in the pitch-black basement.

My alarmingly fast heartbeat declines, and I release a deep breath of relief. Finn said he was tired, meaning he's probably off to bed. All that's left for me to do is sneak up to my bedroom and pretend this never happen—

"What the fuck?"

I'd recognize his gravelly voice anywhere.

No.

This is all in my head.

Finn can't be here.

He can't be right in front of me.

But he is.

He's standing a few steps away from me, the outline of his broad frame all I can see. Not that I need to see his expression to know he's about to rip me a new one.

"So, what? You're fucking spying on me now?" he snarls inches away from my face.

"What? N-No," I begin to say, but Finn interrupts me, smacking his palm over my mouth to shut me up. Next thing I know, he's captured my forearm and hauled me into the wine cellar.

I shriek when he traps me against one of the wine racks, his hard chest meshing so closely with mine that I can feel his body heat enveloping the skin my top doesn't cover.

The small window in the wine cellar emits just enough moonlight for me to distinguish his disarming hazel eyes. I understand when he points to the ceiling with his other hand—more precisely, to the floor above our heads—that he's waiting for something.

We stay in this position, his torso flush with mine, his palm over my mouth, until we hear the front door slam in the distance. That seems to be Finn's cue because he backs away, robbing me of a warmth I ache for instantly.

I'm quick to understand he was waiting for his buddies to leave before raining hell down on me.

How thoughtful.

"You have five seconds to explain yourself." He folds his tattooed arms over his chest.

"I… I heard voices and came down to check," I improvise.

An angry scoff leaves his throat.

He's not buying it, but he doesn't argue.

"How much did you hear?" he asks.

It's a simple question, but secrets and lies plague every word. I see it in his eyes. He's hoping I didn't hear about what he did to get my stuff back. Hoping to keep up the charade a little while longer.

"Everything," I admit.

His jaw goes slack for a moment.

"I should've let them catch you," he spits and walks off.

Wait, he *knew*?

He knew I was here this whole time?

No, that's not possible. He must've had a feeling I was here when I knocked my knee into that stupid plant.

If it wasn't for him telling the guys his dog was to blame, they might've caught me eavesdropping. And he definitely pretended to leave with his friends just so he could bust my ass.

Acting on impulse, I take a jab at him. "That was Xavier Emery, wasn't it?"

Finn stops dead, glaring at me over his shoulder.

"So what if it was?"

It sounds like a warning.

Like he's telling me to watch my fucking mouth.

"He has no idea what you did, does he?" I taunt, knowing damn well I'm only pouring gas onto the fire.

I can't help it.

This guy *infuriates* me.

I hate that I can't figure him out. That he's so far from a normal person my people skills are useless with him. Finn Richards doesn't lie to cover up his sins—like any of us would. He lies to cover up his good deeds.

And I *need* to understand why.

"Damn right, he doesn't." He swivels around to face me. "And it's going to stay that way."

"I could rat you out as soon as summer ends, you ever think about that?" I threaten.

He heaves a quiet scoff. "Yeah, but you won't."

"How do you know?" I yearn for a weakness of some sort. I'll take anything, I just want to see him flinch *once*. Finn takes a few menacing steps forward, and I'm the one who flinches.

"Because I know you, Gem. You talk a good game, but we both know you wouldn't do shit to actually hurt anyone."

It's true, but he can't know that.

"How did she know me?" I change the topic.

He frowns. "Who?"

"Louise. She looked at me like…" I pause. "Like I'd done something to her the other day. I told her my name, and her face changed. Why?"

"I told you not to ask questions you can't handle the answers to." He feeds me the same crap he did that night in the library.

"And I told you you have no *fucking* idea what I can handle." I stand my ground. "Answer me. How did she know me?"

"She didn't know you," he caves. "She knew your name."

Huh?

"Why would you tell her my name?"

He cracks a hint of a smile. "I didn't *tell* her anything."

"Then how did she—"

My heart does a full three-sixty when Finn fills the space between us and shoves my body against the wine rack again, this time with entirely different intentions.

Heat rushes to my cheeks, the sinking feeling in my stomach paralyzing me. This feels final. Like whatever escape route I had before just went up in flames.

Finn shocks me by grabbing a fistful of my hair and pulling—not hard enough for it to hurt, but hard enough to nudge my head forward. Then he positions himself near my earlobe, his hot breath tickling my skin, and whispers, "She knew your name because I fucking *moaned* it."

Pretty sure my soul leaves my body right then.

"You what?"

There's no way.

No way Finn really said that to me.

Did I imagine it?

The answer becomes clear when he pulls away.

"You heard me," Finn grits through his teeth. He sounds angry at himself. Like he's sick of fighting a war he's bound to lose. "You were the one in my fucking head while I was blowing inside another girl."

My jaw crashes to my feet.

"It was *your* perfect fucking mouth wrapped around my cock, *your* innocent eyes looking up at me. Because it's always you these days. It's. Always. Fucking. You." He stresses every word, staring me dead in the eyes before saying, "Is that what you wanted to hear?"

I'm floored.

No better word for it.

"You're disgusting." The lie makes my vocal cords ache.

"I asked you a question." Finn lets go of my hair, bracing his palm against the wine rack behind me and caging me in.

We're so close his lips would graze mine if I just nudged my head forward. He smells as good as the night he found me in his bed, and he's just as devastatingly beautiful, but there *is* one major difference.

He's not the only one I'm scared of anymore.

I'm scared of myself, too.

"I said, is that what you wanted to hear?" he urges, his gaze falling to my lips for a moment that pushes me dangerously close to the edge.

God, I want to kiss him.

I want to kiss him so bad.

What's wrong with me?

"It is, I can tell." Finn flashes a satisfied smirk, and my ego slams the brakes.

"How can you be so sure?"

His confidence doesn't waver one bit.

Then he finishes me off.

"Because you're parting your fucking legs for me."

I'm mortified when I glance down at my thighs.

He's right.

I *am* parting my legs for him. Branding myself as "open for business" without realizing it. I dare hope he'll spare me further humiliation, but, of course, it doesn't end there.

"And because, if I were to kiss the shit out of you right now… you wouldn't stop me."

I should run.

Why am I not running?

"You forget that I hate you."

He laughs a bitter laugh and whispers, "You forget that I can hear your breathing."

Kill. Me. Now.

Again, he's right.

He's got me all hot and bothered.

"You'd let me kiss you, Gem. And what's worse, *you'd like it.*"

I want to yank him to me and find out.

"You're batshit crazy if you think I wouldn't stop you."

"Really?" Finn mocks.

For a fragment of a second, time stands still.

Until Finn strips everything away with three little words.

"Then *stop me.*"

His mouth descends over mine so fast and hard I lose all form of balance.

Finn wraps his arm around my waist before I fall, but my back still crashes against the wine rack behind me, the impact rattling the wine bottles like an earthquake.

I've imagined my first kiss many times before.

The perfect kiss with the perfect guy.

Prince Charming was supposed to be kind, caring, gentle. But the boy ravaging my mouth? The devil destroying each and every one of my expectations?

He's everything but.

Finn is hungry, demanding, possessive in the way he claims

my mouth, and I'm happy to let him lead, despite the ear-splitting alarms blaring in my head. I know it shouldn't be him. He shouldn't be my first kiss.

He's not the guy I saw in my dreams.

And yet… when his tongue pries its way between my teeth and his hand circles my throat roughly, I want Prince Charming to fuck off so I can hold on to my villain a little while longer.

My knees almost cave in when I suck on his bottom lip, nibbling on it clumsily, and a primal groan tears from somewhere deep within his throat.

Tell him to stop.

What are you waiting for?

My body demotes my brain to the sidelines, and I embrace the thousand ways we will inevitably crash and burn, but nothing, not even the gruesome images of our flaming hearts blowing into a thousand pieces, is enough to repel me.

God, he's such *a good kisser.*

I feel like I could collapse at any moment, like my body can't possibly sustain his kiss, and I wind up grasping at his rich-kid shirt like he's a life raft. We're clawing at each other's hair, clothes, faces, chasing a fix that's set on eluding us, and we don't even react when a bottle of wine slips off the rack and hits the floor.

I barely hear the bottle shatter.

I barely notice the liquid pooling at my feet.

All I can feel is Finn disrupting the kiss for a moment, then banding his hands around the backs of my thighs to lift me up into his arms.

My legs loop around his waist as Finn slams our bodies against the rack once more, his palms gripping my ass cheeks for support. Then he's kissing me again. And again. I always thought my first "boyfriend" would take it slow, but now that I'm giving my first kiss to the monster sleeping down the hall…

I don't want "slow."

I want rough.

I want hard.

I want everything I *shouldn't.*

I can't stop myself from whining in disapproval the second his lips disconnect from mine to drag torturous kisses all over my jaw. I hear him laugh a raspy laugh at my desperation before running his tongue up my neck slowly, all the way to my earlobe.

Fucking hell.

I shiver deep in my bones when his teeth sink into my earlobe, and he tugs on it hard, luring a shy moan out of my throat.

One moan.

That's it.

One moan and I feel him harden against my leggings.

Before I know it, he's straining against the fabric of his sweats, and I part my legs like his own personal fuck toy. I hate myself for it, but it doesn't deter me from tightening my ankles behind his back.

I know the friction I seek will put us on a collision course with disaster, but I couldn't care less.

"Fuck, Dia," Finn hisses through his teeth.

Did he just…

He said my name for the first time.

He. Said. My. Name.

Not "Gem."

Not "Sitter Girl."

Dia.

Why does it sound so good rolling off his tongue?

Operating on lust, I begin to move back-and-forth, rubbing myself against him until—

Holy shit.

My mouth dips open at the pleasure zapping through my stomach. He's rock-hard now, his covered shaft hitting every single nerve ending in my clit with each thrust of my hips.

This can't be happening.

I lock eyes with Finn in the darkness of the wine cellar. Only then, when I drink him in, his mouth hanging open, his hazel eyes flaring with bad intentions, do I realize what I'm doing…

I'm dry humping him.

I'm dry humping my boss's son in a wine cellar at three in the fucking morning.

A wicked grin on his lips, he watches his length slide up and down my slit over the fabric of my leggings, then takes a fistful of my hair again, inflicting a smidge more pain than before.

"You like using me, don't you, Gem?" His voice is deep and carnal. "You like using your boss's son's cock to get off. *Say it.*"

My nipples harden at his claims.

"I… I like using you." I falter. Red colors my cheeks when the pressure between my legs becomes unbearable, and I throw my head back with a moan so raw and unfiltered Finn lets out a strangled curse.

"The whole thing. Say it," he insists.

I hesitate.

"But I—"

"Fucking say it or I'll stop."

That's all it takes for me to cave.

"I like using my boss's son's cock to get off," I admit shamefully.

"That's my girl." Finn grunts in appreciation.

What. Have. I. Become.

As if to reward me, Finn grabs himself at the base and slides the head of his cock faster and faster against my clit for several minutes until my thighs clench. I start wiggling in his embrace.

Shit, am I…

Am I about to *come*?

But he didn't even touch me.

Well, not really.

We're still fully clothed, for fuck's sake.

There's no way I'm about to—

"*Finn.*" My mouth drops open.

It sounds like a cry for help, like I don't know what to do with myself *or* this pleasure, and he reads me loud and clear.

"You're going to come, aren't you?" he rasps, harnessing the hold he has on my hair to force me to look at him and squeezing my throat. "You're going to come for me like a good fucking girl?"

His dirty talk tips me over the edge, but as soon as the overwhelming pleasure washes over me…

So does the guilt.

Reality catches up to me, the fear of losing not only my job but also my *heart* soaring in my chest. Finn picks up on my anguish right away, slamming his lips over mine and whispering in my mouth.

"Stay with me."

Breathe, Dia.

Fucking breathe.

"Here and now, Dia. Nothing else," he adds, drilling his words into my brain and watching as I reach the point of no return.

"Here and now," I croak, surrendering to my orgasm and the regrets I know will surely follow. I'm seconds away from coming undone when Finn's sinful mouth trickles open, too.

"Oh, fuck." His jaw flexes as he speeds up his thrusting. "Fuck, Dia," he calls again, his body jerking against mine. "*No fucking way.*"

He sounds like he can't possibly believe what's happening.

Like the thought of him blowing into his sweats without having been touched directly is unconceivable to him.

I'm a goner before I can overthink it.

Finn nestles his face in my neck, breathing faster as we ride out the waves of our orgasms together, knowing damn well that as soon as we plummet back down to earth, *everything* is going to change.

And sure enough, from the moment our breathing steadies and the consequences of what we did sink in, the metaphorical gap between us grows five hundred miles.

He still has his nose buried deep in my neck, but he feels far away now. My stomach twists into a knot as we struggle to catch our breaths. Finn unlinks my legs from his waist and puts me down the next second.

I expect him to ice me out the way he did Louise, but… he tilts my chin forward and kisses me instead.

He kisses me so hard I gasp.

His tongue slips inside my mouth, and while I don't understand shit about what's going on, I welcome his lips without a second thought.

That's when the spell breaks.

He backs away like he just got zapped.

Like he just realized what he was doing, and it wasn't a part of the plan. Slowly, hatred spills back into his sharp eyes, and his features revert back into the scowl I've grown to hate.

"Finn," I whisper, foolish enough to hope we can talk about

what just happened, but he's not having it.

Without sparing me a glance, he adjusts his pants—more precisely, what's left of his hard-on—and turns to walk away.

"Don't follow me," he spits.

Then he's gone.

Eleven

Diamond

How many blisters can you have before your feet just stop working? My first guess was eight, but I'm bordering on ten, and well, *still walking*. Two whole weeks have gone by since my brother decided he wouldn't be driving me to work anymore.

It came out of nowhere. Jesse just strolled into the kitchen one weekend and told me he was done entertaining my "nonsense."

Something about refusing to play a part in my *horrible* decision to see this job through. He said if I wanted to keep working for Mr. Richards, I'd have to find a way to get there myself.

I thought about telling my dads but was nervous Jesse would retaliate and snitch on me for living with a boy. So, I agreed to pretend like my brother was still driving me around when, in fact, I've been walking for an hour every Friday and Sunday.

It's not the hour-long walk that's killing me.

It's the bad-quality shoes. They must've belonged to my sister for five years before being passed on to me, but every cent I've made this far has gone to buying my car.

Shoes will have to wait.

It's near 9:00 p.m. when I amble up the driveway to the Richardses' mansion with my luggage. I slow down at the sight of Finn's car parked by the entrance, my rib cage compressing the loud drum where my heart should be.

Shit, he's here.

I haven't seen him much since the wine cellar incident…

I was thankful for his absence, at first. Finn staying out all the time meant there was no risk of the dry humping fiasco happening again, but it's become crystal clear that he's avoiding me.

He doesn't even come home to *sleep* most days. And when he does, he's gone before I wake up. I knew we'd come to regret the kiss and well… *the other stuff*, but I didn't think he'd fall off the face of the earth.

It's been quiet around the house. So quiet that I caught myself wishing Theo would get into a fight with his parents and move back in a few times.

I suck in a breath as I unlock the front door and push it open. I notice the lights are on in the kitchen and recognize the sound of the fridge closing.

Lexie runs to me on cue, her warm welcome a temporary cure to my anxiety. I pet her for a few minutes before marching myself straight into the lion's den.

Every muscle in my body is tense as I grip the strap of my bag and turn the corner. I find Finn by the sink, pouring himself a bowl of cereal. His hazel eyes flick to me when I walk in, a dash of desire zapping throughout my entire body.

Yep, he's still handsome.

I'd hoped staying away from him for a while would terminate this attraction, but as soon as our eyes meet, my mind opens the door to a dark and twisted memory.

You're going to come, aren't you? His voice echoes in my head over and over. *You're going to come for me like a good fucking girl?*

"What took you so long?" His rude question shocks me.

I blink myself back to reality. "None of your business."

Unaffected by my scathing response, Finn bites back a scoff. "You need some help with that?"

"With what?"

"Getting that stick out of your ass."

I don't let his comment about my bad mood faze me, a hate-ridden smile plastered on my face. "Remind me again why I put up with you?"

Seeming more amused than annoyed, Finn sits on one of the stools around the kitchen island and sticks his hands up. "Can't help you there. I've been trying to figure that out since the day you got here."

"Not that it concerns you, but I'm saving up for a car," I enlighten him.

He doesn't reply, eating his cereal as though I'm a ghost trying to communicate with the living.

All right, then.

I swivel to leave, ready to jog up the stairs.

"Gem?" he calls behind me.

I spin to glance at him, and his mouth opens for a second. I get the feeling that he wants to say something important, and for a moment there, I'm dumb enough to think he might be ready to acknowledge what happened.

"Let me know if you plan on showing up this late every Sunday. I'd rather not starve."

On that note, he continues to eat his cereal and treat me like a piece of furniture. *Of course.* Me getting here late on Sundays means no more meal prep for the week, hence no more food for His Majesty.

Irritated, I don't waste my breath answering and hurry up the stairs. I'm bursting into my bedroom and dumping my belongings on my bed a few seconds later.

Everything is officially back to normal.

And the boy who whispered dirty little secrets in my ear…?

He's not coming back.

***

I'm the worst dog sitter ever.

Seriously, what kind of dog sitter takes a nine-year-old dog on a walk in the middle of a heat wave? To be fair, I didn't know when I decided to take Lexie for a walk this morning that Silver Springs would turn into a furnace.

We've been walking around town for almost two hours. We had to take multiple breaks not to die of thirst, and I'm beginning to wonder if I should just call Aveena and beg her for a ride.

We're all out of water, too.

And we're a thirty-minute walk away from the house.

Not my brightest moment.

I know enough is enough when Lexie starts panting next to me. I'm wearing shorts and a tank top, and I'm practically melting. I can't imagine how hot she must be with all that fur.

I grab my phone out of my pocket, ready to dial Aveena's number, when a text pops up on my screen.

A text from Finn.

We ran into him on our way out earlier. He'd just rolled out of bed, looking like a fucking god, per usual.

I click his message instantly.

Finn: You've been gone almost two hours.

Another message comes through a second later.

Finn: Is Lexie okay?

I swallow a scoff at his bluntness.

We're both *okay. Thanks for asking.*

I text him back quickly.

Dia: **It's hot as shit, and we're all out of water. We might be a while.**

I know he saw the message when the *Read* receipt pops up on my screen, but he doesn't reply. I try Aveena and Jesse a few times, but neither picks up.

Crap, do I call my dads?

If they drop me off at the house and find out I live with a boy, I'm done for. Before I know it, ten minutes have flown by. Lexie slows down as we struggle up a steep hill, her panting becoming more obvious and shallow.

Screw it, I'm calling my dads.

A bead of sweat rolls down my forehead as I unlock my phone to dial my dad's number. Only, a car turns the corner with a loud screech before I can press Call.

I recognize him instantly.

He honks at us the moment he notices us, slowing down by our side, then stopping completely. He rolls his window down and unlocks the doors with a click of a button.

"Get in." Finn gestures with his chin, and as annoyed as I've been with him lately, I've never been happier to see him.

Is that why he didn't message me back earlier? Because he got into his car as soon as I told him we were dying in the heat?

I don't think twice, swinging the back door open and helping Lexie onto the back seat. I climb into Finn's passenger seat next and buckle up.

"Did you just drive around the whole town to find us?" I question as he pumps the gas.

"Lexie has a GPS tracker in her collar." Finn shrugs, his tattooed bicep all I can see as he grips the wheel with one arm.

"Oh." I nod. "Thanks, anyway."

"Didn't do it for you," he says dryly.

If I had a dollar for every time this guy goes out of his way to remind me he *doesn't* care, I might be able to buy him a conscience.

"Whatever," I mutter and stare out the window, still sweating my ass off. Finn's scorching leather seats aren't exactly helping. "Can you turn on the AC?"

"Already have."

"It's not working," I spit. If he's going to be an asshole to me, I might as well be one, too. I attempt to open my window, but Finn's locked them all from his side.

"Unlock the windows," I command.

"The AC's going to kick in. Just give it a minute," Finn argues, but I can't take another second of this heat.

"For fuck's sake," I huff and unbuckle my seat belt.

I'm leaning over him before he can react, my breasts grazing his arm. I hear his breath catch in his throat, but he doesn't push me off.

I can't believe my own actions when I brace my hand on his thigh, not too far from his crotch, acting like I don't realize what

I'm doing. I stretch out my arm and unlock the windows myself. I notice his grip on the steering wheel tightening as I pull away.

I knew it.

He feels it, too.

And he can pretend he doesn't remember that night in the wine cellar all he wants, but his body hasn't forgotten.

Peeling my hand off his leg, I slouch back into my seat and buckle up. I open the window to enjoy the breeze, and to my surprise, Finn doesn't say anything.

Not one word.

A few minutes tick by before I gather the courage to speak again.

"Why'd you call your car Remy?" I ask, nosey as ever.

I've pretty much given up all manners when it comes to this guy. From now on, I'm only treating him as well as he treats me.

Finn presses his lips into a tight line at my question. "Do you know what car you're going to buy yet?"

His sudden topic change doesn't get past me, but I choose not to point it out.

"I do. She's in my dad's employee's garage, just waiting for me to buy her."

"Got any pictures?" Finn asks.

I'm well aware he's just trying to avoid discussing the mysterious "Remy," but I play along, digging through my phone for a picture as he drives. I find one just in time for the next red light and hold up my screen to his face.

Finn assesses my green bug car for long seconds before biting back a laugh.

"What?" I call him out.

"That's… an interesting choice."

"Are you calling my dream car ugly?"

Finn grins, flicks his head in my direction, and gives me a once-over in his passenger seat.

"You bet your sweet ass I am."

Did he just say I had a sweet ass?

Oh my God, Dia, stop.

"Like I said, you hate everything. Speaking of, you still owe me one thing you don't hate."

He shrugs. "Just because your car is ugly doesn't mean I hate everything."

A loud gasp falls from my lips the next second, startling him.

"Did you see that?" I ask.

"See what?" he worries.

"My last fuck just went flying out the window." I gesture, and Finn cracks a laugh that makes me want to search every corner of my brain for another joke.

Anything to hear that laugh again.

"How long until you can buy it?" He revives the conversation when we pull into his driveway, and he slows down by the water fountain.

"I'm five hundred short. Five hundred, then you'll be rid of me. Happy?" I tease, convinced he's only interested because he wants me gone.

His response leaves me breathless.

"That's not why I was asking." He maintains the eye contact.

Unable to think of a single answer, I clamp my mouth shut, quick to understand that he's just dropping us off when he doesn't kill the engine.

"You're not coming?" I unbuckle my seat belt.

"Nah, someone's expecting me."

I'm itching to ask who that *someone* is but decide against it, climbing out of the car and opening Lexie's door.

"Hey, Gem?" Finn calls as we're heading for the house.

I stop to glance back at him. He has his window down, this panty-dropping smile on his face and a world of ulterior motives in his eyes.

"Don't forget to charge it."

Then, without further explanation, he drives off.

Wait, what?

Twelve

Finn

Brody: Did the girl with the flat ass quit yet?

The sky is pitch-black by the time I park in my driveway and read my brother's text. Brody Richards is an idiot. It's common knowledge at this point. I just didn't realize he was a *blind* idiot. The house sitter is a lot of things—stubborn, cunning, feisty—but she's not flat. Not by any stretch of the imagination.

My fingers type a reply too fast for me to catch up.

Finn: Nope. Still here.

My brother's reply pops up on my phone immediately.

Brody: I know something that would send her running home to her lying sack of a brother if you're interested...

Two weeks ago, I would've *jumped* at the opportunity to find out whatever fucked-up secret my brother is keeping. Anything to get this girl out the door, but now...

I'm not even sure it's worth the effort.

I'm starting to get used to having her around, and no one is more shocked than me, but my dad might've been onto something when he hired her.

Her presence allows me to do whatever I want without having to worry about Lexie. I couldn't have stayed at Theo's until midnight tonight if it weren't for her.

The asshole needed me—well, he needed *someone*—even though he'll never admit it. Shit is getting pretty bad over at the Coxes'. I know Theo only invited me to hang because he was hoping his parents would get off his case with me there.

And he was right.

They bit their tongue for most of the evening, and Theo did a marvelous job at pretending like his relationship with his folks wasn't a dumpster fire.

Leaving my brother's message unanswered, I shove my phone in my back pocket and drag myself out of the car. Lexie greets me at the front door, and I'm a tad surprised to see her there. It's past midnight, and she always sleeps in Gem's bed. She's usually sound asleep upstairs by now.

Unless… Gem kicked her out?

I nearly drop my keys when I hear it.

The faint, distant sound of…

Buzzing?

Am I hallucinating?

I notice my breathing quickening as I stalk up the stairs,

tracking the noise to the second floor. I'm at the house sitter's door a second later, the buzzing clearer than ever.

Her bedroom door is open a crack, and under the moonlight, I see her lying in bed, wearing a lace bra, her lower body concealed under the covers, and her pouty mouth hanging open.

Holy hell.

She's using it.

She's using the sex toy I gave her.

I packed a vibrator in a box today and left it on her bed with a note saying to rub one out and fix her mood swings. I was just trying to mess with her—she's been irritable all week—but I didn't think she'd actually touch it.

Well, touch *herself.*

Fuck, I should leave.

But I'm hard.

I'm so fucking hard my cock strains against my pants, yearning for freedom. Her breathing is heavy, her chest hauling up and down as she rotates the toy underneath the blanket and chokes on a moan I'm afraid might kill me.

The hallway is soaked in darkness, and she can't see me watching her. Nor can she see me slipping my hand inside my briefs like a fucking creep.

Jesus, Finn, stop.

But I can't.

I *can't* stop.

I suck in a sharp breath when she palms her left tit over her bra. She's flawless. Point-blank. She's what my sweetest nightmares are made of. An innocent, cunning little thing I'd do anything to taste.

But it's when she slips a hand inside her bra and pops out one of her tits that I full-on *strangle* my cock. Her tit is beautiful, just big enough to fit into my palm, and her nipple… I want to suck that nipple into my mouth.

Fuck, I feel like a criminal.

Like I'm witnessing a show I don't have tickets to, but I'm *incapable* of looking away. I lose myself in her body. Those round, perky tits, her black curls flowing down her shoulder, and that tight stomach.

She's sweaty, the shape of her opened legs evident through the blanket. *This fucking girl.* I fist myself slowly, at first. Then I imagine myself coming all over her pussy, her tongue sticking out, begging me to fill her throat, and I'm a goner.

Next thing I know, I'm jacking off to her, guiding my hand up and down my shaft faster with every stroke. Robbing her of a moment she thinks is private, and the worst part? I'm too engulfed in the sight of her to care.

She nudges the blanket farther down her stomach, just enough for me to see the shape of her hand as she speeds up her circles and grabs her tit again, her back arching a bit.

Fuuuuck.

I lift my palm to my mouth and spit in it, then wrap my hand around my cock again, picking up speed. If she pushed that blanket down one more inch, I'd be coming in two seconds. My dick jerks when she throws her head back with an irritated growl.

She lost it.

The G-spot.

And she's not happy about it.

"Come on." She sounds pained.

I'd sell my fucking soul to help her find it again.

"Come on," she repeats, her breathing labored, and my jaw flexes. If I keep this up, I'm going to blow, and it's becoming harder to be quiet.

"Seriously?" she huffs a moment later.

Any control I might've had over my body is drained out of me when I muffle a groan and withdraw my hand from my cock. I surprise myself by swinging her bedroom door open and catching her in the act. I might not know shit about my next move, but I do know one thing…

I'm ending the night with her legs wrapped around my neck.

* * *

Diamond

Dear Gem,

I'm afraid I must insist you use this gift in the shortest

delays and fix your mood swings.

Urgently,

—Your housemate who can't stand to spend another day with your grumpy ass.

That's what the note said.

Pretty straightforward, right?

Wrong.

You see, what the note failed to mention is that my boss's son would wind up walking in on me with a vibrator between my legs…

I found the toy shortly after Finn dropped us off, and at first, I had no intention of using the damn thing. Until I stepped out of the shower in my nightgown at around eleven and saw the box sitting on my nightstand.

It was obvious that Finn was just messing with me and didn't expect me to use it, which, for some reason, made me want to use it even more. I decided it couldn't hurt to try a toy for the first time, which brings us to the most mortifying moment of my life.

"Finn, what the fuck?" My voice comes out as a shrill and panicky yelp.

I sit up and yank the blanket over my body. I'm wearing nothing but a bra and an opened robe, but I don't want to risk flashing him by closing it.

And what's worse, I was so focused on not showing him the goods that I didn't get the chance to turn off the toy. It's still vibrating and pulsing between my legs, and the newfound angle is, well, a revelation.

Fuck.

Not now.

"Need some help with that?" Finn stands in my doorway, his arms folded over his chest and his shoulder braced against the threshold.

I want to disintegrate when he gives me a slow body scan.

Shit.

That look.

He's looking at me like an animal contemplating his next meal. Like a monster waiting to crawl out from under my bed and scar me for life.

Not to mention he saw my breast.

The horror.

Even if it was just for a few seconds, he—

Wait.

My eyes dart to his pants, to the bulge pushing against the fabric, tearing at the seams. He's hard as steel and not even a little embarrassed by it. My lips part when I realize…

He didn't see me for just one second, did he?

"Have you been watching the whole thing?" I spit, and my cheeks smolder with a mix of rage and shame.

"Eh, more like witnessing it." Finn shrugs, cool as a fucking cucumber, and the pressure between my legs decides *now* is a good time to defy my brain. A quiet moan slips from my lips, cutting through the air.

His eyes immediately flare.

"You think that feels good, Mitchell?" Finn scorns, his use of my last name and the red flags in his voice fueling my vulnerability. "You think this is anything compared to what I would do to you? Anything compared to my tongue and my fingers? *Cute.*"

Oh my…

"You're doing it wrong, by the way," he adds, drilling his focus into the toy working my sweet spot under the blanket.

Is he serious?

"I don't need your tips. Get the fuck out!" I fire back.

"Oh, sweetheart… I'd give you more than the tip."

My mouth goes from slightly ajar to wide open, and I feel so powerless it's dizzying. I can't let him have all the power here. I've done nothing but suffer at his hands these past few weeks—technically, the time in the wine cellar had to do with *another* part of his body—and I'm done.

I'm done feeling like a prisoner to a cruel prince.

I should be the one holding him captive.

In an attempt to turn the tables on him, I do the only thing I can think of: I ignore him. I tear my eyes away, and after making sure that the blanket is hiding my body, I slouch into bed, lying on my back.

Then I guide my hand underneath the blanket under Finn's scrutiny, the tent in his pants doing little to hide the defiling thoughts in his head. I squeeze my eyes shut and pour all of my energy into climaxing.

Only, I've lost the spot.

Again.

"Get. Out." My teeth chatter as I play with myself in front of my boss's son like a sex-deprived sicko.

"And miss the show? Fuck that," Finn grits out, a thousand fires igniting in his gaze.

And he's not kidding.

He parks himself at the edge of my bed, watching me chase an orgasm that's nowhere to be found. I'm going to have to throw him out myself, aren't I?

"Get out." I repeat, but dishonesty drips from my voice.

There's a part of me, buried deep down inside, that wants him to ignore my request. A part of me that wants him to *stay.* I'm quick to close my robe underneath the blanket and remove the toy from between my legs.

I turn it off and toss it on the bed. Then I charge toward him, ready to swing the door open and kick him out.

I've barely opened the door an inch before his hand catches my wrist and he slams the door closed again. I let out a yelp when my chest comes flush with the icy door.

Finn grabs hold of my other wrist and joins my hands behind

my back like he's going to cuff me and throw me into the back of a police car. I'm at his mercy, pinned against the door, and I wiggle left and right to free myself.

"Get off me," I snap over my shoulder, and Finn lets out a low, ruthless laugh that makes me shiver everywhere.

I'm trapped.

He's got me tangled in his web, and there's no way in hell he's letting me go. I inhale a breath when he closes the gap between us, pressing his hard chest to my back to keep me firmly in place.

"Get off," I repeat in a pride-driven attempt to save face. Finn's breath skitters down my spine as he positions his mouth next to my ear.

"*Make me.*"

I oblige, wriggling against him, seeking a way out, but he won't budge. I feel every inch of Finn's hard-on against my ass. The more I squirm, the harder he gets, and I'm terrified…

Because I don't feel trapped *at all.*

I feel alive, turned on, and, mostly, embarrassed by how much I love hearing his groans as I "accidentally" rub against his crotch.

"Look at you, rubbing your ass all over my cock like the filthy fucking liar that you are." Finn grunts against my neck, his grip around my curls tightening. "Tell me you don't want me to make you come right here against that door, I fucking dare you."

"Like you could," I say to provoke him.

He doesn't speak for a bit.

"Was that consent?" he teases, and I chew down on my lip. I don't have the courage to say it out loud, so I opt for a quiet approach, stroking him harder with my ass.

"Fuck, Dia." He sounds pained, as though he can't take another minute of this. I rock back and forth against him, quietly telling him what he already knows.

I, Diamond Mitchell, want my boss's son to do unholy things to me against my bedroom door—let's just say I won't hold my breath for Employee of the Month.

"Fuck, I bet you're soaking wet, too." Finn guesses right, and I respond by spreading my legs for him.

That's it, I must be possessed.

Another laugh rolls off his tongue. "Give me a yes, Gem."

Dia, don't go there.

Don't go down that road with him.

Don't—

"Y-Yes," I choke out.

Too late.

"That's a good girl," he breathes out and drags a finger up my thigh. I can't suppress a gasp when he lifts up my robe, stopping inches from a place no one's ever touched before.

"Wider," he instructs, and I oblige, offering more of myself and quivering with anticipation. I nearly fall apart when Finn jerks my robe out of the way and slides a finger inside my slit.

This is happening.

A guy is touching me for the first time.

And it's not just any guy.

It's Finn fucking Richards.

"So fucking wet." He groans, and my eyes roll back as he guides his index deeper to test the water. He runs his finger up and down my crease slowly. Pleasure thunders through me every time he grazes my clit, but he never stays there long enough to put out the fire.

"Come here," he grunts, his right palm wrapping around my throat from behind. My heart nearly bursts out of my chest when his lips crash down on mine. I kiss him back over my shoulder in an instant, the sensation of his tongue mingling with mine overriding my senses.

Jesus, it is always like this?

Does every boy kiss like that, or *is it just him*?

My questions crumble when Finn thrusts a finger inside me. Just like that, he takes another one of my firsts, filling me with not one but *two* fingers and making me gasp in his mouth. The sensation of fullness is overwhelming, and he's stretching me to the limit, but his thumb landing on my clit and rotating hard and fast trumps the pain in no time.

I can hear my own arousal as we kiss, feel the result of his fingers pumping in and out of me coating the inside of my thighs. Less than two minutes later, I'm backing up into his hand for more. I don't recognize the girl moaning in the dark. She's a stranger to me.

Dangerous.

Impulsive.

Reckless.

She doesn't think, she just *feels*.

And if I weren't so busy riding my housemate's hand and hating myself for it, I'd be trying to exorcize her out of me.

"What do you want?" Finn urges. "You want me to stretch that tight little pussy wider? Tell me."

The promise I made to my brother to never get involved with Finn that first week pops into my mind, and my conscience challenges my heart to a duel…

"You know what I want," I whimper.

News flash: my heart won.

"Fuck yeah, I do."

That's his cue to stop going easy on me.

I smack my palms to the door as if to brace myself for mind-blowing pleasure, and, sure enough, he starts finger-fucking me and rubbing my clit with so much intensity that I cry out, muffling my moans with my hand.

I gasp when his palm leaves my throat, and he jerks my robe down completely. The fabric cascades to my feet, and Finn plants a trail of kisses up and down my shoulder blades. Goose bumps immediately join the party. Next thing I know, he's cupping my breast inside my bra, taking a handful and twirling the pad of his finger around my tight nipple.

Finn's mouth crashing over mine again temporarily makes

me forget that this is the first time I've ever been naked in front of a guy—well, *almost* naked. I'm still wearing a bra.

Things are moving too fast, but the last thing I want is for him to stop. My moaning is hindered when he wraps his hand around my wrist and spins me around, my back slamming against the door with a thud. His fingers slide back into position, and I squeeze my eyes shut instinctively.

I don't have it in me to look at him.

It's one thing to have your boss's son finger you from behind; it's another to have to look him in the eyes while he sets fire to all the promises you made yourself.

From the first time I saw him, I've known I was attracted to him, and while a part of me would go to the end of the world to pretend that's all this is… a stupid, meaningless attraction… I'm terrified I'll look him in the eyes and find out it's more.

Even if it's just more for *me.*

I keep my eyes closed for a while, whimpering and squirming as Finn's thumb works my clit at maximum speed. Then, minutes later, the pleasure reaches its apex, and I begin to tremble. Fireworks explode in my toes, shooting up my legs, and my increasing moans speak for me.

"Yes. Oh, God. *Yes.*" I claw at his chest, digging my nails into his tattooed shoulders.

"No." Finn's firm voice startles me.

What does he mean, *no?*

"What?" My eyes snap open.

"I said no. You're not coming."

Seconds before my orgasm hits, Finn stops.

He just *stops*.

He withdraws his fingers and takes off, walking toward my bed. The pleasure dies down instantly, and my body jerks a few times, the space between my legs feeling awfully empty.

"What the hell?" I whine. "What are you doing?"

He doesn't reply.

"You're such an asshole."

"*Huh-huh*." Finn heaves a laugh.

He's back before I know it, but…

He's holding the sex toy now.

That's what he was doing?

The buzzing of the toy informs me that he just turned it on. My back arches off the door when he positions it onto my clit and selects the highest setting. Top it off with his fingers plunging deep inside me, and I know whatever orgasm I thought was coming before is going to seem dull in comparison.

I'm right back to where I started a minute later.

"Finn!" I sound like I'm begging him, and I hate it.

"Now." He grants me permission. "Come for me, Dia. Come all over my fucking hand."

I squeeze my eyes shut again, but my attempt to protect my heart backfires because he kisses me roughly and says, "Open your eyes."

I pretend I didn't catch that.

"Look at me," Finn urges. "Fucking look at me when you come."

So, I do.

I force my eyes open and take it all in.

Those demon-ridden eyes, that dirty, vicious mouth. The dark aura surrounding him clashing with the light in mine. And my heart cries out in realization as I come on his fingers. He doesn't stop his thrusting until I'm boneless against the door.

Finn gives me a moment to catch my breath and cracks a small smirk, staring straight into my soul before saying, "*That's* how you do it."

He finishes with a thrust that draws a shrill moan from my mouth and pulls his fingers out of me. Then he gestures for me to move, opens the door, and leaves me there.

Just like that.

My thighs covered in my own juices, I pick up my robe that's collecting dust on the floor and throw it back on. My legs are still shaking as I plop down on the end of my bed, losing myself in the verdict I read in his eyes.

It's just an attraction for now. But if I allow myself to dig deeper, to see a good person where everybody sees a monster, it could become more. And there's only one solution.

As soon as I have enough for a car…

I'm out of this house.

Thirteen

Diamond

My dads always told me to be careful what you wish for. That sometimes, getting what you want is the worst thing that could possibly happen to you…

I thought they were exaggerating, but I can practically *hear* the numbers on my phone laughing at me as I stroll up the driveway with Lexie on a leash.

My bank statement says I'm about two hundred short of my goal. A few more days working for Mr. Richards and I'll have more than enough for a car.

And that's a good thing.

I should be happy.

After all, I promised myself, when Finn was taking another one of my firsts, that I'd be out of this house as soon as my wallet allowed it.

But… leaving now would mean saying goodbye to Lexie three weeks earlier. Packing my bags would equal to never seeing her again. I doubt Mr. Richards will want me around once he returns from his vacation.

The house is eerily quiet when we march inside after our

afternoon walk. I only saw two cars parked in the lot on my way in—a red one I know for a fact belongs to Theo and a silver one I've never seen before.

Is Theo back for good?

Or just visiting?

I've barely unleashed Lexie before she aims for her dog bed. She plops down on the cushion and dozes off almost immediately. She seems tired these days, which isn't surprising considering her age, but her energy drop is becoming harder to ignore.

She's been breathing more heavily on our walks, too. Like she's struggling. First time it happened was the day we got trapped in the heat, so I didn't think much of it, but it's been happening more and more. The vet ran some tests for her annual checkup, and we're still waiting for the results.

Hopefully, everything comes back normal.

I pad toward the fridge to grab a water bottle and slow down when I see three pieces of masking tape slapped on top of the door—no doubt courtesy of Finn. Words are scribbled over it, and I recognize his handwriting from the note he attached to the vibrator three days ago.

Theo's moving back in, thought you should know.

P.S. *If he tells you I ate all the cookies you made, he's lying.*

P.P.S. Fine, I ate them.

A scoff shoots out of me, and I press my lips together as if to stop it from evolving into laughter. I'd rather not be on good terms with him when I leave. I couldn't handle my last memory of him being that damn heart-stopping smile.

It doesn't help that he's been surprisingly decent to me since we had *semi-sex*. We exchange small talk and greetings when we run into each other, not to mention excel at pretending like he never finger-fucked me to high heaven.

Shoving Finn out of my mind, I reach for my water and shut the fridge. I'm wandering onto the patio with the intention to bask in the sun for a bit when I realize someone beat me to it.

Lacey Mattson, to be exact.

The girl is well known around school as captain of the cheer squad, Brielle Randall's "friend"—everybody knows they secretly hate each other—and, last but not least…

Theo's groupie.

Rumor has it, she and Theo were friends with benefits for most of junior year until a pregnancy scare quite literally *scared* Theo away. He freaked out, distanced himself, and they've been on and off ever since, occasionally winding up in bed together at parties.

Aveena, who's lived in Silver Springs much longer than I have, says Lacey's been obsessed with Theo since the third grade, but post-puberty, Theo could never see her as more than a convenient side piece.

Now that I think about it, I'd bet good money she's the one Theo ran off with the night of Brody's party. Their fuck buddy relationship would also explain her presence here.

In a purple bikini, Lacey relaxes by the pool on a sun lounger. A messy bun sits on top of her head, her phone next to her on the lounger. She peels her eyes open when she hears the glass door close. Lacey blinks at me for a moment, her sun-kissed face indecipherable.

I'm not sure what to do.

Do I introduce myself? Ask her what she's doing here? If my interactions with Brielle and Louise are anything to go by, Easton High's cheerleaders aren't big on non-popular humans.

I assume she's going to ignore me the way every member of the cheer squad would, but then…

"Hi, I'm Lacey."

I immediately scan the backyard as if to make sure she's talking to me. She chuckles at my behavior, sitting up straight.

"Yes, you." She laughs again. "You must be the house sitter—Diana, is it?"

If it were any other cheerleader, her question would feel like an insult. A sick, twisted way of making me feel inferior by calling me the wrong name, but that's not the vibe I get here. It sounds like an honest mistake, and I decide to treat it as such.

"Diamond," I correct her with a smile. "But most people call me Dia."

"Shit, sorry." She gestures for me to come closer. "Get over here. I'll be damned if I don't at least *meet* the superhuman who's been putting up with Finn Richards all summer."

I chuckle, stalking toward the sun lounger beside her.

"Sit." She pats the empty chair, and I comply, the pit in my throat warning me to stay alert. As though she could switch on me and reveal her true colors at any moment.

Because a girl who has absolutely everything in life can't possibly be this nice, *can she*?

"Girl, how do you do it? I have to know." She nudges me with her elbow.

"I need a car. That's how," I admit.

She grins. "For what it's worth, you have all my respect. Theo told me Finn's been a major ass to you."

"Speaking of, do you happen to know where the guys are?" I sit cross-legged on the lounger.

"Nope." Lacey reclines back down, then lowers her sunglasses in front of her eyes. "Theo told me to meet him here, then he took off with Finn like two minutes later. They haven't been back since."

"Wait, he asked you to come here, then he just left you?"

She nods.

"Dick move," I comment, and she chuckles.

"Believe me, I'd be *very* offended if Finn didn't have a heated pool."

I laugh. "Any idea where they went?"

She shrugs. "I think I heard them say something about settling a debt. No clue what it means, though."

Settling a debt?

Must be Theo's debt. Fat chance that the son of a millionaire would settle for *anything.*

"Your hair is gorgeous, by the way." She peeks at me. "Seriously, I'd die for those curls."

"Oh, wow, I… thank you," I stammer, taken aback by the compliment.

I wait for the conversation to die.

Only, it doesn't.

We discuss Finn being an asshole some more, then Theo's parents being harassing bullies that kick their son out to the curb on the regular. We laugh and talk for over fifteen minutes, and I come to the conclusion that Lacey Mattson is an overall decent person. She might be a privileged white girl with a perfect body and perfect, wealthy parents, but she's a *nice* one.

An alarm on her phone marks the end of our conversation.

"Ah, shit." She checks her phone. "I have to get home. I'm throwing a party, and my girls are coming over so we can get ready together."

"Go. I'll tell Theo you had to run." I smile.

"You're an angel." She deactivates the alarm, pushing off the lounge chair.

She's barely taken two steps toward the house before she

stops. My first thought is that she forgot something until she spins around, her clear eyes gleaming with an idea.

"Do you want to come?" She doesn't seem to be joking.

My brain functions ditch me.

"T-To the party?"

"No, to Disneyland—*yes* to the party, dummy." She cracks a laugh. "It'll be so much fun. I'll introduce you to my people, we'll dance and have a great time. What do you say?"

She's trying to convince me.

I repeat, Lacey Mattson, captain of the cheerleading team, is trying to convince me, *has-one-friend* Diamond Mitchell, to come to her party. It's not like I've spent all of my high school years wishing I'd score an invite or anything.

"Sure, why not?"

"Great," she squeals. "Give me your number. I'll text you the address. Although you can probably catch a ride with Theo later."

The text containing her address pops up on my phone a minute later.

"See you tonight." Lacey offers me a parting smile and trails off. I can't move a muscle, watching her leave and wondering if I imagined it all…

Except, I didn't.

I didn't imagine a thing.

And tonight?

I'm going to my first party.

* * *

"Wait for me!" My voice carries throughout the house as I hurry down the stairs with my heart in my throat. Theo texted me that they're heading out soon, and I sure as hell didn't spend *three* hours getting ready to miss my ride.

I catch my reflection in the hall mirror.

I'm confident enough to say that I look good. I straightened my hair, which thanks to my thick curls took a decade, and went all out on the makeup—mascara, eyeliner, lipstick, *the whole deal.*

I'm bursting into the kitchen a moment later, wearing high-waisted jeans and an off-the-shoulder top I wasted forty minutes picking out. Finn and Theo surround the kitchen island, eyes pointed at their phones. Theo is the only one to look up when I come in.

"Damn, Dia. It's a party. Not prom," Theo teases, and I flip him off, fueling his smile. Finn's gaze snaps to mine at Theo's remark, and I see his throat bob as he gives me a once-over.

I almost expect a compliment until his features harden.

"You're not coming."

It's cute that he believes that.

"Try and stop me."

Finn shocks me by smashing his phone facedown on the counter. "Did I fucking stutter? You're not coming."

"Yes, I am." I match his tone. "Lacey invited me."

He scoffs. "That's called pity. Nobody wants you there."

My stomach sinks at his cruelty.

"You *do* realize that knowing you don't want me there makes me want to go even more, right?"

Fuming, Finn doesn't argue, rolling his fists into firm balls and letting out an irritated "I'll be in the car."

The front door slams behind him, and Theo and I lock eyes, startled by his outburst. He left me a funny note on the fridge just a few hours ago, and now he's making a scene because I want to go to a party I was *invited* to?

Why is he so hell-bent on keeping me away from this party?

Theo plucking his keys out of his pocket and gesturing to the door halts my spiral. I have no idea what this night has in store for me, but hey, it can't possibly be worse than the way it started...

Can it?

***

Lacey: Text me when you're here.

Clutching my phone into my fist, I shadow Theo and Finn inside Lacey's house and consider two equally plausible possibilities.

One: Lacey invited me here because she genuinely enjoys my company and wants to be my friend. Or two: my life just turned into a bad remake of *Carrie* and Lacey invited me for the sole purpose of humiliating me.

Maybe Brie put her up to this?

Or could it be Louise?

Last I checked, neither loves me very much, and considering that Finn moaned my name while in bed with Lou and that I cockblocked Brie and Finn on my first day on the job, I wouldn't like me either. All I know is I don't belong here, and it took me marching into the most chaotic party in history to realize it.

The house is jam-packed, dense smoke and a mixture of sweat and vomit triggering my gag reflex as we push through the crowd. The music is also ear-splitting, but I'm not nearly as bothered by it as I am by the suffocating heat.

"Cox, Richards, get your asses over here. We need you." A basketball player in the middle of a beer pong game calls on Theo and Finn from the moment we enter the room.

"I'll text you when we're leaving," Theo, being the designated driver, tells me before setting off to meet his buddies. Finn follows suit without so much as a *glance* in my direction.

I watch Finn's friends hype up his arrival, hitting his shoulder as though he's a god amongst men. That's when I realize I'd rather risk being humiliated by Lacey and her mean friends than spend the entire night alone.

I would've invited Aveena, seeing as she's my only friend in the world, but I know Vee would rather choke at every meal for the rest of her life than show up to a party. That, and the smell of alcohol makes her queasy.

I'm on my own, for better or worse.

"I'm here," I text Lacey, my stomach twisting into a tight knot. Her response comes through right away.

Lacey: Where?

I message her back.

Dia: Kitchen.

Less than a minute goes by before her voice slashes through the music.

"Dia!" I spot her waving at me by the door, a bottle of rosé in her right hand. I slap on a smile, nudging my worries aside and making my way over to her.

"About time." She chuckles drunkenly, cluing me in as to how much she's had.

Short answer? *A lot.*

I'm surprised when she loops her arms around my neck for a hug. Maybe I was paranoid? Lacey isn't Brie. Or Louise. From what I can tell, the girl has more kindness in her pinky than her cheerleader friends ever will in their entire body.

I'm not saying she doesn't have her moments—she's been known to get into it with Brie once or twice—but she's like a breath of fresh air from the mean-girl stereotype.

"Let's get you a drink." She grabs my forearm to guide me

to the wine cooler that's filled with random drinks in the kitchen.

"You like vodka?" Lacey grabs a vodka bottle out of the cooler and hands it to me. I have the reflex of uncapping the bottle and sniffing it. My nostrils burn at the scent.

Jesus.

"I guess…?" I cringe, and Lacey laughs.

"The look on your face. I'm not going to make you drink it plain."

She's not?

"Come on." She leaps to her feet and heads for the fridge. "Bloody Mary all right?"

This one is a no-brainer since I've had this drink virgin at my dad's restaurant more times than I can count.

"Absolutely." I nod, and Lacey pulls tomato juice out of her fridge door. I watch as she gets to work, biting my tongue when she pours a little bit too much vodka in there for my taste.

She tops it off with a celery stalk, wedging it onto the rim of the glass, and hands me the drink.

This is weird.

Being here.

Being offered my first real drink by Lacey Mattson.

I can't help feeling like I should be doing this with Aveena… but then again, my best friend promised herself to never drink after witnessing her father's struggles with booze.

I used to praise her for it, admire how she refused to make the same mistakes as her dad, but now? I realize I've been beating myself up for wanting different things. I thought if she didn't need alcohol, or boys, or parties in her life, I shouldn't either, but…

Maybe I should be free to decide what I do and don't like for myself. Free to make my own mistakes and learn from them.

Lacey claps in excitement and singsongs, "*Try it. Try it.*"

I cave to her request and bring the drink to my lips. The first sip is overwhelming, the underlying taste of vodka stronger than anticipated, but I quickly adapt.

"Is it good?" Lacey questions.

"Delicious. You've got skills," I compliment, and she flips her hair over her shoulder for effect, making me chortle.

"Come on, I'll introduce you to my girls." Lacey takes my arm again, ushering me to the living room, where people are dancing carelessly. My legs weigh a thousand pounds when I see Brielle, Louise, and another cheerleader named Hadley chatting from afar.

This is it, isn't it?

The part where they humiliate me in front of everyone?

"Found her," Lacey informs the girls.

Brielle and Louise transfer their focus onto me, the shock in their gazes a clear sign that they weren't expecting to see me here.

"Everyone, this is Diamond." Lacey drags a sip of rosé right out of the bottle. "But she'd rather you call her Dia."

Louise's mocking scoff drives my heart to my stomach. "And

I'd rather drink *spit* than be a part of this conversation."

Then she walks off.

So… safe to say she's not the forgiving type?

No one speaks for long seconds.

Until Hadley chimes in.

"Don't mind her. She's a bitch when she drinks." Hadley's smile is full of apologies, but I'm too focused on her gorgeous, natural ginger hair to reply.

"Please, she's a bitch when she *breathes*," Lacey counters, and Hadley and I chuckle. I always thought Hadley Queen was amongst Easton High's most down-to-earth and somewhat "normal" cheerleaders.

Her mom owns a convenience store downtown. They're comfortable but not rich like Lacey or Brie. And definitely not *gross* rich like Finn. She quit the cheerleading team last year to help out her mom after her twin brother passed in the one and only holdup Silver Springs has ever had.

Word on the street is that she won't be here much longer, though. Her mom put the store up for sale after the incident. She couldn't bear to work where her kid died any longer.

"You go to Easton, right?" Hadley asks.

I nod.

"But you didn't grow up around here, did you?" She says it as a fact. I bet she knows every person she went to kindergarten with like the back of her hand. Small-town perks.

"Yeah, my family moved here freshman year."

"Fascinating," Brie huffs out.

I thought maybe Brie would abstain from treating me like shit since I know her darkest secret and could ruin her life, but *nope*. Still a bitch.

"You guys want shots?" Lacey ignores Brie.

Without awaiting our response, Lacey leads us to a room that seems like your typical man cave—flat-screen TV, reclining leather chairs, sports posters, and minifridge in the corner.

"I think I left some Jell-O shots in here." Lacey flings the fridge open and pulls out a tray of cherry-flavored shots. "Shit, we're missing one." She distributes the shots amongst us until we're down to the last one. "Go ahead." Lacey inches the tray closer to me.

"Don't you want it?"

"Nah, you live with Finn. Trust me, you need it more than I do." She laughs, and I blink a few times, the room spinning.

Man, my tolerance is *crap*.

"Actually, I'm good." I force a smile.

"Is she above drinking or some shit?" Brie lets out defensively.

"What? No, I—"

"Jesus, Lace, where'd you find this girl?" Brie releases a scornful laugh, which results in every girl in the circle staring at me. Why do I feel like I'm failing some kind of test right now?

"I…"

"Come on, don't be a prude," Brie pushes me, and I feel like they're deciding whether or not I can sit with them ever again. You'd think my armor is made of glass by how fast it crumbles under their scrutiny.

In the snap of a finger, I abandon my convictions and grab the Jell-O shot. The girls cheer me on as I tilt my head back and down it in one go.

"That's what I'm talking about," Lacey sneers, throwing her arm around my shoulder for a hug.

Axel Fletcher swings the door open the next second. "Fucking finally," he says when he sees us. "Randall, Queen, you're up for beer pong. Last chance."

"Shit, *coming*." Hadley drags Brie with her, following Axel back to the kitchen.

"I want to dance!" Lacey says as soon as the girls are gone and guides me back to the living room. We dance away the next hour, passing her bottle of rosé back and forth and making up dance moves so ridiculous my stomach eventually starts to ache from laughing.

"I have to pee so bad," I confess, my gaze combing through the room for the bathroom. I spot a long line of drunk kids spreading down the hallway and groan. "Ugh, this is going to take *foreverrrr*."

In case that wasn't clear, the "tipsy" ship has sailed for me.

One more sip and I'm officially entering "drunk" territory.

"Come—" *Hiccup*. "—here." Lacey lures me in closer, her breath thick with alcohol. "We have a guest house out back. The key is under the mat. Use the bathroom in there."

"You're the best." I immediately tear through the crowd in search of the door leading to the backyard. I find it fast enough but spend five minutes looking for the damn key under the mat to the luxurious guest house.

It's almost pitch-black outside. Lacey's house is isolated from others, located by the woods and a creepy hiking trail I know kids love to walk at night to scare each other. There are also old, abandoned railways around here.

I eventually find the key to the guest house inside a decorative plant and head out when I'm done, making sure to lock the door. I've just placed the key under the mat when I hear two people arguing.

"A payment plan? Who the fuck do you think I am? A bank? A fucking *charity*?" a man spits aggressively, and in any other scenario, I'd run back to the party, but…

The voice I hear next roots me in place.

"I told you I'll get you your fucking money."

That voice.

It belongs to Finn.

What the hell is he doing back here?

That's what Lacey meant, isn't it?

When she said the guys went to settle a debt? Finn owes someone money. He must've gone and tried to convince that someone earlier. I take it the guy coming back for round two means it didn't go over so well.

Is Finn buying drugs? And how in the hell is the son of a *millionaire* in debt in the first place?

Hesitant, I peek from around the corner of the guest house to see better. I spot two silhouettes under the moonlight, one I recognize as Finn's and one belonging to the sketchiest guy I've ever seen.

The stranger is wearing shabby jeans, a black hoodie, and a stalker baseball cap. He's shorter than Finn by at least four inches and looks like he hasn't showered in months.

"Do you think I don't know where you *live*?" Sketchy Guy threatens. "That I don't know Daddy's swimming in cash?"

Finn seems to decide the conversation is over because he throws the beer in his hand back for a sip and turns to leave.

Sketchy Guy is not having it. "She's cute. The girl you pulled up with—black hair, tight little body. *Good choice*."

He saw me?

It dawns on me instantly.

Is that why Finn didn't want me at this party?

Because he knew he'd have… company?

"She your girl?" Sketchy Guy hounds, but Finn carries on walking. "What do you say I pay her a visit and take what you owe me?"

Finn stops instantly.

Next thing I know, he's tossing his beer onto the grass and charging back to the creep with such speed that his "dealer" backtracks into a tree.

"Watch your fucking mouth," Finn grits out, the darkness in his voice shaking me to my core.

"Damn, struck a nerve, didn't I?" Sketchy Guy snorts. "So she *is* your girl?"

Finn remains quiet for a moment.

"House sitter," he admits.

The guy cackles. "Daddy's employee, huh? Man, that's got to suck. Living with a girl like that and not being able to do shit about it."

Except… he *did* do something about it.

In the wine cellar.

Against my bedroom door.

"Tell you what." The guy steps closer. "You want me to consider your payment plan? You get back in there, bring sitter girl to the woods, and I'll destroy that tight little asshole for you."

That's what sets Finn off.

I have to cover my own mouth when Finn's hand circles the guy's throat and he smashes his back to the tree, hoisting him up a few inches in the air without breaking a sweat.

"You want to say that again?" Finn gets up in his face. "Come on, try me. Talk about her again, *see what happens*."

Sketchy Guy tries to claw at Finn's shirt, face, throat, gasping for air.

Finn couldn't go for a punch like a normal person.

He's *strangling* him.

"If you ever lay a finger on her—" Finn squeezes the guy's throat so hard, he makes a disturbing wheezing sound that makes my skin crawl. "—if you even think of going near her, or looking at her, or *breathing* in her direction, I'll kill you with my bare fucking hands, you got that?"

Sketchy Guy's gasps become more and more desperate, his attempts at freeing himself lacking in strength as he suffocates.

He's going to kill him.

I don't think, jumping out from behind the guest house and belting Finn's name at the top of my lungs. His head whisks over his shoulder at the sound of my voice, and he releases the guy.

I can't tell what he's thinking when he sees me standing there, watching the darkest side of him take over.

Coughing his lungs out, Sketchy Guy seizes the opportunity to book it into the woods. It's so dark out we almost immediately lose sight of him.

"*Fuck*!" Finn snaps and glares at me like this is my fault.

Like he's mad at me for stopping him from choking someone to death. He doesn't speak for long seconds, dragging his palms over his face with a sigh.

"What the hell was that?" I shout.

"Mind your own damn business." Finn plucks his beer from the grass before disappearing into the woods.

I have no clue if he's chasing after Sketchy Guy or just in the mood for a midnight stroll, but as my housemate dives deeper into the forest by Lacey's house, there isn't a doubt in my mind.

Wherever he's going…

I'm going, too.

Fourteen

Diamond

I've always been terrified of horror movies.

Grew up admiring the girls that can power through them without shitting their pants, but me? I'm not brave. What I am, though… is *stupid.*

The kind of stupid that follows her boss's son into a forest in the middle of the night, only to lose him two minutes later with no service on her phone.

On the bright side, no need to watch horror movies if you're living one.

I've been wandering around the trail by Lacey's house for thirty minutes now. I'm constantly looking over my shoulder, half-expecting an axe murderer to jump out of a bush and chop me up into pieces.

I realize I've been walking in a circle when I recognize the maple tree on my left—it's the third time I've seen it.

Two initials are carved into the trunk.

H + N.

So, not only have I lost Finn, but I've also lost my way.

Nice going, Dia.

I've refused to stray from the hiking trail in fear of getting devoured by some animal in the woods, but I can't keep going in circles. Maybe the only way out is through?

Stepping off the path, I grab my house keys out of my pocket and trap one into my fist. Not that I expect a *key* to stop a bear from eating me alive, but it's the best defense I've got. Plus, wild animals aren't the only thing I'm worried about. Finn's sketchy "friend" might be roaming these woods, too.

Tears forming in the corners of my eyes, I trudge through the forest with my phone flashlight on. I understand I've reached the town's abandoned railway when I almost trip over the track, thick roots and weeds twisting around the rusted steel.

I have no clue where this leads.

Odds are, following this track will only drag me deeper into the woods, but I don't see a better alternative to find cell service. I walk for fifteen minutes and stop when I emerge out of the woods and spot the town's wooden trestle bridge ahead of me.

Silver Bridge.

It was named after the town. Back when people still thought the railways were a good idea. The train was to be a fast and affordable way to get to neighboring towns. A sign of growth for Silver Springs. Little did we know, our annual death toll would start to grow, too.

Silver Bridge quickly became a gathering spot for the youth. Kids would meet there at night to watch the town lights, which, admittedly, are *breathtaking* from up here. They'd hang out, get drunk, then run out of the way when they heard the train coming.

Thirty-seven kids died on Silver Bridge the first year.

Some fell off the bridge into the rocks; others were crushed by the trains. They put up countless warning signs, but teenagers forged ahead anyway, convinced it wouldn't happen to them.

To this day, hundreds of people have died here—most of them minors. The town pulled the plug on the project after the bridge claimed the mayor's kid's life.

No one really comes here anymo—

Wait.

Is that a shadow?

Yes, it is.

There's someone here.

A man.

Standing disturbingly still on the bridge.

The moon, sea of stars, and distant town lights allow me to see the stranger's feet extending past the edge of the structure, eyes riveted to the horizon. I stiffen up when the guy's focus drifts to the abyss beneath him and he assesses the compacted rocks responsible for numerous funerals.

He's looking at a three-hundred-foot fall.

Three. Hundred. Feet.

But he doesn't back away.

He doesn't even *flinch.*

I'm alone with this stranger in the woods, with no cell reception and absolutely no way to call for help if the need arises, but I can't just leave this guy here.

I have to do *something.*

"Hm, excuse me?" I call.

It feels like the air has been sucked out of my lungs when the stranger flicks his head in my direction, and I realize that the boy on the bridge isn't a stranger *at all.*

"F-Finn?" My voice cracks.

I've seen many emotions on Finn Richards's face since the day I moved into his house—anger, hatred, desire—but this one? This one I've never seen before.

I've never seen him *hurt.*

It's in his eyes.

In the way his mouth falls open for a short moment. He looks shocked, a little bit drunk, but mostly, he looks sad.

Broken.

I don't know squat when it comes to reading this guy, but I know he didn't expect to see me here. And he sure didn't expect me to follow him to the deadliest spot in town.

Finn slaps on an impenetrable poker face, sips on the beer he was holding when he took off earlier, and diverts his attention back to the shimmering lights ahead of him.

This moment.

This scene.

It brings me back to that night in the library. Back to begging Finn to get off the window, wondering why in the *hell* he would put himself in danger like this.

That's the missing piece to my puzzle.

It all starts to make sense from there.

My brother's overprotectiveness. The things he said to me in the car all those weeks ago. He said Finn was a fucked-up masochist. That he was dangerous but not to others.

To himself.

That's what he meant, isn't it?

This isn't the first time Finn's played with fire like this. I heard the stories but never believed them. Finn was quite the topic sophomore year. Word on the street was Finn had been arrested for car theft, underage drinking, vandalism—all before the age of seventeen. It's also been said that he'd end up in the hospital weekly…

If the rumors are true, this boy has been digging his own grave *his entire life.*

"What the hell are you doing?" I was aiming for a firm voice, but it comes out as a plea. He doesn't answer, keeping his eyes glued to the skyline.

I'm worried he's giving me the silent treatment until he downs what's left of his beer and shocks me with a simple question.

"Do you like the ocean?"

I try to convince myself that I became hearing-impaired in the last two minutes. That would make a lot more sense than my housemate asking me if I like the goddamn *ocean* right now.

Finn waits a beat for my answer, then carries on when it

becomes obvious that it's not coming.

"She didn't," he says, his voice barely above a whisper.

I put the pieces together right away.

He said *she.*

And there's only one woman that's ever mattered to this guy.

His mom.

"She was terrified of it, actually." He pauses. "She could barely get in the pool with me."

I know he's probably just sharing because he's drunk, but I'll be damned if I don't learn what I can while it lasts.

"She hated boats, too. Even after my dad tried to name one after her." A deep laugh rips from his throat, and the sound alone makes my bones quiver. "God, she hated that fucking thing."

I hold my breath with all my might, scared that I'll say the wrong thing and the spell will break.

"It took me a year to convince her to get on it."

My heart immediately splits down the middle.

"I thought…" The pain in his voice tears me apart. "I thought if she just tried it *once…*"

He never looks at me as he divulges his darkest secrets, staring blankly into the night as if he's somewhere else.

Out of his body.

Out of his head.

Out of this shit town.

"One time." He proves me right. "One fucking time. That's

all it took."

Oh my God.

The one time she got on the boat, she drowned?

I'm startled when he chucks his beer down the bridge with all his strength. I hear the glass shatter against the rocks, and all I can think is…

That could be his skull.

Just one wrong move and he's dead.

And the worst part?

I don't think he wants to die.

I'd bet my soul that he'd never *actually* jump off that bridge.

He's tempting fate. Giving the universe a chance to do it for him. Waiting to see if karma will take the bait and punish him for what he did. Because deep down…

He thinks that's what he *deserves.*

I stop inches before the bridge begins.

"It wasn't your fault," I croak.

Finn's eyes cut to mine, and I can practically *see* his walls going back up.

"Don't fucking do that," he snaps.

"Do what?"

"Look at me like I'm a wounded puppy you want to nurse back to health."

I ignore him. "Get off the bridge."

"Just fucking go, Dia." He shuts me out, diverting his focus to the emptiness beneath.

I spend the next five seconds searching for a way to get him to open up again, then a few more seconds disapproving of the only plan I came up with.

He got mad earlier.

No, he got *murderous.*

When the sketchy guy talked about touching me, he went crazy. Part of me would like to believe he did it because he cares about me. Even just a little bit…

So, I use the only leverage I have.

Myself.

My heart pounding in my ears, I step onto the bridge.

Don't look down.

Don't look down.

Finn's rough voice cuts through the air instantly.

"Dia, what the fuck?"

Bingo.

I keep my head high, locking eyes with him across the bridge.

"What the fuck are you doing? Stay back," he barks, extending one arm out like that's going to stop me from getting any closer.

"What? So, it's perfectly fine when *you're* standing on a deadly bridge, but I can't?" I point out.

Fuming, he stares daggers into my forehead.

"Why are you doing this to yourself?" I question.

"Dia, I swear to God, if you don't turn your ass around right now—"

I cut in. "Answer the question. Why are you doing this to yourself?"

"Dia, stop!" he snaps, fear gleaming in his eyes, but I don't heed his warning.

"Tell me why!"

That's his snapping point.

"Because it should've been me."

His voice is so piercing I stop dead. Just like that, the boy who claims to feel nothing drops his heart at my feet.

"She saved me." He sounds like he's *this* close to falling apart, and my whole being aches to put him back together. "She saved my fucking life, and it wasn't…"

Worth it?

I want to finish for him but decide against it. A million questions clash in my head, the obvious one being what exactly happened that day? I want to know how she saved him, what caused the accident, but I also know the last thing Finn needs right now is an interview on the worst day of his life.

"And I know it's fucked-up—" He shoves a hand through his tousled hair, gripping a handful like he's trying to get his mind straight. "—but I need to know how she felt. Did it hurt? Was she scared? Did she… *hate* me?"

My first instinct is to hug the breath out of him. Problem is, my pity won't help him. I'm sure the boy who watched his mother die has had more than enough people pity him in his lifetime. What he really needs is for someone to open his eyes.

"You're full of shit, you know that?"

He looks at me, shock all over his face.

"You act like you don't want this, but you like feeling this way, don't you?" I close in on him and watch his shoulders sink under the weight of the truth. He doesn't speak, but the resentment in his eyes conveys the impact of my words.

"Why else would you keep putting yourself in these situations?" I come to a stop before him. "You like punishing yourself. *You get off on it.*"

He sucks in a breath when I cross the void between us and press my hand to his torso. I feel his chest heaving up and down, his heart hammering against my palm.

The near proximity forces him to lower his head to look at me, the lines I drew between us getting blurrier and blurrier. The moonlight gleams in his eyes, and for a short moment, I almost forget we're *three hundred feet* away from imminent death.

"You feel that?" I apply pressure to his chest. "The air filling your lungs?"

He waits for me to carry on.

"That's privilege… And what you're doing right now? It's wasting that privilege."

There are tears in my eyes, but somehow, they feel foreign.

Like they don't belong to me.

Like I'm feeling everything he *refuses* to.

"What happened to your mom…"

From the moment I bring up his mother, he pulls away.

Emotionally, physically—in all the ways that matter.

He starts closing himself off.

Looking away.

He starts to *run*.

Because that's what he's always done.

"Hey, stay with me." I recycle the line he used on me the night he took my first kiss and surprise myself when I grab his face between my hands. "What happened to your mom was *not* your fault. Do you hear me? It wasn't."

He doesn't want to hear this, but he needs to. He needs to hear it before he does something stupid again and gets himself killed. I'm not nearly foolish enough to believe that I can save Finn Richards from his demons, but maybe, if I'm lucky…

I can get him to save himself.

"Don't you get it? Every time you put yourself in danger like this." I fail to swallow the pit in my throat. "Every time you punish yourself because you think that's what you deserve… you risk throwing away the *one* thing she died to save."

I know I'm getting through to him when he squeezes his eyes shut as if to stop himself from showing vulnerability.

"Don't you dare throw it away," I choke out.

He peels his eyelids open at my words, and I flinch. His eyes… They're bloodshot, battling tears. Seeing him so vulnerable, so *hurt*, feels like a violent blow to the stomach. I could wish on every damn star in the sky for a colder heart, a soul that doesn't suffer when his does, but it wouldn't change the fact that I care.

Somewhere along the way, I started *caring* about this idiot.

In spite of everything.

In spite of the whole world telling me he's a monster.

We don't separate for long seconds, my hands cupping his face in the darkness, his breath crashing against my mouth as he stares me in the eyes. Relief creeps in when Finn presses his forehead to mine and whispers a small, heartbreaking "Let's go."

Snapping out of it, I nod in agreement and slowly withdraw my hands from his face. My breathing unsteady, I pivot and start leading the way back to solid ground.

I'm two steps ahead of him when I hear it.

The loud creaking of wood behind me. The devil laughing on my shoulder when part of the bridge collapses from under him. But the sound I hear on repeat? The noise I know will haunt me forever? Is the scream leaving my lips…

When he *falls*.

Fifteen

Diamond

I couldn't tell you how many times I've wanted to kill Finn Richards… How many times I've pictured myself pushing him off a bridge for his cruel pranks. But now that he's *really* hanging on to a bridge, gripping the edge with his body suspended over a massive void?

I know my parents were right.

Be careful what you wish for.

My screams sound like distant echoes when I kneel on the remaining part of the bridge. The snapping sounds erupting around me make it clear that the bridge is a ticking time bomb, but all I can think about is the rude boy holding on to a life he wasn't sure he wanted two minutes ago…

There's fear in his eyes.

Panic.

Regret.

Part of me wonders if this is the ultimate punishment for him. Getting a peek of death after flirting with it for years, only to realize it's the worst preview he's ever had.

A wave of nausea rolls through my stomach when I see the emptiness beneath him, the sharp rocks just waiting to crush every bone in his body.

If he hadn't caught himself, he'd be dead right now.

Both his hands clutch the structure, but it seems slippery. From the moment he removes one hand, I'll have limited time to bring him up.

"Give me your hand," I shout, stretching my arm out as far as I can go. I have to lie flat on my stomach in order to reach him. Finn is petrified. He doesn't even blink.

"Finn!" I cry out, choking on the pit in my throat. "Finn! Give me your hand. *Please.*"

His arms begin to shake under the weight of his body, and the little self-control I have left spills out of me in the form of tears. He needs to snap out of it.

"Trust me. Please. You have to trust me." I release the most piercing plea of my life.

His eyes jerk open at the scream leaving my mouth. He's never fully trusted anyone, or trusted *life*, since it took his mom away, but he has to believe not everyone is going to let him down. He has to believe in me.

"Finn!" A sob escapes my throat, kicking him into gear, and he squeezes his eyes shut for a second. I have hope again when he throws his arm in my direction, aiming for my hand.

My scream echoes in the night.

He missed.

He's hanging from one hand now, his other arm drooping by his side.

"Again!" I stretch my arm out all the way down to my fingertips. Finn nods and flings his available arm up with all his strength, letting out a deep wail of rage, fear, and pain that makes me ache bone-deep.

That's when his hand locks with mine.

And I know it all comes down to this moment.

The adrenaline kicking in, I pour all I have into pulling him up and cry out in pain when sharp debris cuts into my arm. Still, I don't let go, ignoring the blood dripping down my skin. I choke on a sob when we fall backward onto the bridge and he collapses on top of me.

We did it.

The bridge trembles at the impact of our bodies crashing together, and the noises multiply at an alarmingly fast rate.

We have to get the hell off this bridge.

I don't waste a second lifting to my feet, trapping Finn's hand into mine and dragging him back to solid ground. We've barely charged off the bridge before half the structure caves in. The whole thing comes undone and crashes against the razor-sharp rocks below. I feel Finn's hand *strangling* mine as we watch one of the deadliest bridges in North Carolina go down.

Then it starts to creep in.

This really happened.

My knees fumble at the thought, and my entire body begins

to shake. I spin to look at Finn, and the look on his face… That shit rips my heart up into a million pieces.

He's pale, his hand limp in mine, with his mouth hanging open as he stares at the massive hole where the bridge once stood.

It's hitting him, too.

He almost died.

For real, this time.

After playing with death for ten years, he finally got his wish. I'm furious at him for putting himself in this situation in the first place, but it doesn't even come close to the worry I feel for him.

"Are you okay?" I'm still sobbing as I clutch his face between my hands and scan him for an injury. Meanwhile, the cut on my arm is bloody and stinging like a motherfucker, but I can't bring myself to care.

As though he's in some sort of trance, Finn doesn't speak or acknowledge me, staring blankly ahead of him.

Then he falls to his knees in the dirt.

I wonder what to do for a bit but quickly drop to my knees as well, positioning myself in front of him so he has a clear view of *me* rather than what's left of the bridge.

Under the moon and distant town lights, I swear I can see part of his demons burst into flames. My tears pick up again, my body making a decision my brain didn't get a chance to veto. Without a warning, I throw my arms around his neck, mesh my body to his, and hug the hell out of him.

I hug him so hard I'm surprised he's able to breathe, but he doesn't push me away, stiff in my arms.

I'm not even the tiniest bit offended that he doesn't reciprocate the hug. If anything, I only hold him tighter, giving up my pride entirely so that he knows he's not alone.

He doesn't welcome my embrace, and I eventually take the hint, but as soon as I start to move away, his arms close around me and he hugs me back.

He holds me to his chest for dear life, one of his hands darting to the back of my head as he nestles his nose in the crook of my neck and inhales sharply.

We stay in this position for long seconds—two kids hugging in the dirt next to a collapsed bridge in the middle of the night.

Yes, I know it'll take a lot more than a near-death experience to completely heal this guy. To put an end to his self-destructive behavior. But tonight, he chose to hold on instead of letting go. Tonight, he chose to live in a world where his mom isn't.

And it's not perfect…

But it's a start.

* * *

Finn

The grass is wet when I plop down on the ground in my backyard. Normally, I'd pass on freezing my balls off, but my clothes are already drenched from getting caught in the rain. Worst-case scenario, the flu knocks me on my ass for a few days, and I get a break from the train wreck that's my own head.

Sounds like a win to me.

It must've started hailing less than two minutes after we pulled ourselves off the ground and decided to head back to Lacey's. The woods were cold and gloomy, but I much preferred the darkness over having to look Dia in the eyes.

She saved me.

She saved my fucking life.

Meanwhile, I've done nothing but try to ruin hers.

She disappeared up the stairs to take a shower from the moment we stepped foot inside the house. She was so cold her teeth were chattering, her delicate body shaking like a leaf.

But me? I was numb.

Tragically and miraculously *numb.*

She's probably in bed by now. I should do the same, but I doubt I'd get much sleep, anyway. And even if I did, I'd just have nightmares about the look on her face when the bridge collapsed.

The clock showed 5:00 a.m. by the time we managed to find Theo passed out with Lacey in her bedroom. Turns out I lost my phone while fighting for my life, and Gem's phone was dead. Lacey said Theo was hammered and to take his car, that she'd drop him off tomorrow.

It'll be morning soon, and knowing this day will be over in a few minutes brings me a strange amount of relief. I brace one leg against my chest, the other lying flat in the grass, and stare at the horizon for at least ten minutes before the patio door creaks open.

I guess she's not in bed, after all.

I keep my focus on the sky, willing the sun to do its fucking job and mark the beginning of a new day. Hesitant footsteps approach me, and a small gasp slips from Gem's lips when she sits on the wet grass by my side. I notice her shoulders are wrapped in a thick blanket, her curls still damp from the shower.

"I'm taking Lexie to the groomer tomorrow." She tries to make conversation.

I nod in response.

I don't fucking know how to talk to her anymore. A normal person would opt for "thank you for saving my life," but it doesn't feel right. It doesn't feel like *enough*.

I was supposed to hate this fucking girl.

I was supposed to send her packing, and now?

Now I'm glad my mediocre father hired her for the summer.

That's right, I'm *glad*.

What the fuck happened to me?

When I don't answer, she picks up a dandelion poking out from the freshly mowed grass and offers it to me.

"Dandelion for your thoughts," she says quietly.

I crack a smile and flip my head in her direction. Her big brown eyes are still a tad red and puffy from crying. Her mouth is pink, swollen from her nervous lip biting on the drive home. She looks up at me through a curtain of thick eyelashes, and I clench my fists to keep my impulses in check.

Fuck, the things I want to do to this girl…

Too bad I can never touch her again.

I see it now.

She's too pure.

Too good.

Too innocent.

For fuck's sake, she risked her *life* for me. When the bridge first caved, she could've left me there. Me, her boss's asshole son who loves making her life miserable. She could've run. No one would've ever known. I'd just be another sad story in a small-town newspaper.

But she didn't.

She stayed, knowing damn well the bridge wasn't going to last much longer. And she may act tough, but there is nothing but light in Diamond Mitchell's heart. I would break her in a second if I got my hands on her again.

And she doesn't deserve to be broken.

Not her.

"Sorry, I'll leave you to it," she mutters following my lack of a response.

She's pushed to her feet, ready to head back to the house, when my hand darts upward and I catch her wrist midair. I didn't even mean to do it. Nor do I mean to sound like a world-class pussy as I mumble, "Thank you."

She's stunned but snaps out of it fast enough.

"For what?" she questions like she *genuinely* doesn't know.

"Saving my life," I clarify.

I can feel my fingers tugging on her wrist, willing her to sit back down, and wonder why my body is a defying asshole that won't listen to my brain. Taken aback by my silent request, she complies, regaining her seat by my side.

She cracks a smile once she's sat down in the wet grass.

"What else was I going to do? *Let you fall?*"

"You could've," I point out. "After everything I've done to you, I wouldn't blame you."

I expect her to feed me another nauseatingly nice line, but instead, she smacks me in the back of the head.

Shocked, I blink at her.

Did she just *hit* me?

"*That's* what you deserve for everything you've done to me." She shrugs. "Not death."

With that said, she directs her focus to the distant light and rosy colors casting over the hill. The sun should be rising at any moment now.

She hit me.

She hit me in the fucking head, and I'm *smiling.*

This girl is a goddamn mystery to me.

I scoff. "You're something, Mitchell."

She flips her head to look at me. "A good something or a

bad something?"

The kind of something I want to break and protect all at once.

"Jury's still out." I gently bump my shoulder into hers.

"Don't make me regret dragging your ass off that bridge, Richards," she teases.

We don't speak for a few seconds, staring into the distance.

She breaks the silence. "I have a question."

"Shoot."

"What was that shady meeting in the woods about?"

"I owed the scumbag money," I say.

"No shit." She snorts. "What I meant is *why*? Aren't you rich?"

My entire body contracts at her question.

I can't be honest.

I want to, but I can't.

She might think she's seen the worst of me with the thermostat and clothes-in-the-fountain pranks, but she has no idea. God, she has no *fucking* idea how far I was willing to go to get rid of her.

Everything I did was to hurt her.

But that was before she saved my life.

She can never know what I did with that money.

"I'm not rich. My father is."

She nods. "What was the money for, anyway?"

"I think it was for weed? I honestly can't remember," I lie through my teeth.

"Also, why were you on that bridge?"

I laugh at her bluntness. "You said *one* question."

"People lie. Get over it." She grins, blissfully unaware of the irony of the situation.

"What can I say?" I shrug, lying on my back in the grass. "Shit is no fun unless it almost kills me."

She follows my lead, lying down next to me and whisking her head to the side to look at me. "Yeah, but why Silver Bridge? It was like you knew where you were going. You booked it into the woods and went straight there."

"That's where my parents met," I admit, wedging my arm under my head for support.

Silence.

She doesn't know what to say, so I spare her the trouble of coming up with a botched version of "I'm sorry your life sucks so much."

"Those woods, the bridge—that's where it all started." I laugh. "Funny, isn't it? All they fucking do is talk about people dying on that bridge. Meanwhile, it's the only reason I was born."

Any other girl would pity me, but we're talking about the girl who called me out on my shit when I was standing on the edge of a fucking *bridge,* so I'm not surprised when she skips out on the pity party.

"How did it happen? Their first meeting?"

I grin. "It was the Fourth of July. Every year, kids would

meet on Silver Bridge to watch the fireworks. Best view in town."

She listens carefully.

"She'd just moved here. My dad spent the night getting shitfaced to work up the courage to ask her out. And when he finally got the nerve to walk up to her, he wound up projectile vomiting all over her shirt."

A small laugh slips past her lips. "Way to make a good impression."

"Hey, he must've done *something* right, or I wouldn't be here." I scoff and fidget with the silver chain around my neck. It's twisted and uncomfortable as shit.

Gem watches me struggle for a moment before stepping in. "Let me do it."

She inches closer, pressing her tits to my arm, and starts to untangle the chain I never take off. My gaze finds her mouth instantly. She sinks her teeth into her plump bottom lip as she focuses on the task at hand.

Not going to lie, she's fucking cute when she's serious.

What the fuck did I just think?

"Did your mom make that?" She pulls away, snapping me out of it.

I'm not sure I want to go there with her.

Or anyone.

I don't reply right away, debating on letting her see even more of my darkness. To be fair, she's already seen more in a single night than most of my friends ever will.

"I noticed Xavier has one, too," she adds.

"Yeah. She gave us matching chains on my eighth birthday." I pause, a bitter scoff surging in my throat. "Right before she got on a boat to her death."

My dark humor seems to startle her because she doesn't laugh. Instead, she stares at me with soul-withering pity, the look in her eyes making me want to take a page out of my old man's handbook and hurl everywhere.

"On your birthday?" she croaks.

I cringe.

I'm not surprised. That's the common reaction when I tell people my mom got on the boat as a birthday present to me. It's not like I can blame them, either. Imagine your mom dying on your birthday because she agreed to get on a boat for you.

Hell, *I'd* feel bad for me.

"Is that the day she got you Lexie?" Dia asks.

I arch an eyebrow.

"Theo told me she was a gift from your mom," she says.

That blabbermouth.

"It was the day before, actually."

A smile stretches over her lips. "You must've been so happy."

I nod. "Over the moon. I'd been begging my parents for a dog since I was old enough to know what a dog was."

"How did they tell you?"

I'm the one smiling now.

"My mom said a surprise was waiting for me in the backyard. I was so fucking excited. They'd left Lexie on the patio, but while they were gone, she started chasing a squirrel and wandered off. I ran out of the house and found a dead squirrel. *Happy birthday to me.*"

She chuckles. "How did you react?"

I laugh. "I definitely wondered if my mom was gifting me a dead animal for a second."

Memories flow through me.

"But then I saw her."

I'll never forget seeing Lexie run toward me that day. I immediately knew this adorable pup slash squirrel killer was going to become my best friend.

"That's why you're so protective of her. Because your mom gave her to you," she gathers.

"Hard not to be. I promised my mom I'd look after her, no matter what. I swore I'd protect her. *Always.*"

There's a moment of silence.

"Your dad's name is Hank." It doesn't sound like a question but a statement.

"Yeah?"

"And your mom's name was Nora, right?"

I nod.

Instantly, her eyes light up.

She saw their tree, didn't she?

The one with their initials carved into it?

That's the only thing that makes sense.

"You know people say the bridge is cursed." I change the topic before she starts interrogating me again. "Legend says every lost soul who walks the bridge will come to meet a tragic end."

"What do *you* think?" she asks.

I shrug. "Normally, I'd say it's a load of shit, but… after what happened tonight, a curse isn't that far-fetched."

"That's the thing with curses." She rolls onto her side, giving me her undivided attention. "They can be broken."

I do the same.

"Only heroes break curses, Gem. And I'm no hero."

Our eyes lock, and I search her face for a glimmer of doubt.

There's nothing.

Everyone in this godforsaken town looks at me like I'm damaged. Beyond help.

Everyone but *her*.

"Have you learned nothing from fairy tales, Richards? We rarely become heroes until the end of the story."

My mouth falls open.

She had to pull my ass up from a bridge I got on *voluntarily*, and she still has faith in me. She sees something that's not there. Man is it going to hurt when she falls from her cloud.

"My turn," I speak up. "Why'd you follow me?"

She pauses for a second, specks of fear floating in her brown eyes.

“I was just curious.”

I snort. “Bullshit.”

“I’m not lying.” She flips onto her back.

“Wrong answer. Try again.” I nag the truth out of her.

“Jesus Christ, fine. I was worried about you. I worry about your reckless ass—big deal.”

I knew that already, but it sure feels good to hear her say it.

“Look, Gem… If you’re obsessed with me, just say so.”

She lets out a bitter laugh.

“Oh, that’s grand coming from the guy who nearly choked someone to death for talking about me.”

Shit. She’s got me there.

Finn, 0.

Gem, 1.

“I wouldn’t have killed him.”

That’s a lie.

I wouldn’t have killed him *intentionally*, but I blacked out when he talked about doing these things to her. Who knows what would’ve happened if she hadn’t shown up.

“If you’re obsessed with me, just say so.” She gives me a taste of my own medicine.

I’m prepared to talk back when she pushes a strand of her hair behind her ear.

My fists immediately close into tight balls.

What the fuck?

What is *that*?

There's a cut on her arm. A long, deep red lesion stretching all the way from her wrist to her elbow.

"Who did that to you?" The words are out of my mouth before I can blink.

She glances down at her arm, instantly sitting up and covering the injury with her palm. "Oh, that? It's nothing. I've had that forever."

She's full of shit.

It looks fresh.

God, I did that to her, didn't I?

She must've hurt herself when she was trying to lift me up. I'm quick to sit up and snatch her arm into my hands to get a closer look.

"Don't fucking lie to me," I grit out.

She understands she's busted right away. "It doesn't even hurt."

In response, I slightly squeeze her arm near her wound, and she flinches.

Liar.

"I never should've gone to that fucking bridge." I drop back down onto the grass with a sigh.

Why the hell am I this mad?

Why the hell do I *care*?

"Don't do that." She lies back down, guiding my face to the side. Our eyes meet again, but mine are searing with rage.

"Don't beat yourself up. If I knew the place my biological parents met, I'd be there in a heartbeat," she confesses.

I jump at the chance to change the subject to get my mind off her wounded arm. Before I go out and strangle someone else.

"You don't know much about them, huh?" I ask.

"Try *nothing*," she corrects. "Don't get me wrong, I love my parents to death, but I still wonder, you know?"

"Why don't you just ask them?"

"I guess I don't want to seem like an asshole? They did everything for me, and here I am, wanting to know more about the dirtbags who gave me up." She pauses. "Well, technically, my mom died, so she couldn't take care of me, but my dad didn't exactly scour the planet to find me."

"Maybe he doesn't know."

"Is it bad that I hope you're right?" She chews on her bottom lip, and my dick jerks in my pants.

Fucking hell, I thought I had this whole "stop imagining her tits bouncing in my face" thing nailed down.

Clearly, I was wrong.

"Nah. If he knew, he's a shitbag who abandoned his daughter. If he didn't, there's hope," I reassure her.

She smiles a grateful smile, as though she needed the validation that she's not a terrible person. Funny thing is, she's the least terrible person I've ever met.

The sun is near rising, the sky a blend of pink, orange, and red. We spend the next minute watching Mother Nature do her thing.

"You said something earlier…" Her voice is shaky, as though whatever she's about to say scares the crap out of her. "That shit is no fun unless it almost kills you?"

I nod.

She inhales a sharp breath to keep her anxiety in line. "Is that why you kissed me? That night in the wine cellar? Because I taste like *poison*?"

Fair question, but I'm a tad shocked that she had the guts to bring it up.

"I kissed you because you're the only fucking thing that doesn't…"

Her mouth trickles open at my admission.

"Wait, are you saying absolutely nothing brings you joy?"

"I'm saying the things that bring me joy also bring me *guilt*."

I assume her newfound courage has run out until she places her trembling hand on my stomach and sucks in a quivery breath.

"Even *this*?"

I'm positive I'm dreaming when her fingers slip toward my crotch. My gaze connects with hers, the promises I made myself about never touching her again bursting into flames.

Technically, she's the one touching me.

That doesn't count, does it?

Her cheeks are bright red, her pupils are dilated, and her

chest is moving up and down at an alarming pace.

She wants this.

My dick swells up when she starts playing with the waistband of my pants.

No. Fucking. Way.

I said I was done.

That she was too good, too pure for me.

That she didn't deserve to be broken.

"Dia," I warn in a weak attempt to scare her off, but she bats her eyelashes at me, so painfully clueless as to the dangerous road she's venturing on.

"W-What about *this*?" she stammers, slipping her hand inside my pants and luring a groan from somewhere deep within my throat. "Does this make you feel guilty?"

Baby, you have no idea…

All bets are off when she cups my cock over my briefs and squeezes. Her touch is timid and gentle. She palms me so softly it's maddening.

Don't do this to her, my conscience shouts, but my body refuses to pull the panic cord.

And my mouth?

My mouth is a backstabbing traitor.

"Fuck, you're killing me." I throw my head back, hating myself because I know how this story ends. I'm going to take everything this girl has to give.

Until there's nothing left.

Until she's just as empty as I am.

She pulls her hand out of my pants, resting her fingers flat on my abs. "Is this okay? I can stop, I—"

I don't think my next move through, grabbing her fist and shoving it inside my briefs. Her clumsy little hand wraps around my cock instantly, my hips jerking forward at the contact. She starts rubbing me up and down, her grip growing tighter and tighter as she guides her fist to the head of my cock, then back to the base.

"Oh, fuck," I groan through gritted teeth. She doesn't seem to know what she's doing—it must've been a while since she was with a guy—and it turns me on even more. I wince when she squeezes me a tad too hard.

"Did I hurt you?" She panics, the strong, sassy girl whose loud mouth I've grown to appreciate buried deep under a mountain of insecurity.

She starts to move her hand out of my pants, but I might die of a serious case of blue balls if she stops now.

"Don't fucking stop." I'm practically begging her at this point, and maybe I'd give a shit if her hand didn't feel so good.

The worst part is, it feels good because it's *her*.

She continues her frankly awkward hand job for a few minutes, and if it were any other girl touching me, I'd probably find her technique to be on the "meh" side.

She's holding back, a prisoner of her own head.

She needs to stop overthinking it.

She gasps when I reach for the back of her hair and smash my mouth against hers. There's a desperation in the way I kiss her, and it feels like a sin. Like I'm corrupting an angel, securing her a spot in hell. *Dragging her down with me…*

I nibble on her bottom lip for a bit, massaging her skull to help her relax, and she gradually eases her tight grip on my cock. My tongue darts out to lick the seam of her mouth as she opens up for me, moaning against my lips while I tug on her wrist and yank her closer.

I've got her pinned to me in an instant, her right leg draped over my thighs as she continues to *try* to jerk me off in my briefs.

"Tell me what to do," she croaks inside my mouth.

I could come just from that.

Fuck yes I'll show you what to do.

Still kissing the hell out of her, I nudge my pants down with one hand, the other lost in her curls. My cock bobs against my stomach, the tip slapping my abs when my underwear slides off. I'm so hard it's torture.

She disrupts the kiss the next second, ogling me with this curious look in her eyes. I know damn well it's not because of my size—let's just say I've never had a problem in that department—which leads me to believe mine is the first dick she's ever seen.

Shit, is she a virgin?

Nah.

Not possible.

I always assumed she'd been with at least one guy. I mean, for fuck's sake, *look* at her, but her clumsy hand job and the way she's devouring my cock with her eyes?

I'm starting to think she's not just *rusty*.

Wait… what if the wine cellar was…

No, there's no way that was her first kiss.

The questions slip my mind when she swallows hard and circles my shaft with her fist.

"Now what?" she asks.

"Spit in your hand," I instruct, and her cheeks flare, but she obliges, spitting inside her palm and lowering her fist back onto me. I groan as she speeds up and down my length, the sensation already a hundred times better than when I was trapped inside my briefs.

I picture myself fucking each and every one of her holes, delving into her possibly virgin cunt, and shit…

I start shaking.

Throbbing between her fingers.

"Fuck, Dia. I need your mouth. Give me your mouth, baby." I sound like a little bitch in agony to my own ears and have no doubt I must sound even worse to her. I don't really expect her to do it. If I'm right and she's a virgin, she might not be ready for a blowjob.

I nearly lose my mind when she kneels by my side and sucks the head of my cock into her mouth.

Yep, I'm done.

RIP, my balls.

She's shy in the way she blows me, taking me deeper inch by inch until she accidentally chokes.

"That's right, baby," I grunt, twisting her slightly wet hair around my fist.

She moans at my comment, and I have to tap into *every single drop* of self-control in my body not to fuck her mouth. I mentally take back everything I said about her being a virgin when she twirls her tongue around me.

There's no way she could suck my dick like that.

This can't be her first time.

I see the sun rising in the background as her head bobs up and down with each stroke of her tongue. I want to slap myself when I forcefully push down onto her head and make her gag.

What the fuck am I doing?

She immediately pulls back, her glare suggesting I've gone too far. "Do that again and I'll bite it off."

I withdraw my hand from her hair on cue. "Shit, I'm sorry. You want to stop?"

I expect her to leave me hanging or make good on her promise and bite my dick off, but she doesn't, hesitant to accept my apology. But I'm already losing my hard-on. Knowing I forced her into something she wasn't into is enough to kill the mood, and she notices my cock shrinking.

"I didn't say I wanted to stop. Just don't push on my head again." She draws the line and guides her tongue back to the head of my cock.

My erection is back in a microsecond, and *fuck,* I never thought I could be so turned on by a girl telling me off. Most girls I've been with didn't set limits. They'd look up at me with my balls in their mouth, choking on all sorts of daddy issues, practically begging for a *sliver* of my affection.

But *she* wouldn't bend her morals for my approval, and that shit right there is the sexiest fucking thing I've ever seen in my life. I throw my head back when she does the one thing I didn't see coming.

She deep-throats me *willingly.*

That's when I understand. It's not that she *didn't* want to do it; she just didn't want to feel like it was taken away from her. I shiver when she glances up at me, a raging fire and this unmissable satisfaction in her gaze.

She's eating that shit up.

She *loves* having me at her mercy.

I know I'm seconds away from blowing when her fist joins her tongue.

"Fuck, Dia, I'm going to blow down your fucking throat." I clench my jaw, giving her a chance to pull away before it's too late. I figured the least I could do is warn her so she can make the decision for herself, but she doesn't budge.

Instead, she chokes on my cock again.

"Then do it."

Holy. Fucking. Shit.

Next thing I know, I'm unloading into her mouth, pumping my hips with greedy thrusts and soiling the innocence I swore to protect less than an hour ago. I don't think I've ever come so hard in my life. Seriously. The colonel might go on strike after this.

I'm still convulsing when she detaches her mouth from my tip with a pop. I watch her swallow my cum as she wipes a drop from her mouth with her index.

Good Lord, where have you been hiding this girl?

On her knees, she sits back onto her heels, her black curls a gorgeous mess and her full lips glistening with need. We trade looks, and the fear cutting through her eyes tells me everything I need to know.

She's not the only one who disconnected from reality for a moment there. Neither of us speaks for a while, and this silence feels decisive. I've barely shoved my semi-hard dick back into my pants before she lets out, "This is the part where you run."

And she's right.

I *always* run.

I ran the day in the wine cellar.

I ran the day I fingered her against her bedroom door.

If the last ten years have taught me anything, it's that I'm damn good at bolting whenever it gets real. But there isn't one bone in my body that wants to bolt right now.

Without a warning, I grip her wrist and yank her back down on the grass with me. She falls onto my chest, her head pressed against my pec as I lace my inked arm around her waist. Not a word is spoken for the next thirty minutes.

Then I notice her breathing become regular.

She's got her nose nuzzled into my neck as she sleeps peacefully in my arms like a lamb to the slaughter. She says *I* should run. But tonight proved I'm willing to stain even the kindest, most virtuous souls just to get my fix…

And if anyone should be running?

It's her.

Sixteen

Diamond

There's something wet on my cheek.

I try to open my eyes, but the light is blinding, and I wonder how I was even able to sleep in the first place.

Shit, my back hurts.

My eyes snap open as I sit up straight, my senses slowly reconnecting with my body. The first thing I see is Lexie tilting her head to the side before sweeping her tongue across my cheek.

I'm surprised to find myself sitting on the grass in the backyard, but not nearly as surprised as I am when I look down and spot Finn sleeping soundly next to me.

It all comes rushing back.

The bridge.

Finn falling.

The… other thing.

Holy shit.

Part of the blanket I had wrapped around my shoulders last night covers Finn, the other half spread over my lap.

We fell asleep.

But why is Lexie in the backyard?

Someone had to let her out—

"What in the fuck?" A masculine voice sends me into cardiac arrest. I flick my head back to see a hungover Theo advancing toward us. He looks like he crawled out from the fiery pits of hell.

He must've just gotten home. Lacey said she'd be dropping him off in the morning. I elbow Finn in the ribs as though we've been caught red-handed, when in fact, we're both fully clothed.

He groans and stirs a bit, still half-asleep.

"Finn!" I give his shoulder a vigorous shake. He peels his eyes open and winces at the sun, blocking the light with his palm.

He notices Theo a few seconds later but doesn't react, his expression a frustrating enigma. Moving the blanket off his body, Finn yawns, taking his sweet time stretching as though he doesn't have a worry in the world.

We were just caught cuddling in the backyard, which is not a big deal in itself, so why do I feel like Theo knows everything?

Ironically, Theo seems *clueless.*

I thought maybe Finn had told him we'd done things before—it's no secret that guys like to run their mouths—but Theo doesn't seem to be in on it.

If anything, he looks like he had no idea Finn and I could even *bear* to be in each other's presence for a few minutes, let alone a whole night. Red stings my cheeks when Theo's shock shifts into a suspicious smirk.

"Well, well, what were you two doing?" he asks the burning question, and I peek at Finn, dreading his response.

I'd like to say I don't expect last night to have meant something, but from me saving Finn's life to us spilling secrets in the dark to the particularly filthy blowjob, it *was* pretty damn intense. Finn catches me eyeing him but pays me no mind, rising to his feet.

Then he flashes Theo a cocky smirk and says, "Take a wild fucking guess."

Theo's eyes convey his understanding.

And my throat hurts like a bitch.

Of course.

That's *all* it was to him.

"I'm going to hit the gym. You coming?" Finn ambles to the house without sparing me a look, and Theo follows suit.

"It's eight in the fucking morning the day after a party and you want to work out? Dude, you need help," Theo scorns.

I'm still seated on the grass, watching them walk away, when Finn stops by the sliding door and shoots me a glance over his shoulder. I'm almost foolish enough to believe he's going to make this up to me somehow.

Maybe smile.

Anything to help shake off the feeling of being used and thrown away. But his features remain as cold as can be.

"Don't forget to take Lexie to the groomer," he reminds me.

After making it clear that I was never anything more to him

than his errand girl, he trails back inside.

I'm stunned, embarrassed, but mostly…

I'm livid.

I can't believe I gave this asshole so many of my firsts, and for what? He couldn't care less about me. The sad truth dawns on me as I push to my feet and ball up the blanket into my arms.

I have to leave.

I stayed for Lexie before when I thought Finn was a terrible owner, but Theo was right—the only fucking thing Finn Richards loves in this world is his dog.

She's safe with him.

My heart, however?

Not so much.

* * *

A week later

I did the right thing.

Words I've been force-feeding myself since the day I packed my bags in a hurry and left the Richardses' house. I called Finn's dad to quit when I was walking home. Except, I didn't have the guts to turn in my resignation and ended up faking a bad cold instead.

My performance earned me seven whole days of lying in bed doing absolutely nothing. I told my parents I was sick, too. I knew my dads would get suspicious if I quit now with only two weeks of work left, and I couldn't handle the questions.

I've had a lot of time to think while a prisoner of my own bedroom, and I've come to the conclusion that I can't stomach the thought of never seeing Lexie again.

I miss her.

I miss her so much it hurts.

I'm going to offer to watch her for free once Mr. Richards gets back into town. Chances are, Finn will be crazy busy with basketball as soon as school picks up. I'm sure I can figure out a way to see her without running into him.

Granted, I doubt I'll be able to avoid him *now*.

Mr. Richards called me this morning to tell me a friend of his was in town and I could take an early leave if I wanted to. At first, I was worried maybe he wanted to get rid of me and he wasn't satisfied with my house sitter services. But then he gave me a huge bonus for work well done.

I've decided to go back to the house to gather the rest of my stuff and see Lexie again before I officially close the book on this summer.

Hey, Finn might not be the one, but at least he helped me gain a bit more experience. And he might've taken most of my firsts, but he'll *never* get the big V.

My new car roars loudly as I drive up to the house for the last time. I finally had enough to buy my bug car from Brenda a few days back, and my dads drove it home to surprise me. She's a bit noisy, but she only has to last me through senior year—the plan is to ditch the car expenses when I go to college.

Duke will be expensive enough as it is.

The house is quiet when I cross the threshold. No sign of Finn or Theo. I couldn't be more excited for Lexie's warm welcome, but she doesn't rush to the door like she always does. Struggling to rise off her bed, she drags herself down the hallway with obvious difficulty.

She looks exhausted.

She's been more and more tired lately.

"Come here." I meet her halfway and kneel in front of her. She puts all of her weight on me when I extend my arms around her, and she rests her head on my shoulder.

Something's wrong.

"Lex, are you okay?" I ask like I expect her to answer me.

I notice some sort of discharge around her eyes, and it takes all I have not to hop on the internet and scare myself to death by searching the cause. We didn't hear back from the vet following her annual tests, and I assumed everything was okay, but I'm starting to worry the tests just haven't come in yet.

I spend most of the day lying on the couch with Lexie, trying to call her ridiculously expensive vet—*trying* being the key word here. The line is busy every time, and I must leave over seven voicemails asking for a callback.

Lexie goes outside to do her business once or twice, retreating to the couch like clockwork. She also doesn't eat *at all* throughout the day. Around dinnertime, I start to wonder if I should just get in my car and drive to every vet in a two-hundred-mile radius until someone agrees to see her.

I'm pushing off the couch, prepared to pick Lexie up and carry her to my back seat, when I hear the front door slam. A masculine voice erupts in the hallway, and I tense up, praying for the newcomer to be Theo rather than Finn.

Lexie barely opens her eyes, too tired to acknowledge the company.

"Absolutely, we'll be there. Thank you." I recognize his voice before he even steps foot into the kitchen.

Finn walks in just in time for me to see him hang up the phone. He makes a beeline for the kitchen, too engulfed in his own thoughts to notice me standing in the living room, and plants both his palms onto the kitchen island.

His head hanging low, he releases a deep, heavy sigh like he's on the verge of losing it and squeezes his eyes shut to keep himself in check.

Only… he *fails*.

Every hair on my body stands on end when he lets out a rough, frustrated growl and chucks his phone against the kitchen wall with all his strength. His phone screen smashes on impact, chunks of glass flying everywhere. He just got that phone a few days ago after losing his first one on the bridge.

His outburst holds anger, desperation, fear, and all it takes is one look in Lexie's direction for me to understand the root of his breakdown.

It's her.

It's got to be.

I'm aware I should say something, make my presence known, but part of me is terrified of talking to him when he's in this state. I've dedicated the last week to convincing myself that Finn Richards is a heartless scumbag who only cares about himself, and I don't know if I can handle him proving me wrong.

The choice is taken away from me when he angles his head toward the living room and notices me.

Color drains from his skin.

"You're back," he says, his voice raspy, but I get the feeling that he knew that already. He probably saw my car parked out front but didn't think I'd be in the living room to witness his breakdown.

"I am."

"Why?" he immediately asks as though he can't make sense of my return. Maybe, deep down, he *knows* the way he treated me a week ago was unacceptable.

"To get my stuff," I admit.

He nods but doesn't answer, throwing open a closet and grabbing a broom to fix the mess. I'm fuming, loathing my foolish heart for wishing he'd ask me to stay or apologize as he cleans up the glass.

"There's something wrong with Lexie," I inform him. Maybe a subject change will prevent me from falling apart.

"I know." He sighs. "I've been trying to get her an appointment with her usual vet for two days. I found another vet willing to see her tomorrow afternoon."

That's who he was on the phone with when he came in.

"Thank God," I breathe out.

Finn makes his way to the couch to pet Lexie. "Has she been sleeping all day?"

"Yep. I haven't left her side."

"Go. I've got her for the night." He gestures to the stairs.

I don't want to leave her, but I'm also desperate for a shower. "Are you sure?"

"I've slept with her on the couch all week. Yes, I'm *sure*."

Reluctant, I approach the stairs at a snail's pace, his silence when I told him I came back to get my stuff plaguing my mind.

He really doesn't care, does he?

"I'm leaving tomorrow night, by the way," I explain, aiming for a semblance of a reaction. "Your dad told me a friend of his was in town and I could take off earlier if I wanted."

I *think* I see a streak of pain rip across his hazel eyes.

"Okay." He shrugs.

Okay.

That's how the story ends?

O-fucking-kay?

The words burst from my mouth seconds before my toe meets the first step. "Okay? That's all you have to say to me?"

I spin to find him staring at me, a hint of shock in his gaze.

I sound pathetic, needy even, but I can't help myself…

It was real.

The night in the library.

In the wine cellar.

In the backyard.

It was all real.

There was a connection. And no, it wasn't love. No, it wasn't a fairy tale, but it was *something.* My pulse wilding out in my neck, I give him one last chance to make this right.

He shoves a hand through his hair, glancing at his feet as he exhales. "What do you want me to say, Dia? It's called a summer job for a reason."

Then he stakes me in the chest with the final straw.

"After summer… it *ends.*"

***

There are many things I won't miss about working for Mr. Richards. For starters, I always *hated* having to walk to the nearby grocery store when I didn't have a car.

Sure, it's just a ten-minute walk, but carrying those heavy bags felt like a whole damn workout. I remember thinking I'd never walk there again after I bought my car, and yet, *here I am,* braving the scorching heat for a final trip to the grocery store.

I needed to get out of the house.

Do something productive and move my body instead of

sitting on the couch worrying about Lexie's appointment this afternoon.

Not to mention I was alone and bored out of my mind. Finn texted me he was taking Lexie for a walk a bit before I woke up, and Theo's been MIA since yesterday—he's probably with Lacey working on another pregnancy scare.

Glancing at the grocery bags in my hands, I try to drum up an excuse for my good deed. I won't be living with Finn much longer. Realistically, I won't even be there to eat the food I bought, but I couldn't take off knowing the guys are two weeks of ramen noodles away from starving. I even made a few casseroles and left them in the fridge this morning.

I'm a minute away from the house when I check my phone screen and notice I have a new voicemail.

From Lexie's vet.

Shit, how could I have missed this?

I don't waste a second unlocking my voicemail and pressing the phone to my ear.

Static.

A beep.

Then a woman's voice.

"Hi, this message is for Diamond Mitchell. This is Charlotte's Vet Centre. We have you as Finn Richards's emergency contact."

Wait, what?

Finn chose me as his emergency contact?

"We weren't able to reach him. We're calling to follow up on Lexie's blood tests and tell you we've found a rather..." She pauses. "*Abnormal* amount of white blood cells in her blood count, which could suggest something is amiss. Further tests are required to know exactly what's going on. Please contact us as soon as you can at—"

I don't hear a *word* of what she says next, my eyes glued to the Richardses' mansion across the street.

The front gate is wide open. And there's a puddle of *something* smeared all over the street, covering most of the sidewalk and snaking up the asphalt driveway leading to the house.

One of the grocery bags slips from my hands, its contents crashing against the concrete with a loud clatter.

Because the puddle isn't water...

Or mud...

It's blood.

Seventeen

Diamond

A million scenarios flock to the front of my mind as I shadow the trail of blood up the driveway. There's only one vehicle in the lot. Finn's. The black car is exactly where it was when I left for the grocery store.

He's home.

He's been home this entire time.

God, what if this blood is his?

Panic blazes through my entire body like lava when I reach the top of the hill, the gruesome scene before my eyes compressing the oxygen out of my lungs.

It's everywhere.

On the stairs.

On the porch.

On the doormat.

Blood creates a path toward the front door, a bloody handprint smacked in the center of the glass.

Do I go in?

Call the police?

What if someone's hurt in there?

Oh, God. Lexie.

She's already so weak and vulnerable.

My pulse shooting up with each step, I reach for the knob, careful not to touch the bloodstains on the door, and push it open. The house is dead silent as I venture into the hall and follow the continuing blood trail into the main areas.

I want to call Finn's name, or Lexie's, but I can't decide if making my presence known to a possible serial killer is the right move. I've barely stepped into the kitchen to grab a knife when I look out the window and spot them in the backyard.

Then my soul leaves my body.

I see Finn on his knees on the patio, his shirt, hands, and forearms covered in blood, but the worst part is…

Lexie is lying in his arms.

She's not moving, blood pouring from her stomach.

No.

Oh, God, no.

"Lexie!" I'm running to Finn's side in a heartbeat, falling to the ground and scraping my knees against the concrete. My white dress immediately soaks up the blood pooling at my feet.

"Where are your keys?" is the first thing Finn says to me.

His skin is pale, and his eyes are bloodshot.

He's in shock.

My silence infuriates him. "I said, where are your fucking keys? I can't find mine. I can't find my keys. Give me your keys," he repeats like a crazy person.

Lexie's still breathing, but barely.

"What happened?" I cry out, the taste of my tears coating my throat, and remove the jacket I threw on top of my dress earlier. I apply pressure to Lexie's wound with my jacket, unable to breathe from crying so hard. She whines in pain at the contact, each of her exhales a struggle.

Meanwhile, Finn is completely *out of it.*

"Give me your keys. We need to take her to an emergency vet. We need to—"

"Finn! What the hell happened?" I snap him out of it.

"I… I don't know. We were coming back from our walk, and some asshole hit her," he says frantically.

"She got hit by a car?" I blurt at the top of my lungs.

Finn gives a small nod, the trauma in his eyes making it clear that *this* is the absolute maximum amount of pain a human being can handle.

"Then he just took off," he adds.

My palm flies to my mouth at the realization…

This was a hit-and-run.

Finn had to drag her all the way back to the house in his arms after she got hit in front of him. He probably ran inside the house, looking for help when he couldn't find his keys.

"Did you call the cops?"

"They're already on their way," he confirms. "Give me your fucking keys, Dia!"

My crying turns hysterical when Lexie becomes cold, her brown eyes filled with tears. Her whimpers decrease in volume, and I grab her face between my hands for a moment. She's scared. Looking at me as though she's waiting for me to save her. To ease her pain.

She's not going to make it.

And we definitely don't have thirty minutes to get to the vet.

Panic overtakes Finn completely. "Dia, for fuck's sake, we're wasting time."

"Finn." I grip his face. "Look at me. She'd be dead by the time we got there."

But he doesn't like my response.

"No. No. You're lying." He shakes his head. "She's going to be fine. You're going to be fine, baby. She's going to be fine, right?" He's *begging* me to lie to him.

I realize time is running out when her breathing becomes shallow and desperate, her body trembling. A tear escapes her eye, and I pet her in an attempt to bring her a sliver of comfort. She licks a tear off my cheek to comfort *me*, which only makes me cry harder.

Memories of the times she cuddled up next to me when I was sad twist my heart in my chest. All the nights she spent sleeping by my side. All the laughter, the walks, the smiles.

This dog is the reason I made it through the summer.

Howling with sobs, I kiss the golden retriever on the top of the head and whisper, "Goodbye, sweet girl."

"No, she's not fucking dying," Finn snaps.

I want nothing more than to spend Lexie's last moments holding her, but looking up at Finn? Seeing the heartbreak in his eyes? I know he needs to say goodbye more than I do. He needs to be with Lexie while he still can.

"You have to say goodbye!" I yell, and Finn blinks at me, fighting tears with all his might.

"Stop! Stop fucking saying that. She's going to be okay. She… *She can't die.*"

I've never seen this boy cry before—hell, I've barely ever seen him *feel*—but his pride doesn't matter right now.

"Finn, don't let her go like this," I urge, knowing we'll be out of time soon. "She *needs* you."

That's what does the trick.

Emotions trickle back into Finn's eyes in a matter of seconds, the walls he built around himself coming undone brick by brick. It's like ten years of repressing his feelings just came to an end when he looks up at me and the truth crashes into him.

His baby girl is going to die.

The dog his mom gave him when he was eight.

She's going to *die.*

Fear sinks its claws into him as soon as he's shoved back into the real world.

Then he loses it.

He lets out a heart-wrenching scream of agony, tears streaming down his cheeks as he nuzzles his face into Lexie's neck.

"Please don't take her away. *Please…*" He sobs into her fur, holding her to him with all he has. "I'm so sorry, Lex. God, forgive me."

He says it like all of this is his fault.

Like he *failed* her somehow.

Panic overwhelms him when her eyes start to close, her breathing slowing down as she lets out a final whimper.

"No!" Finn cradles her head to his chest. "No, no, no. Don't leave me, Lex. Please."

Then she's gone.

She just… died in his arms.

And as police sirens echo in the distance, slowly increasing in volume, I know for a fact…

A part of Finn just died, too.

***

"They're done." My voice is but a whisper when I hang up the phone with the crime scene cleaners Mr. Richards hired—tragically, there was enough blood to qualify for their services.

Finn doesn't move an inch, his eyes drilled to the time on his car dashboard as he mutters something beneath his breath.

I think he's counting?

Keeping track of how many hours it's been since she left us?

The answer is *fifteen.*

Fifteen hours since a pet disposal service loaded Lexie's body up in the back of a car and took her away. They'll be cremating her first thing tomorrow.

Finn hasn't shed a tear since the police ripped him off her corpse. It's like he switched to autopilot, permanently shutting off whatever valve was blown open when he fell apart in the backyard.

The whole town knew about the hit-and-run by lunchtime. It started with a few nosey neighbors, then snowballed into a hot piece of gossip for widows and grannies to dissect over tea.

My dads have been blowing up my phone, asking me why Finn was rumored to have witnessed the atrocity when he was supposed to be gone for the summer.

I ended up telling them he'd come back into town the day before, which they found somewhat acceptable considering tomorrow's my last day, anyway. I know I'll have to come clean, eventually, but I can't deal with them right now.

The Richards estate was surrounded by police less than a minute after Lexie took her last breath. You'd think the Silver Springs Police Department deployed every damn car they had at once. And the worst part?

It wasn't even about Lexie.

They couldn't have given two fucks about the family dog bleeding out in front of us. The reason so many of them turned up is because the "accident" seemed personal.

Calculated.

Finn said he noticed a gray car with tinted windows following them for most of their walk. To make it worse, Lexie wasn't in the best shape, so he couldn't exactly book it down the street to lose him.

He'd just convinced himself he was being paranoid when he and Lexie began crossing the street to reach the house. Then the driver pumped the gas and plowed into them at full speed.

Finn barely managed to jump out of the way.

Sheriff Daniels let slip that this isn't the first time Finn's family has been targeted. Apparently, there were quite a few incidents following Nora Richards's disappearance—damage done to the property, attempted break-ins, even kidnapping threats on the kids.

Something about Mr. Richards offering a million-dollar reward to whoever found his wife, back when they still had hope she'd be found alive. Her body hadn't turned up, and they thought maybe, *by some miracle*, she'd swam to safety or been dragged to shore by the current.

The massive media coverage and large sums of money being dangled in front of less fortunate folks eventually earned the family a little too much attention.

Some believed the family had the reward stashed somewhere in their mansion. Others thought they'd make bank by breaking in and stealing whatever expensive shit they could get their hands on—even better if that "expensive shit" turned out to be one of the kids... No wonder the police are paying *extra* attention to this case.

Mr. Richards was furious when he heard. He booked a flight home as soon as the cops contacted him. From what I could gather, he's willing to move heaven and earth to find the bastard who did this to Lexie.

"Finn? Did you hear me? We can go home." The lie immediately begs to die on my tongue.

Home.

I'm not sure this house will ever feel like his home again.

"It's almost midnight. You need to get some rest." I brace a hand on his shoulder, and he flinches, shooting me an accusing glare that implies I've pulled him out of his safe place.

That place in his head where he likes to hide.

The dark corner where nothing hurts, nothing bleeds, and nothing dies.

He doesn't want to come back, but he's been hiding in that very place since his mom's accident. I managed to pull him out that day on the bridge. Then again this morning when he said his goodbyes to Lexie.

I won't let him go again.

"Finn?" I whisper, pushing my luck and reaching for his hand that's nervously fidgeting on his lap. "Can you take me home? Please?"

I convinced him to go for a ride while the cleaners got to work, and we've been parked in the springs' parking lot for hours. To think the town owes its name to those springs. Hell, they're famous in North Carolina, but barely two hours here and I've seen enough of them for a lifetime.

Finn's hand is icy, and I envelop his knuckles with my fingers, aiming to transfer some of my warmth to him. He doesn't react or reciprocate the gesture, but he looks alive again, like he just took a dive back down to earth, which is more than I could say a minute ago.

At last, he gives a small nod, returning to a world he'd kill to escape, and ignites the engine.

The drive home is as stressful as it is quiet.

Neither one of us says a word, but the fear we share is palpable. We're both terrified to march into the house and realize today was *real.* That Lexie is not going to come running to us the moment we burst through the door.

Because she's gone.

Because she's *dead.*

We must stay in the driveway for over five minutes, both lacking the strength to make the first move. Until the urge to pee forces me to take action, and I jerk the car door open. Finn doesn't follow, but I don't push it.

He'll come inside when he's ready.

The blood on the doorknob is gone.

So is the bloody handprint.

But the images in my head are too fresh to erase.

Air gets caught in my lungs when I walk into the pitch-black house. The smell of bleach burns my nostrils as I venture into the hall and flick the light on. I focus ahead of me, making a beeline for the kitchen.

I'm scared to see something of Lexie's.

Scared I'll crumble under my grief.

Her bed that's full of her favorite toys catches my eye when I turn the corner.

I can still see her, ogling me with her big, brown eyes and tongue sticking out. I see her swinging tail as she runs to me and licks my face, overwhelmed with joy. My eyes immediately fog with tears, and I charge toward the bathroom to avoid Finn walking in on me mid-breakdown.

I must stay in there, crying into my hands, for over five minutes. Until I hear the front door close.

Finn found the courage to get out of the car. That's a start. But I know the hard part is what comes next—seeing her things, feeling her absence, cohabiting with her ghost.

I start wiping the mascara and makeup staining my cheeks but stop at the sound of rapid footsteps tearing through the first floor. What's got him in such a hurry?

There's clatter.

Furniture moving around.

As much as I want to go out there, I'd prefer not to be a snotty, weeping mess in front of him again.

I need to be strong.

One of us has to.

I manage to get a grip on my feelings a few minutes later,

padding out of the bathroom and into the kitchen. He's not here. Glancing around the room, I venture into the kitchen.

"Finn?"

No response.

My jaw nearly hits the floor when I look out the window and find him standing still in the backyard, a pile of unidentified things at his feet. I notice he's holding something.

A red can.

My heart stops.

Is that… *gasoline?*

On high alert, I slide the patio door open and speed over to him, not the tiniest bit surprised by the lack of emotion on his face. His hazel eyes are vacant, cold, *haunting* as he stares ahead of him and ponders his next move.

"Finn, what are you doing?" A mix of panic and shock steals my voice. He doesn't acknowledge me one bit, as though he's in some sort of trance, and begins pouring gasoline all over the pile of things before him.

That's when I realize…

They're Lexie's things.

Her dog bed, her favorite toys, her blankets.

Everything they ever bought for her.

"Finn." I tug at his shirt. "Finn, don't do this."

Nothing seems to be enough to earn me his attention.

"Finn, *goddamn it.*"

Only then does he look at me, the gutting pain I saw in his

eyes when Lexie took her last breath nothing more than a vague and distant memory.

"She won't be needing it anymore," he drones.

Then he spins and bolts back toward the house. I match his every move, begging him to snap out of it as he starts searching the kitchen obsessively.

"What are you looking for?" I yell even if, deep down, I already know the answer. He finds what he was looking for seconds later. I leap into his way as he races toward the backyard door with a box of matches in his hand.

He's so out of it I wouldn't be surprised if he accidentally set the house on fire.

"Look at me." I grip his collar, stumbling backward when he attempts to continue walking. A glimmer of hope soars in my chest when his hand flies to my lower back to keep me from falling. There's still humanity left in him.

Even if just a drop.

He keeps his eyes fixated on the pile of stuff in the backyard, dodging my gaze like it's a loaded gun.

"Look at me!" I yell before cupping his face with both hands and allowing our eyes to lock. "This isn't going to bring her back."

He swallows hard.

I see you.

You're still in there.

Come back.

"Neither will keeping her shit in the house," he says, his voice flat, and detaches my hands from his jaw.

I stop him from pulling the back door open.

"Finn, please. This is insane."

"Get out of my way," he warns through gritted teeth.

"No!" My scream is shrill, near deafening. "This isn't the right way to cope, and you know it."

"Then how?" he snaps, the raw desperation and misery in his voice stabbing me in the heart. "How do I keep going? Fucking how? She's *dead*, Dia. I was supposed to protect her. I… I promised my mom…"

With that said, he picks me off the ground by the waist and moves me out of the way like I'm weightless.

He's out the door before I know it.

I trail after him toward the pile of memories on the ground, my sight made blurry by my tears as he slides the box open and lights a match. From there, I wait. It's all I can do. I hold my breath and squeeze my eyes shut, waiting for him to destroy a huge part of his life to avoid dealing with it.

Only, he never does.

I peel my eyes open to see Finn with his arms hanging down his body limply, the lit match trapped inside his trembling fist.

He can't bring himself to do it.

"*Fuuuuck*," he shouts.

He's mad at himself.

It's like he thinks his inability to erase her makes him *weak*.

Then, in a blind rage, he puts out the match and tosses it onto the grass. I've barely had a chance to catch my breath before he takes off toward the house again.

I don't miss a beat, shadowing him to the stairs—I swear my job description should've been "Chasing after Finn Richards." I follow him up to his bedroom, where he yanks his closet open and pulls out a baseball bat.

We lock eyes, but he's too far gone to see the plea in mine.

I shriek when he takes a swing into the framed picture of him and his basketball team on the wall. The picture smashes into a thousand pieces, glass flying everywhere, and I have the good sense of backing away to avoid the fallout.

He's operating on crazy as he smashes everything in sight—furniture, lamps, you name it. Before I can blink, Finn is darting out of his bedroom in the direction of the double doors down the hall. The library.

Ruining his own stuff wasn't enough.

He needs to ruin his dad's, too.

I stood by and let him go apeshit on his room because I knew if he didn't let it out now, he'd drown in grief, but I can't let him lose what's left of his father's trust.

There are first editions books in there. Priceless art pieces and collector items Mr. Richards must've spent a *fortune* and years of his life amassing. Finn might not see it through the veil of rage blinding him, but he told me once that all he'd ever wanted was his father's respect…

I can't let him do this.

I pick up the pace behind him, nearly tripping over my own feet to reach the library before he does irreversible damage. He's bursting through the doors the next second, already rampaging through his dad's possessions by the time I get there.

I've tried begging him, screaming his name, standing in his way earlier. *Nothing worked.* No, if I'm going to stop him from tearing every book in here to shreds, I need to do something drastic.

I tense up when he takes the bat to a crystal liquor bottle on a golden trolley, the smell of booze flowing to the entrance of the room. I understand he's found his next victim when he speed walks to a porcelain vase displayed on a pedestal by the fireplace.

Just as he's taking a swing, I let out a shrill, guttural "Stop!"—the kind that could break windows—and make a decision I know for a fact won't go down as my finest moment.

It all happens in a matter of seconds.

I jump in front of the vase in a desperate, impulsive attempt to bring him back. I see fear in his eyes when he realizes his target isn't the vase anymore.

It's me.

I curse my lapse of judgment as soon as I realize he might not be able to stop himself and squeeze my eyes shut, preparing for impact. I wait and wait, but nothing happens.

My entire body quivering with fear, I force my eyelids open, only to see Finn holding the bat in the air less than an *inch* away from my skull. His mouth is open, an expression of pure horror plastered to his face.

He almost hit me.

The thought must be too much to bear because he stumbles back a step, a million apologies in his gaze. I can tell it's becoming harder and harder for him to retreat to his safe place. Soon, he won't be able to bury his emotions at all.

"I'm so sorry," he chokes out, lowering the bat.

Struggling to catch my breath, I lift my hand to my chest to calm my pounding heart.

"It's okay," I promise and close in on him slowly, never disconnecting my gaze from his as I reach for the bat in his hand.

He lets go of it without a fight, and I lob it to the side.

"No, *no*, it's not fucking okay. I almost…" He stumbles backward again, eyes burning with pain, and scans the library with an expression of disbelief.

It's like he can't believe he did all that.

His hands fly into his hair, and he grips strands of it between his fingers before falling to his knees on the library rug. This is the third time I've seen this boy on his knees since I've met him.

Once was at the bridge after he almost died.

The second time was earlier today when Lexie was fading away in his arms.

But somehow, this time feels different.

This time, it feels like he's surrendering.

To his pain, to the grief, to *me.*

Then he starts to hyperventilate, grief spilling down his beautiful face, soaking his cheeks, his jaw, his mouth. I'm on my knees by his side in seconds, leading his forehead to my chest and holding him tighter than ever before.

He starts shaking in my arms, his body howling with years of ignored trauma. Like it all just came rushing back at once, and for the first time since the accident, the truth caught up to him.

He lost his mom.

And Lexie.

And I don't think he's ever truly let himself feel it until now.

His despair wets my shirt, but I don't move a muscle. Not that I *could* get away even if I wanted to. He holds me like his life depends on it, his face nestled deep into my neck and his tattooed arms strangling my waist. The storm gradually clears up as his breathing stabilizes.

"I'm here," I whisper through my own tears.

"You shouldn't be," he says bluntly.

Shocked, I pull back an inch, and he looks up at me through bloodshot eyes. I can't bring myself to answer, but he reads my confusion loud and clear, slipping out of my arms.

"You shouldn't have come back."

His words feel like knives.

Even after all of this, he's still pushing me away?

"Why?" Pain drips from my voice.

In response, Finn traps my face into his palms and stares me dead in the eyes, something dark and possessive flickering to life in the backs of his irises.

"Because now, I'm never letting you leave again."

His mouth slams down on mine so fast and hard I lose track of my own thoughts. Finn doesn't give me a chance to sign on the dotted line, concluding our transaction with a kiss. The way he ravages my mouth is definitive.

Binding.

His lips sliding against mine feel lethal, like an alcoholic's first drink after years of sobriety, but I want—*need*—more and let him know with an unintentional moan. He's got me begging for his touch as he nicks my bottom lip and parts my teeth with his tongue.

I swore on my life I was giving up on this boy.

But his kiss is like ointment to an infected wound, a distraction we both desperately need after the hell we went through today. This is harmless. We're just making out. As long as I don't give him the big V, it doesn't have to mean anything…

Right?

My patience skips out on me when he licks the seam of my mouth, grazing my tongue with his until I'm gripping the back of his head to deepen our connection. Finn groans into my mouth, handing the lead over to me as our tongues mingle.

His words play in my head like a broken record.

Because now, I'm never letting you leave again.

Does he mean that?

Is he just using me to get over his grief?

I find comfort in knowing that, no matter what happens here tonight, I'll be gone tomorrow.

I gasp when Finn pulls me to his body with a jerk and pins me down under him, his hard chest caging me in. The night I found him standing in the window, he told me all about the naughty things he wanted to do to me on this rug. And here we are now, making out like animals in the exact same spot.

"Do you have *any* fucking idea how excruciating the past week has been?" He sounds irritated. "How many times I almost got into my car to drag your stubborn ass back home?"

My mind starts racing.

He missed me.

He *missed* me.

He was just too much of a stubborn ass *himself* to admit it. He's inching closer, seeking another kiss, when I stretch my arm out to push him away.

"Then why are you such a dick?" I spit, throwing his behavior in his face. "You did everything you could to convince me you didn't care. Why?"

"Because I didn't *want* to care," he snaps, regret lacing every word. I'm baffled by his reasoning. That's why he pushed me away every chance he got?

To convince himself he didn't care?

"God, Dia, you drive me fucking insane." He leans in, guiding his lips to my neck and sucking on the sensitive spot beneath my collarbone. "I can't sleep. I can't eat. All I can do is think about you. And fuck, I'm tired. I'm tired of *hiding*." My head falls back at the sensation, and it takes all I have not to surrender to him again.

Memories of the vile words he said to me invade my brain, the countless daggers he drove through my chest hard to ignore.

"Not good enough." I attempt to move out from under him, but he's not having it, trapping my arms on each side of my head and keeping me anchored to the rug.

"What do you want me to say?" The desperation in his tone makes me so happy it should be illegal. "That I'm an asshole? That I don't deserve you? Fine, I don't." He rests his forehead against mine, breathing heavily. "I don't deserve you, Diamond Mitchell. I don't deserve your compassion. I don't deserve those big, brown eyes. Or that smart fucking mouth. I don't deserve any of you."

"No, you don't." I choke, wiggling to free myself again, which results in Finn tightening his hold on me.

"But I want to try!" he blurts.

I blink up at him in shock.

"I want to try to be worthy of you. I… Fuck, just let me *try*."

His mouth is on mine before I can argue, his tongue peeking between my teeth and stripping me of all my defenses. He kisses me like he's taking an oath, making me a promise with his mouth.

I pull away. "They're just words, Finn."

"Then let me show you." There's something about the way he says it. A hint of danger. I tense up when his fingers travel down my stomach, leaving a trail of goose bumps behind and stopping near the button of my jeans.

He's undoing my zipper in no time, dragging slow kisses all over my stomach and hip bones. I gasp when he tugs on my jeans, yanking them down my legs swiftly.

"I'm sorry, I'm so fucking sorry," he chants, repeating his plea over and over as his fingers snake up my thigh toward my red thong. Shivers scatter down my spine when he spreads my legs wide open and presses his mouth to my center.

His mouth is hot, *heavenly*, as he licks me up and down over the fabric, applying more and more pressure to my clit and soaking my underwear.

From there, I'm a goner.

"You want my forgiveness?" I bite back a moan.

His eyes snap up to me.

"Then earn it."

At first, he's shocked, but his surprise is quickly replaced with a cunning smirk. I know he heard me loud and clear the second I look down and see raw desire and determination staring back at me.

"Yes, ma'am."

What did I just get myself into?

I'm confident the neighbors heard me moan when he nudges my panties down my legs in one go and licks me up and down, minus the barrier. He starts slow, barely flicking my clit with his tongue, and I whine, my body contracting with need.

He laughs.

"You want more, baby?" he whispers, his breath fanning my center, and I squirm.

"Fuck you," I snap.

"You first," he fires back.

Motherfucker.

"If you want more, take it." His tongue grazes my clit again.

So, I do.

I let out a curse, grip the back of his head, and bury his face deep in my slit. He replies with a carnal groan I feel in my bones. I understand he wasn't kidding about earning my forgiveness when he slides his palms under my ass, his fingers digging into my flesh possessively, and sucks my clit into his mouth so hard my hips buck forward.

Good Lord.

It's raw, and messy, and dirty, but I can't get enough. I'm clutching his hair between my fingers before I can stop myself, bucking my hips again to give him better access.

"That's it, baby. Fuck my face," he growls, licking me so fast and relentlessly my eyes roll back. My pride kicks in a few seconds later, and I bite down on my lip to smother my moans.

He notices instantly.

"Don't even think about it. I want to hear you." Finn's voice is low, gravelly as he takes the choice away from me and squeezes two fingers inside me, stretching me as punishment.

The more I try to fight back, the harder he goes, pumping his fingers in and out of me and tugging at my clit with his teeth. I can feel his fingers sinking into my waist, marking me with his ownership as he devours me without a *smidge* of restraint.

"Forgive me. Please forgive me." He twirls his tongue around me again and again, but I can't bring myself to answer.

My moan evolves into a complaint when he uses his grasp on my waist to spin me around and pin me facedown against the rug. It feels itchy against my bare skin, but my focus quickly diverts to Finn's hands slipping between the rug and my body to angle my ass up. I start to panic when I hear him pull down his zipper.

"Finn," I warn.

"Just trust me."

On that note, he slaps my ass, drawing a moan out of me, and guides the head of his cock to my core from behind. He's hot and throbbing and *shit*, I almost wish he'd push inside me.

Only, he doesn't.

He just uses his cock to rub me in quick, rough circles. I cast a glance over my shoulder and find his jeans around his knees as he jacks off hard and fast, lustful eyes glued to the show between my legs. His groans of pleasure are the best part. An indescribable feeling soars to life in my stomach as I watch him work us both.

Shit, I'm going to come.

I roll my hips greedily, wanting more friction. His tip inches dangerously close to my entrance with each back and forth of his cock against my clit.

Finn throws his head back with a growl.

"Fucking hell, Dia, how much self-control do you think I have?"

But I can't help myself.

"Oh, God, yes!" I cry out, the pleasure reaching its apex. I feel him lean over me the next second, his chest blanketing my back as he grits out in my ears,

"Say that you forgive me."

I don't say a word.

Truth is, I can't forgive him until I see who he is when the sun comes up tomorrow. Will he be back to his cruel self?

Push me away like I have the plague?

"Say it." He's begging me.

I keep my mouth shut.

And in response?

He stops.

He pulls away, leaving me hanging with an uncompleted orgasm wreaking havoc on my sanity. My entire body trembling in anticipation, I cave to his request, tasting the bitterness of defeat.

"I forgive you." It comes out as a whimper.

My heart swells up with shame from the moment I let him off the hook. Groaning in satisfaction, Finn doesn't waste a second flipping me onto my back and settling between my legs again.

I'm afraid the pressure is going to rip me in half when he clamps his mouth shut on my clit once more, nibbling, licking, teasing until I'm right back where I started. My mouth spills open as I come, a prisoner to his tongue and tattooed arms.

I'm shuddering with spasms, damn near disconnecting from my body as my orgasm hits at full capacity. Finn doesn't let my convulsing faze him, eating and fingering the living hell out of me until he's got me panting on the library rug. It takes me over five seconds to stop shaking.

As soon as I can breathe again, Finn climbs up my body, tilts my chin forward, and crashes his mouth to mine. I'm quick to pull his shirt over his head, exploring his pecs and abs with my fingers. His bare cock comes flush with my entrance, our chests heaving in harmony. He could push inside me so easily right now, and I'm terrified…

Because I want him to.

This may be a huge mistake. I may regret giving up my V-card to a boy as broken as he is, but I want to feel him inside me. I want to feel *all* of him before I leave this house behind.

There's a chance we'll go back to being strangers after this. Just two faces in a crowded hall—me, the invisible girl watching from the sidelines, and him, the basketball star, high up on his throne. There may not be a tomorrow for us.

And I'm okay with that.

As long as I have him *now*.

"Fuck me," I croak into his mouth.

Finn stops kissing me on cue.

He draws back, staring down my face to figure me out.

"Jesus Christ, Dia, don't toy with me."

"I'm not."

"What?" He still doesn't believe it.

"You heard me." I snatch his face and kiss him again. "I want you to *fuck* me. Right here. Right now. Then we can go our separate ways."

The lust in his eyes immediately morphs into a combination of shock and irritation.

"Is that what you think I want?" he says quietly.

My lips part.

"To fuck you and *walk away*?"

I can't speak, but he doesn't expect me to, slamming his mouth to mine again. I only realize what's happening when he pulls away and reaches for his jeans on the ground. He plucks a condom out of his pocket, and while I hate that he's the type of guy to carry protection around at all times, I swallow the pill the best I can.

He's barely rolled the latex down his shaft before he's positioning his hard, veiny cock between my legs.

"I meant what I said," Finn rasps inches away from my mouth. "You sealed your fate from the moment you walked your cute little ass back into my house."

Then he thrusts into me.

And a tear rolls down my face.

Not because it hurts.

Or because I'm sad.

But because this... *us*... it's too damn much for my heart.

"Oh, fuck." Finn stills himself, pure agony in his eyes as his jaw muscles quiver. "Fuck, Dia, I can't..."

He stretches me painfully, burying himself to the hilt, and I twist under him in an effort to adjust to his size.

Shit, he's big.

"Don't move," he commands.

We stay in this position for a bit, his cock unbearably stiff inside me until I can't take it anymore.

"Finn, please," I moan.

His mouth descends over mine, probably to wash away the pain, and thankfully, it works. I lose myself in his kiss, nibbling on his lower lip. His breathing is deep, unsteady, like he's pouring every ounce of his focus into holding it. Finally, after a few seconds of intense making out, he parts from me.

"We're good," he says.

He pulls out completely and thrusts back in without a warning. His cock slices into me like a knife, and I wince, my body tensing.

This hurts.

I don't want it to hurt, but it does.

This is still my first time, and Finn isn't exactly average size.

You'd think my thoughts are stamped across my forehead by how fast he stills again.

"I'm hurting you, aren't I?" He knows right away.

I'm tempted to lie but decide against it. I don't want my first time to consist of me struggling to hide my pain, mentally begging him to slow down. His eyes light up in understanding before I get the chance to confess.

"Tell me you didn't…"

Give me your virginity, is what he meant to say, but I can read between the lines.

"I did," I choke out.

He doesn't speak for a while.

"Fuck, Dia, you should have told me." He presses his forehead to mine.

"Like I told you when you took my first kiss?"

I can't believe I just said that.

His eyes widen at my confession.

He remains silent for a while, memories clashing in the backs of his eyes until he whispers, "All of them?"

I know what he means without further explanation.

"All of them," I admit.

My first kiss.

My first blowjob.

I gave him my first *everything*, and he didn't even know it.

I dread his reaction, waiting for him to scold me for my lack of communication, but he goes straight for my lips instead, kissing me senseless.

"I'm the first guy who's ever been inside you?" he asks despite knowing the answer. He just wants to hear me *say* it.

"You are."

He looks so deeply into my eyes I'm afraid he can see through my lies. Truth is, I don't want this to end tomorrow. I have feelings for him.

And it's *killing* me.

He snaps me out of it by circling my throat with his hand and leaning forward to whisper in my ear, "You mark my fucking words, I'm also going to be the *last*."

He curls his fingers under the hem of my Radiohead T-shirt and jerks it over my head—I threw on the first outfit I could find earlier. He's unclasping the magnet of my bra, which is conveniently placed at the front, a heartbeat later.

This isn't the first time Finn has seen my breasts if you count the time he watched me like a creeper while I was using the sex toy he gave me, but I still battle the urge to hide.

I have a large birthmark above my right breast, and I've always felt insecure about it. I'm seconds away from covering up when Finn banishes my worries with one flick of his tongue. His mouth latches onto my nipple, sucking, tugging, gently biting until my body relaxes.

"Your birthmark is so hot." The pad of his fingers skim over the mark I spent so much of my life despising.

He starts fucking me again.

Harder.

Faster.

But the sensation of his mouth on my nipples overrides the discomfort I was feeling a moment prior.

Okay, I'm starting to feel good.

Really good.

And judging by the look on his face, the way he clenches his jaw as he moves in and out of me, I'm not the only one. I'm barely aware of my legs wrapping around his waist, holding him as close to me as possible.

"How does it feel to know no one is ever going to fuck you but me?" he grits out as he picks up the pace, pumping his hips faster. "All your firsts are mine, you hear me? All. Fucking. Mine."

I want to argue and say he already has them all, but his finger dipping downward to rub small circles around my asshole proves me wrong. The sensation makes my stomach contract despite a voice in my head warning me as to his intentions.

"Never going to happen, Richards."

He smirks. "We'll see."

My breasts bouncing with each of his speedy thrusts, I dig the heels of my feet into his back. He complies with my silent request, fucking me harder.

"Shit, that feels so good," I moan.

Finn groans as he pounds into me for several minutes like he's trying to fuck any boy I've ever looked at out of my head.

He hoists my leg up on his shoulder to ram himself deeper inside me, triggering his own undoing in the process.

"Oh, fuck." His jaw contracts as his thrusting grows jerkier, uneven. "Fuck, Dia."

Seeing the pure ecstasy on his face lifts me up higher than ever before. It's intoxicating, ten times better than experiencing it myself, and I clench around him, nudging him over the edge.

His mouth comes down on mine as he peaks, pumping into me one last time before blowing into the condom with a grunt. He collapses on top of me a few seconds later, and his words rush to the front of my mind, twisting my heart into my chest.

He says no one else is ever going to touch me.

That I'm his.

And in that moment, as the boy I'm afraid to love plants luscious kisses all over my neck, branding me with promises of a tomorrow…

I almost believe him.

Eighteen

Diamond

The next day rolls around faster than I would've liked.

The room is quiet when I begin to stir, the morning sunrays caressing my face and easing me out of slumber, but there's something in the air.

Something… *off.*

It feels like a pile of bricks is sitting on my chest when I jolt my eyes open, sitting up in bed and scanning the room.

Finn's room.

It feels like barely two hours ago, Finn and I were naked on the library rug, his length still deep inside me. I remember the fear rising in my throat when he spilled into the condom and pulled out.

I had to tap into every drop of courage in my body to look him in the eyes after that. I thought this was the part where he picked up his baseball bat and smashed my heart into a thousand pieces.

Instead, he took my hand, pulled me to my feet, and threw me over his shoulder to carry me to his bed.

We cuddled the rest of the night.

The same way we did when we fell asleep in his backyard. We must've spent three hours kissing and bickering—he strictly *refused* to let me leave his bed to get dressed—before we passed out around seven. It was great, but… leaving me alone to wake up in his bed after he popped my cherry?

Not so great.

He bailed.

We had sex and he left.

As if it wasn't bad enough, his side of the bed is made. Almost like he woke up, saw me sleeping, and thought, "*Eh.* Let's just pretend she's not there."

I don't know what I'm supposed to do from here. Just take off? I did say I was leaving no matter what. I'm stupid enough to search the sheets and nightstand for a note. I even check my phone for an apology text message.

Nada.

I'm about to go comb through the library for my clothes when I hear heavy footsteps hurrying up the stairs.

He's back?

I manage to convince myself that he didn't run out on me. Maybe an emergency came up, or maybe he *did* chicken out, but then he came to his senses. All of that fades at the sound of a deep and croaky voice.

"Stop fucking with me, Richards. I know you're here," a man calls from down the hall.

My breathing halts, my heart pulsing dangerously fast.

It's not Finn.

It never was.

He's not coming back for you, Dia.

My survival instincts scream to *hide*, to throw on whatever clothes I can find and climb out the window. Who cares if I break my leg? It can't possibly be worse than getting ambushed by a stranger while butt naked in a boy's bed.

"Hey, motherfucker, I'm talking to you." There's anger in the man's voice. Whoever this is, he's no friend of Finn's, and he sure didn't stop by for a cup of tea.

I spot Finn's closed door and feel the adrenaline kick in. Maybe if I run, I'll have time to lock it. That should buy me some time so I can figure out my next move.

My phone.

I need my phone.

Last I recall, it was in my jeans pocket.

Except… my jeans are in the library.

Along with my bra, panties, and what's left of my dignity.

I'm trying to see clearly through the thick fog clouding my thoughts when the floorboards creak a few feet down the hall.

He's almost here.

Dia, do something!

I can't move, the fear paralyzing me from head to toe. By the time I snap out of it, gearing myself into fight mode, my window of opportunity is already gone. The oxygen leaves my body when Finn's bedroom door squeaks open…

And an oddly familiar guy appears in the doorway.

I'm petrified, unable to move or speak, but my memory is all I need to place the strange man standing before me. It's the guy Finn was talking to the night of Lacey's party.

The guy who told Finn he'd rape me in the woods before almost getting choked to death.

It's not his face that gives it away—it was dark that night, and I didn't get a good look at him—it's his shabby, over-worn black jacket. He's not wearing a stalker baseball cap this time, but he *is* wearing the same vomit-inducing odor. He's standing in the doorway, but I smell him from here.

I'm clutching the blanket to my chest so tightly I can barely feel my knuckles anymore. As for him? The only thing he seems to be feeling right now is satisfaction.

His lips twitch into a crooked smile as he looks me up and down, delighted by his discovery. The slight tremble of his body and dark circles under his eyes do little to hide his demons. My best guess? He's a drug dealer slash drug addict, and he's desperate for his next fix. That sure would explain why he's been bugging Finn for his money.

"Well, well. What do we have here?" The creep, who can't be much older than twenty-nine but looks forty due to substance abuse, lets out a wheezy laugh and ventures deeper into the room.

A feeling of helplessness crushes every bone in my body when he closes the door and locks it. It's the way he looks at me.

Like I'm some poor, defenseless animal who wandered into his trap.

"House sitter turned *dick sucker*." He cackles. "It's quite the résumé you've got there, sweetheart."

His comment makes my skin crawl, and I direct my energy into hiding my distress from him.

"Where's your boyfriend?" He glances to the undraped window on his left as if to make sure Finn's car isn't pulling up. If he really knew Finn, he'd know he isn't the dating type, but I decide to use his ignorance to my advantage.

"He's on his way. He went out to get us breakfast. He should be home any second," I lie.

"Is that so?" he mutters, his devious smile growing in size.

He's not buying it one bit.

Was he just testing me?

No, he clearly didn't know Finn was gone or he wouldn't have called his name earlier. That's when I realize I did this to myself. *I'm* to blame for his skepticism.

Why?

Because I'm crying.

Tears are streaming down my face uncontrollably, but I'm so crippled by fear that I didn't even notice. No wonder he doesn't believe me. If Finn really *was* on his way home, a few minutes away from bursting through the door and rescuing me, I wouldn't look scared for my life.

"Heard your boy had a big day yesterday." The man starts to

pace around the room, analyzing the things on Finn's desk, then picking up the framed picture of his mom for a closer look. "Such a shame about that dog—Lexie, was it?"

The words are barely out of his mouth before he intentionally drops the picture on the floor, not even flinching when it explodes into a thousand little fragments.

That picture has to be the only thing Finn didn't smash when he went into a blind rage yesterday. The rest of his room looks like a category four hurricane went through it.

"For what it's worth, she didn't have much time left, anyway. She looked like shit," the guy adds, and I go from terrified to fuming with anger.

First, he doesn't deserve to say her name. And second, he shouldn't know that. He shouldn't know *anything* about her. It's not like they mentioned her health issues on the news.

"Must've been a pain cleaning all that blood." He chuckles, twisting the knife into my wound. My emotions are clearly plastered all over my face because he scoffs.

"Oh, chin up, baby. There would have been a lot more if I hadn't missed."

My throat closes up.

If he hadn't missed…

He's talking about Finn, isn't he?

Finn told the cops he barely had time to move out of the way before the car hit Lexie. But she wasn't the target—*Finn* was. Lexie was merely collateral damage.

I zone out as I relive Lexie's last moments. He apologized to her. When she was dying… Finn *begged* her to forgive him.

Did he know?

That's why he was blaming himself, isn't it?

He knew he played a part in it.

"Enough chitchat." The guy begins to approach me, cutting off my air supply in the process. "Be a good girl and deliver a message for me, will you?"

My gaze roams around the room for some sort of weapon as he advances toward the bed. On autopilot, I grab the empty glass of water Finn got me when I got thirsty last night, ready to smash his head in, but his wrist flies out to catch mine. He easily overpowers me, ripping the glass out of my hand and chucking it away. His hand wraps around my throat before I can blink, pinning me down to the mattress.

"You fucking bitch," he growls and spits in my face.

My tears soak my mouth as his saliva rolls down my cheek, carrying the smell of his rotten breath.

"You're going to tell your boy that if he doesn't get me my money by end of day tomorrow, I'll get someone else to settle his debt." He inches closer, squeezing my throat until I'm gasping for air. "Maybe *you*."

He pauses, enjoying my struggle as I try to claw at his face and arms. He slackens his hold on my throat for a few seconds, just long enough for me to inhale a shallow breath, and then he does it again.

"Although, if I'm being honest, I'm not sure he would care. Looks to me like he got what he wanted, then tossed you aside like garbage."

I never back down, putting up the fight of my life, but nothing is enough to get his dirty paws off my neck. Tears cast a thick mist over my eyes as one of his hands falls to my covered breasts, the thin blanket the only thing standing between him and my naked body.

I almost wish he'd suffocate me as he groans. "Let's see those tits."

Just close your eyes.

Close your eyes and leave this place, Dia.

His fingers curl under the blanket, but just as he starts to lift it off my body, his phone rings.

I never believed in miracles.

Until now.

Cursing beneath his breath, he uses his free hand to jerk his phone out of his pocket and press it to his ear.

"What?" he barks into the phone.

I can't make out what the person on the other end is saying.

"*Now?*" Sketchy Guy snaps. "I'm a little busy."

Whoever he's talking to doesn't seem to like that answer because I hear yelling.

"No, don't fucking call him. The shit is mine."

Drugs, probably.

The arguing continues for a few minutes, until Sketchy Guy

releases a heavy sigh.

"Fucking hell, fine. I'm on my way."

On that note, he hangs up the phone.

The monster looks down at me, his jaw tight as he spits, "You'll see me again."

He lets go of my throat and leaves.

I barely hear my sobs through my excessive coughing, but I do hear the sound of his car outside. The roar of the engine dies down shortly after.

The next few minutes are a blur. I feel like a ghost watching myself from the outside as I run to the library to pick up my clothes from the floor. I'm sobbing the entire time I pack my belongings.

I notice all of Lexie's things were left by the dumpster down the street as I'm getting into my car. So, Finn didn't have time to leave me a note, but he found the time to go through his entire house to throw out Lexie's toys at the butt crack of dawn?

I make sure to block his number before pushing the gear into drive, my brother's countless warnings about Finn playing on a loop in my head.

And I didn't listen before…

But I'm listening *now*.

* * *

Finn

Don't call her, don't call her, don't call her.

Don't *fucking* call her.

I fidget with my phone for long seconds, the urge to select her contact info tearing at the stitches of my ego. I've never been one to blow up a girl's phone, begging for a minute of her time, and I sure as shit am not about to start now.

Eh, who am I kidding?

I've been staring at her phone number like a delusional little bitch for two days. I keep waiting for her to give me a sign of life, but she's gone radio silent since the day I skipped out on her while she was asleep.

She must think I'm an asshole.

That I *chose* to leave her.

She was still naked in my arms when I got the call. Sheriff Daniels was on the other end, insisting that I show up to the police station to discuss a promising lead on the bastard who murdered Lexie.

I was dumb enough to think I'd be back before Dia woke up. Worst-case scenario, I'd shoot her a text and clear things up, but I hadn't charged my phone, and the stupid thing died on me as soon as I got to the station. The interrogation lasted fucking forever, and by the time I came home, she was gone.

She'd packed her things and left.

To be fair, I left first. Why can't I just text her? Get over myself long enough to apologize?

Short answer?

My pride is a pain in the ass.

It won't stop calling me weak for wanting something that might not want me back. After all, she said we should go our separate ways after we fucked, but does she seriously think she can just walk out of my life?

After I buried myself inside her on the library floor?

This girl…

This fucking girl…

She haunts me.

I can still see her, legs spread out, pussy glistening as I worked her with my cock. Her shy little moans as I took her virginity, promising to never let another guy touch her.

And I meant it.

She's insane if she thinks I'm going to pretend I never had her tits in my mouth when I see her at school in a few days. What's her plan? Move on? Meet a nice guy?

Give him the rest of her firsts?

Dream the fuck on, baby.

My best friend making his way to my car halts my spiral.

Xavier's been back from camp less than twenty-four hours, and he's already cleaning up my mess. He came over to my house the second he heard about Lexie and somehow got roped into getting my ass out of trouble—the way he always does.

To be fair, my best friend thinks he's Dr. Phil or some shit. He knew something was wrong as soon as he came in. I eventually caved and told him about the police's discovery.

Turns out the car that was following Lexie and me was stolen. It was found abandoned by a dirt road with only one thing inside…

A baseball cap.

What's worse, I've seen that cap before.

On the scumbag dealer my brother hooked me up with at the beginning of the summer. Had I known Brody's guy was such a nutcase, I would've never borrowed money from him in the first place.

I haven't been able to stop wondering if the lowlife could have something to do with what happened to Lexie. I even set up a meeting to "pay him back," which is really just code for "uncover the truth."

Xavier and I are meeting him behind the abandoned movie theater across town in ten minutes. The place is a dump. No one will see us there. But most importantly…

No one will hear him scream.

A torn expression on his face, Xavier opens the door and slides into my passenger seat. My mouth goes dry at the stack of money in his hands. He just sold one of his autographed basketball jerseys for me—the thing was worth a pretty penny.

All so that I could pay back some fucking nobody.

I'm aware there's a good chance the money will never make it into the guy's hands, but we wanted to be prepared. Just in case the bastard is genuinely clueless and the person responsible for Lexie's death is still out there.

"That's all of it." Xavier hands me the cash.

"Thanks, man." My voice is laced with shame.

He slouches into his seat. "Don't mention it."

I'm good at that.

Not mentioning things.

Like the fact that I fucked his girlfriend.

Twice.

To think I was this close to doing it again the day Dia burst into my life. I crack a smile remembering how she kneed me in the balls without blinking, promising that the only thing her mouth would ever do for me was telling me to *fuck off.* I hated her for that back then, but now?

I realize I got off easy.

If there was such a thing as karma, she would've ripped my balls off my body right then and played Ping-Pong.

I'm a terrible friend.

Xavier Emery has done nothing but put out fires in my life since we were kids, and in return, I betrayed his trust in the worst way possible. One of those days, I'll come clean. Tell him the truth and let the chips fall where they may.

But for now, I need him.

I need him to be my conscience—since the only person who's ever managed to calm me down is currently ghosting my ass—and stop me if things go too far. If I find out the motherfucker is responsible for Lexie's death, I won't be able to stop myself from killing him.

That's where Xavier comes in.

The drive to the abandoned theater is a quiet one. We barely exchange glances, worst-case scenarios thrumming through my system. We park in the back alley behind the run-down theater and wait for the scumbag to show his face.

I alternate between bouncing my leg nervously and checking my phone every five seconds, hoping Dia might show me some fucking mercy and send me a text.

It doesn't have to be a novel. I'll take anything. She can tell me to fuck off for all I care.

As long as she texts me.

Jesus, I'm such a pussy.

Xav lets out a scoff. "Fuck me, Theo was right."

I look up from my phone.

I don't even get the chance to ask him what he smoked before he adds, "Dude, just call her already."

Wait, Theo told him about me and Dia?

Jesus, am I the only person on this goddamn planet that *didn't* know I had it bad for Diamond Mitchell?

"Call who?" I act clueless.

I knew from the moment Lexie left us that I didn't have the strength to push Dia away anymore, but admitting that I'm whipped to *myself* and admitting it to my friends are two very different things.

"Oh, for fuck's sake. Give it to me." Xav huffs and reaches

over to my side. He's grabbed my phone before I can react.

At first, I think he's messing with me.

Until he holds up the phone and presses the Call button.

Shit.

"You bastard." I climb over the center console to try and steal my phone back. Xavier dodges my arm, wrestling me for a bit before putting the phone on speaker and smothering a laugh.

"It's ringing." He turns up the volume.

And he's right.

It does ring.

But just once.

Then it's straight to voicemail. The automated answering machine informs us that Dia hasn't recorded her outgoing message yet. The loud beep cuts through the air, and I've pissed off enough girls in my life to know what this "one ring" bullshit means.

She blocked me.

And, judging by the nauseating look of pity on my best friend's face, he knows it, too. I'm quick to jerk the phone out of Xavier's hands and hang up.

I'm almost happy to see two shady guys turn the corner the next second—yes, as in I'd rather talk to a possible *murderer* than acknowledge that the only girl I've ever given a shit about just offered me a one-way ticket out of her life.

I specifically told Baseball Cap Dude to come alone, but then again, the bastard is no genius.

"Remember what we talked about?" I gesture to Xavier's phone in his pocket with a flick of my chin.

Xavier nods, quick to unlock his phone as I assess the guys before me. The rando tagging along is on the buff side and more imposing than his buddy, but I have no doubt Xavier and I could take them. I notice they both have their hands tucked into their pockets, as if to make sure they have quick access to something.

I can't tell what they're packing.

Knives?

Guns?

Whatever it is, they're not playing, and they've got us at a serious disadvantage. Doesn't matter. I came here to get a confession, and I'm not leaving without one.

They stop a few steps away from my car, watching us intently as though they're afraid we're going to slam the gas and run over their empty fucking skulls.

My fists clench as my focus drifts to the guy I nearly strangled to death the night of Lacey's party. Then the little doubts left in my mind go up in smoke.

He's not wearing his baseball cap.

I make the first move, pushing my door open and stepping out of the vehicle. Xavier follows my lead, not far behind me as I round my car and make a beeline for them.

"I see you brought a friend," I drawl.

Baseball Cap Dude flashes a rotten smile. "Consider him my insurance policy."

I almost laugh.

He's batshit crazy if he thinks this guy, or a *hundred* guys, could ever protect him from me.

"Where's my fucking money?" He cuts to the chase.

"Admit it first."

My response throws him off his game. He casts a glance toward his friend, who's just as much of a brainless fuck as he is, and cocks an eyebrow.

"Admit what?" he asks.

I scoff. "Spare me the bullshit. I know you killed my dog. Did you really think I'd never find out?"

I expected many, many reactions from him, but I definitely didn't expect him to laugh in my face.

His cackle ticks me off. "Is that a trick question?"

His buddy laughs along with him.

"Why else would I confess to your whore? I *wanted* her to tell you I'd run the bitch over. Not the brightest crayon in the box, are we?"

My *whore*?

What the hell is he talking about?

The shock in my eyes must give away my confusion because his lips curl into a twisted smile.

"Your side piece didn't tell you?" he realizes.

My side piece?

Wait…

Is he talking about Dia?

"I'm guessing that means she also didn't tell you about our little *run-in*?" He smirks.

No.

Fuck.

They had a "run-in"?

When?

"You should've seen her." He cracks a wheezy laugh, relishing in a memory I want to shove up his ass. "Naked in your bed, helpless, *vulnerable.* Poor thing was heartbroken, thinking you abandoned her."

I can't breathe, the blood sizzling in my veins.

"I get why you like her. She's a hot piece of ass. And fuck, *those tits.* I just might have to track her down and finish what I started once we're done here." He whisks his head back to tell his buddy, "You feeling a threesome? Girl's got two holes for a reason."

Then I lose it.

Plain and simple.

He touched her.

He. Touched. Her.

I'm barely aware of how fast I tackle him to the ground. There's nothing around me, no voice of reason blaring inside my head, no survival instincts warning me about the weapon in his pocket. There's just red. And blood.

His blood.

"You motherfucker, you think you can touch her? You think

you can *hurt* her? You're dead. You're so fucking dead," I shout to the point of straining my voice as I crash my fist into his jaw.

Over.

And over.

And over.

Until he's but a bloody, panicky mess under me. I grip his collar so hard, I squeeze the breath out of him but never stop pummeling his face with blows. His groans of pain do nothing but fuel my rage.

He forced himself on her.

Because I wasn't there.

Because I walked out on her.

Images of her waking up to his disgusting, sweaty body weighing her down blur together before my eyes, but nothing compares to the blinding pain I feel when something sharp slices through my forearm.

Then it's not just his blood anymore.

It's mine, too.

A lot of it.

He stabbed me in the forearm.

The pain is enough to snap me out of whatever trance I was in. I have the reflex of removing the knife from my flesh—which, I'll admit, was a stupid idea because the bleeding immediately worsens.

I take a look around to see Xavier rising off the ground where the guy that was supposed to be Baseball Cap's backup lies unconscious. Xav has the guy's gun in his hands. I didn't even *hear* them fight. My arm hurts like a bitch, but I try and ignore it, watching as the pathetic piece of shit beneath me chokes on blood, red staining his yellow teeth.

I can see everything I lost in his eyes.

Lexie.

Possibly Dia.

"Finn." There's a hint of worry in my best friend's voice.

"Which one was it, huh? Which one of your disgusting fucking hands touched her?" I lob the knife away and flip the bastard around, blood dripping down my wrists. I straddle his back, pinning both of his arms to each side of his body.

He starts to beg, choking down apologies, the blood in his mouth muffling every word.

"I'm sorry, what was that?" I take pleasure in his misery.

"Dude, he's had enough," Xavier intervenes.

I ignore him.

"Oh, well. Guess I'll have to take them both."

He's twisting beneath me, trying to escape his fate, but I have him helpless and vulnerable—just like she was. I scan my surroundings and spot a heavy-ass brick coming apart from the crumbling building just inches to my left.

Score.

"This is for Lexie."

The grown man screams like a little girl when I smash his knuckles with the brick. I can't stop myself, eating up his agony, his whimpers, the sound of his bones *breaking*.

"This is for touching her," I add, and repeat my actions until all of his fingers are fucked-up. I feel myself fade with each passing second.

It's the blood.

I've lost too much.

Still, I keep going. I'm about to divert my focus to his other hand when I feel Xavier pulling me off the guy's body.

I'm too weak to fight him. Just like I was too weak to fight *for* her. But not anymore.

"You touch her again, I'll cut them off. Do you fucking hear me?" I shout as Xavier drags me to the car against my will.

Xavier throws my ass into the back seat of my car and plops down onto the driver's seat before charging out of there at maximum speed. My leather seats are immediately covered in blood, and I fall onto my back to avoid looking at the wound.

"Did you get it?" I ask.

"Yes, I got it, you fucking psycho." Xavier sighs and pulls his phone out of his pocket, his other hand on the wheel.

Then he stops the recording. His disapproval of my methods makes me laugh, but it doesn't dim my relief in the slightest.

Because I won.

I got my revenge.

I got my confession.

And now?

Now I get my girl back.

Nineteen

Diamond

I thought I was prepared to go back to school.

I've walked these halls many times before, so why does this feel like a first? Why does this feel so *different*? My lungs squeeze the air out of my body as I push through the crowd with Aveena. Thank God for breaks. I might need a minute to recover from first period.

I seriously considered turning around and driving back home when I stepped into English lit this morning.

There he was.

Sitting at the back of the class, Theo, Axel, and a few of his basketball buddies huddled up around his desk like groupies. I didn't have the strength to look at his reaction when I came in. Mostly because my heart couldn't have handled it if he'd had *none*. Nearly all desks were taken, leaving just two seats in the back right next to the guys.

Some might call it fate. I call it a sick prank from the universe.

Aveena, being painfully clueless as to what happened this summer, didn't think twice, leading the way toward Finn and his fan club. I know I should've told her, but a part of me fears her judgment. Not because I'm afraid she would think less of me, but because I do.

I think less of me.

I can't imagine how that conversation would go. Hey, Vee, remember the asshole basketball player I said I wouldn't touch with a five-foot pole? Well, I let him screw me on the library floor. Oh, and I gave him all of my firsts.

Not exactly a flattering story.

I spent the whole class feeling this weight on my shoulders. Like someone was staring at me. I wanted it to be Finn. But I eventually convinced myself it was all in my head.

Why would he be looking at me now? He chose to let me go. Didn't try to contact me for *five* days after I woke up naked in his bed—granted, I blocked his number, but if he really wanted to, he would've found a way.

His excuse would have to be airtight for me to even consider forgiving him. As far as I'm concerned, the guy better have been bleeding out in the hospital.

"You want to tell me what that was about?" Aveena's voice lures me back to reality.

"What do you mean?" I arch an eyebrow, edging my way to the locker we share. We've shared a locker since freshman year.

"I get that Mrs. Callahan is evil incarnate and all, but you *bolted* out of there." She cracks a nervous laugh to conceal her worry. "And that note…"

If she wasn't sure something was going on before, she definitely is now.

She must've seen Theo, who was sitting behind me, tap my shoulder halfway through the homework assignment. I didn't even turn around, but I heard him whisper, "*From Finn.*" Believe me when I say I've never been so scared of a piece of paper.

I reached over my shoulder and grabbed the crumpled note. Finn's familiar handwriting felt like a punch to the stomach.

Talk during break?

I don't know what he has to say to me.

Probably "thanks for the sex, let's pretend it never happened," but I'm not ready to face him. So, when class ended, I leapt off my chair and practically *raced* to the door.

I caught feelings. No matter how much I wish I didn't, and I'd rather never talk to him again than have him look me in the eyes and tell me the past two months meant *nothing*.

I glance at her. "It was just a stupid note. Didn't mean anything."

I'm aware I owe her an explanation, but Easton High's crowded hallway isn't the place to tell her about my summer fling with the school's delinquent.

"Really?" Aveena slows down, eyes glued to something in the distance. "Then why is Finn Richards leaning against our locker?"

I flick my head to see Finn waiting for me, shoulder braced against the metal, his tousled brown hair a mess and his gorgeous hazel eyes stuck on me. He seems tense, holding pressure in his shoulders.

I only realize my mouth is open when Aveena nudges my jaw shut. "My house, tonight. I want to know everything."

I nod and exhale a gust of air, setting off to meet him.

This is it.

Time to get my heart broken.

Heads begin to turn before I've even reached Finn's side. I stop in front of him, whispers rising in the halls when he grabs my forearm and starts dragging me through the crowd. I assume he doesn't want people to see him stomp all over my heart as he guides me to an isolated corner by the cafeteria.

We stand there, staring each other dead in the eyes for a few seconds, waiting for whoever holds the courage to speak first.

"Let's just get this over with." I blow out a breath.

The corners of his lips twitch into a smirk.

"*Gladly.*"

I nearly drop my phone when his mouth collides with mine.

My back hits the wall with a thud, but all I can hear is the sound of angels singing as one of his hands flies to my face, the other spreading in my hair to deepen the kiss.

I gasp at his mouth moving with mine, and Finn uses my shock to slip his tongue past my teeth. I'm mad at him. I'm furious that he left me, but I'm also tragically happy that he's kissing me.

How *pathetic* is that?

My hands are on his shoulders before I can overthink it, and I feel his entire body relax at my touch. Is that why he seemed so tense earlier? It's like we've both been holding our breaths since the last time we kissed, and as heated memories of him moving inside me submerge my brain…

So does the pain of waking up alone.

No, no, Dia, snap out of it.

I smack my hands over his chest before he can rob me of my common sense and push him away. He barely stumbles back a step, stunned by my rejection, but he hasn't seen anything yet.

Without thinking, I take a swing and strike him in the face.

Hard.

"You left me!" My voice cracks.

He's fazed by my slap but quickly regains his composure, his hands flying to each side of my face again.

"No, no, I didn't. Look at me." He cages me against the wall, giving me no choice but to meet his eyes. "I didn't fucking *leave* you. I went to the police station. They called me before you woke up. I had to go, Dia. I had no choice."

A tear rolls down my cheek.

Is that really why he left?

Because the police asked him to?

"I'll prove it to you. Want me to call the sheriff? I will." He pulls his phone out of his pocket frantically. "He'll tell you I was there. He'll—"

My palm covers his to stop him from bothering the police. I have no idea why, but I believe him.

I believe he didn't leave by choice.

"Then why didn't you tell me? Why didn't you send me a text or leave a note or—"

"Because I'm a fucking idiot," he cuts me off. "I thought I'd be back before you woke up. And then my phone died, and I couldn't reach you. I'm so sorry." He exhales, pressing his lips to my forehead, then kissing every inch of my face in a gesture so disturbingly sweet that it throws me off. "I'm sorry."

If I didn't know any better, I'd say the time we spent apart *finally* woke him up as to what he wants.

"And the five days after that? What's your excuse?"

"Well, for starters, you blocked my number. And second…" He pauses as though he's debating on telling me the truth.

"What is it?"

He doesn't speak right away.

Then he drops a bombshell on me.

"I may have gotten stabbed a little…"

I know I said he had to have a damn good excuse like bleeding out in the hospital, but it never occurred to me that I could be *right*.

"You what?" Panic overtakes me. "Where? How? Why didn't you tell me? Why didn't you—"

"Hey, I'm fine." He halts my spiral. "He got me in the arm.

Didn't hit anything vital. They kept me at the hospital for a few days, gave me some stitches, some painkillers, and sent me on my way."

"How did you even get stabbed in the first place?" I can't help lifting up the sleeves of his varsity jacket, scanning his skin for an entry point of some sort.

My throat burns like hell when I find a stitched wound with clean-cut edges on his veined forearm.

It's true.

He got stabbed.

What. The. Fuck.

He exhales another long breath. Why do I feel like it's about to get worse?

"I found Lexie's killer."

I immediately recall what the creep told me the day I got assaulted. I never told Finn about the guy's confession. I thought he knew already.

I thought the only reason Finn apologized to Lexie before she died was because he *knew* he'd played a part in her death by borrowing money when, really, he was just as clueless as I was.

"Finn, I have to tell you someth—"

He interrupts me. "I know it was the scumbag from Lacey's party."

He does?

"He's the one who stabbed me. Before that, he told me what he did to Lexie and…" He chews on his bottom lip. "…what he did to *you*."

My cheeks turn scarlet.

"How much did he tell you?"

"He said he couldn't wait to finish what he started, so I assumed he hadn't…"

I lower my eyes to my feet, feeling dirty, soiled, *ashamed*. I know none of it was my fault, and it could've been so much worse, but I can't help feeling embarrassed.

"He didn't." I swallow hard. "He was going to, but he got called away. He did say I'd see him again, though. Let's hope he doesn't come back for round two."

Anger flashes in Finn's eyes, but he quickly gets a grip. "Read my fucking lips—he's *never* going to touch you again."

"How do you know?" I stress my bottom lip.

He laughs. "Kind of hard to do with broken fingers."

My head snaps up. *What did he just say?*

Jesus, he said it like he was talking about the weather.

"You broke his fingers?" I blurt.

"Damn right. Then I delivered his recorded confession to the cops on a silver platter. His prints were all over the car that hit Lexie. Turns out they already had a few warrants out for his arrest."

"But… won't he snitch on you for what you did to him?" I realize.

"Bastard tried." Finn shrugs. "We passed it off as self-defense. Made up a story about him coming at me to finish what he'd started. At this point, it's his word against mine. I'm no fucking saint, but I've never been accused of attempted murder."

I didn't think I'd *ever* be happy about a car trying to run Finn over—okay, maybe I would've been at the beginning of the summer. It's one thing to kill a dog, another to kill a dog while *trying* to kill its owner. I have no doubt Mr. Richards's million-dollar lawyers are going to do everything in their power to throw the monster in jail.

"He's going down?" Tears flood my eyes at the thought of Lexie's murderer rotting in a cell.

"We got him, Dia. We fucking got him." Finn catches a tear rolling down my face with his thumb.

For a moment, I forget all about the five excruciating days I spent convinced he didn't care about me and throw myself in his arms. I push to the tips of my toes, mashing my chest closely with his and reveling in the smell of his cologne.

Lexie is going to get *justice*. This is the best outcome we could've hoped for in this situation.

Finn doesn't waste a second wrapping his arms around me, holding me so tightly it's hard to breathe. His fingers brush hair off my neck as he drags a few desperate kisses up and down my collarbone, inhaling my scent like he's trying to memorize it.

Everything is perfect.

Until it's *not*.

"Finn?"

Finn pulls away from me like he just got caught committing a federal crime. I whisk my head to see Xavier, Theo, and Axel ogling us from around the corner.

"Dude, come on, not on school property. At least take the girl home." Axel laughs into his fist.

I wait for Finn to tell him to fuck off, but he doesn't react.

That's what he wants people to think, isn't it?

That I'm a hookup?

Because no matter how many times he promises to never let me go, Finn Richards still has an image to maintain. He's still hiding behind his heartless persona, protected by a façade I thought I'd knocked down.

"Let's go," Xavier intervenes before it becomes awkward. "Fletcher, *let's fucking go*," he repeats and ends up having to force Axel away. Finn's gaze finds mine as soon as we're alone again.

I see it in his eyes.

He knows he fucked up.

I might be able to forgive him in unusual circumstances like him getting stabbed, but I don't think I can handle a guy being ashamed of me.

"Dia..." He tries to step forward, but I step back.

"You can't even hug me in public," I whisper, more to myself than him, and turn to leave. "I... I have to go."

His hand flies to my wrist in a split second, and he spins me around, yanking me back to his chest.

"Hold on a fucking second. What does this mean?" he begs,

searching my eyes for a clue.

"It means you were right." It takes all the courage in my body to detach from him. "It's called a summer job for a reason. After summer, it *ends*."

Then I leave him there.

As I head back to my locker with a crumbling heart, I realize why being back between these walls feels so different.

It feels different because *I'm* different.

This summer changed me.

Finn changed me.

But in the end...

I couldn't change *him*.

* * *

Finn

The cafeteria is so loud I can barely hear myself *think* as Xavier and I edge through the crowd to meet the guys. Theo, Axel, and a few players from the team are already seated at our usual table, cracking jokes about people I know for a fact don't hold a candle to me.

Truth is, *I'm* the biggest joke around. No, I'm a whole-ass comedy show for pulling away when she hugged me this morning. Why the fuck did I pull away?

It's so easy when we're alone. When I have her backed up in a corner, big brown eyes blinking up at me, but in front of my friends? In front of the world? That shit feels like running through a battlefield naked.

It's like I don't want people to know that I care. And it's not because I'm ashamed of her. If I'm honest, it's not even about Dia at all. *It's about me.*

I spend the next five minutes playing with my fork and staring at the unappealing food on my plate. I'm briefly brought back to reality by Theo apologizing for his absence the day of Lexie's death.

Something about his psycho parents taking his phone and locking him inside his room for twenty-four hours when he stopped by to get some of his stuff.

I nod, accepting his apology, regardless of the fact that I didn't need it, and retreat to a faraway world. I've almost successfully drowned out Axel's sexist jokes when he says the one thing that could capture my attention.

Her name.

"Fuck, she's hot. Dia, is it?"

My eyes lift from my food tray to Axel leaning back into his seat, staring at the cafeteria entrance. I follow his eyes to the large wooden doors, spotting her immediately.

She's walking with Aveena Harper, outshining every fucking girl in the room with her plump mouth and lustrous curls. I didn't know Dia was friends with Aveena.

Aveena's mom and mine were tight when we were kids. Xavier and I would hang out with her every weekend and pull a bunch of sick pranks on her to make her life miserable. He refused to say it out loud, but Xavier had the biggest fucking crush on her. I remember giving him so much shit for it.

I can't tear my eyes away as Dia saunters farther into the cafeteria, looking for a place to sit. And I'm not the only one staring. The whole table is.

Hell, any guy who has *eyes* is staring.

We must be pretty obvious because Aveena elbows Dia, gesturing toward us with her chin.

Dia's head snaps up.

And our eyes lock across the room.

A twinge of pain colors her dark eyes for a fleeting moment, but she's quick to bury it, looking away. She finds two available seats shortly after.

"Look, Richards, it's your girlfriend." Axel scorns.

My fists contract into tight balls. That's what I was afraid of. The guys thinking that I'm whipped.

And honestly?

They might be right.

"She's not my girlfriend," I grumble.

He snorts out a laugh. "Do you hug all your fuck toys, then?"

My fuck toy.

He thinks she's my fuck toy.

If anyone's a toy, it's me.

The girl's got me wrapped around her fucking pinky at this point. I may not be ready to show her off to my friends, but what she doesn't understand is I've never met *anyone* I wanted to introduce to them. She might've given me her firsts, but she's a first for me, too.

"She was there when his dog died. They caught the guy, and she was happy. End of story." Xavier drums up an explanation that's sure to get Axel off my back. Part of me wants to thank him while the other wants to break his nose for fighting my battles.

"Right, your dog." Axel clamps his mouth shut. "Sorry, man."

I don't reply. Axel rises off his chair the next second, and it's like a billion sirens just went off in my head.

"Where are you going?" I nearly blurt.

He glances at me over his shoulder. "To talk to her."

"Why?" I don't miss a beat. I can feel everybody's eyes on me, but I don't give a damn.

He smirks. "Use your imagination."

He turns to walk away.

"Sit the fuck down, Fletcher," I stop him again.

"Dude, either she's your girl or she's not. Make up your fucking mind."

And he's right.

I have no business keeping guys from talking to her. No business trying to mark my territory if at the end of the day, I'm not the one taking her home.

"So, what's it going to be?" Axel cocks an eyebrow, and I get the sense that he's challenging me or some shit.

But I say nothing.

He flashes a satisfied grin. "That's what I thought."

Then he's making his way over to her table.

I wish the guys would start talking about something. *Anything* as long as it distracts me, but they keep their mouths shut, watching Axel shoot the shot I couldn't.

I grab the plastic knife on my right, pretending to cut through my food, but it's no use. My eyes are back on her in a heartbeat. Axel stops by her table, planting his palms on the edge and telling Dia something I can't hear. Judging by the look of disgust on her face, she's not into it.

Or him.

Until her eyes light up in realization, and she finds me in the crowd. She catches me staring, and just like that… she learns the rules to a game I didn't even know we were playing.

She goes from unresponsive to Axel's flirting to involved in the conversation in an instant, batting her eyelashes at him as he spews to her what I'm sure is a bunch of crap.

In that moment, I want nothing more than to rise off my seat, march over there, and drag her into a bathroom stall to remind her who she belongs to.

I nearly go blind from rage when she grabs Axel's phone to add her number into his contacts. My mind starts to run wild with images of Dia spread out on his bed, moaning Axel's name, her tits bouncing as he takes the rest of her firsts.

"Finn, what the fuck?" I recognize Xavier's voice.

Will she even remember me when he's inside her? Will she—

"Shit, dude, you're bleeding."

A hand shakes my shoulder vigorously, pulling me out of a dark place. I'm back in the crowded cafeteria in the snap of a finger. A small gust of air leaves my lips when I look down and see the plastic knife I was holding a moment prior digging into my hand. I was clenching my fists so tight I didn't even realize…

There's blood all over my napkin, some in my food, some on my cafeteria tray.

I'm so fucking jealous I made myself *bleed.*

It's almost like my body is trying to punish my brain for being a coward and letting this happen. I glance around the table to find the guys watching me like I'm an alien.

All of them but Xavier.

In his eyes, I see a glimmer of understanding.

Then he nods.

And I know that nod is his way of telling me "Who do you think you're kidding?"

He's telling me to go for it, and as I watch Dia force herself to laugh at one of Axel's jokes, the words the moron said to me play on a loop in my head.

"Dude, either she's your girl or she's not. Make up your fucking mind."

Well, I just did.

I made up my mind.

And, before the day is over…

Everyone in this goddamn school is going to know Diamond Mitchell is mine.

* * *

Diamond

There are only twenty-four hours in a day.

Six of which the average student will spend at school.

But as Aveena and I amble out of Easton after the longest day of my life, I catch myself wondering if I accidentally entered a time loop. I swear I've been stuck in this building for *ages*, dreading every class break and bending over backward to dodge Finn in the halls.

It wasn't too hard to avoid him in the afternoon—we didn't have any classes together, and our lockers are in different sections—but avoiding my *guilt* was a very different story.

I've never been one to play with someone's feelings. Until Axel Fletcher came over to my table at lunch and started feeding me ridiculous lines about my eyes. I was this close to shutting him down when I looked over at Finn and saw the rage in *his* eyes.

He was pissed.

He was jealous.

And I liked that.

So, I played along. Faked a smile and listened to Axel's garbage pickup lines. I even added a fake number into Axel's phone to make it look like he had a chance.

All so that Finn would wake the hell up.

I'm not sure I like this version of me.

"My mom and sister are out all night. You're coming over," Aveena states as we stride across the parking lot together.

"Do I have a choice?" I crack a smile.

"Nah. Girls who don't tell their best friend about their scandalous summer romance don't get choices," she teases.

I check my phone as I walk, hoping for the mercy of a text from Finn.

No new messages.

Disappointment sinks in my stomach like a rock, but I don't let it faze me, refreshing my texts obsessively. Maybe he doesn't know I unblocked his number? I'm halfway to my car when Aveena grips my arm and stops dead at something in the distance.

I look up.

And understand why he didn't text me.

I didn't get a text because I'm getting the *real deal.*

Finn is leaning against my bug car with his head hanging low, his tattooed arms crossed over his chest and his brown hair cascading in front of his eyes. The strap of his sports bag dangles from his shoulder, and I assume basketball practice is kicking off tonight.

"My place, seven o'clock." Aveena flashes a knowing grin and takes off toward her car.

You'd think Finn has some sort of Dia radar because as soon as she's gone, he looks up, hazel eyes capturing mine across the parking lot.

"Richards! The fuck are you waiting for? Coach wants to talk to us before practice," a voice I'm positive belongs to Axel calls behind us.

I flip my head to see Theo, Xavier, and Axel watching us from the crowded school stairs with gym bags of their own and their backs pressed to the railing.

I almost expect Finn to desert me again—he's proven to be particularly skilled in that department—but he doesn't waver one bit, dead set on maintaining the eye contact.

"I won't bite, Gem." His lips twitch into a small smirk.

But he's lying. He might not bite, but I'm afraid if I get any closer, he'll sink his claws into me, making good on his promise to never let me go.

I can feel a thousand eyes on me, the weight of unwanted attention slowing me down as I approach him. My demeanor is cautious, apprehensive, when I come to a stop before him.

"What do you want?" My shoulders shrink under half the school's scrutiny.

In response, he lets out a scoff.

It's low, deep, captivating.

But it's also mocking.

Like he's surprised that I'm even *asking.*

"I think you know exactly what I want."

My heart hammers in my chest.

"But only if you can hide it, right?" I meant to sound confident, but it comes out as a whisper.

Finn pushes off my car, slowly stalking toward me. He stops a hair too close for my heart's liking, but my pride forbids me to move away. I shiver when he tucks one of my curls behind my ear.

"Do I look like I'm hiding?" He arches an eyebrow.

He's got a point.

The school parking lot isn't exactly *private.*

"You did earlier," I remind him.

I know I made my case when a sigh leaves his lips.

"You're right, that was shitty of me."

Shitty?

Dude, you tore my heart to pieces.

"I'm sorry." He holds my stare. "And not just for today. I've been hiding since the night you kneed me in the fucking balls."

I wait for him to carry on.

"I'm a coward, Dia." He exhales. "I've spent ten years of my life pretending like my heart was rotting at the bottom of Lake Belmont with my mom."

I suck in a breath at his admission.

This is the first time he's brought her up while sober.

"I did everything I could to convince people it drowned with her that day. And it worked. Too well, actually. Because I started believing it, too."

You could hear a pin drop in the school lot.

Most kids have dispersed, but the cheer squad and the basketball team decided to park their asses in front of the school and enjoy the show. Finn's not loud enough for them to hear him, but that doesn't mean those nosey bastards aren't trying.

"Then you showed up one day, shoved your fist through my chest, and pulled that shit out. You reminded me I had a heart, Dia, but I didn't realize how beat up and damaged it was until you walked away from me this morning."

My throat feels like it's being squeezed.

"I guess what I'm trying to say is… it's not going to be easy. I'm probably going to hurt you, and sometimes you're going to call me an asshole and we're going to fight, but *fuck*, for once in my life, I want to fight. I want to fight until we get it right."

I can't speak.

"Fight for me, Gem. And I promise to fight like hell for you."

I only realize I'm crying when salty tears slide down my lips.

"What… What does this mean? I… Do you want to date?"

His hands clutch my face, and he drills his gaze into mine.

"I don't know what to call it. I mean, just two months ago, I couldn't even fathom *wanting* to be with someone. This is all so fucking new to me, but I think… I think if you give me time, we'll figure it out."

So many thoughts spin around in my head, the primary one being that I don't really have a choice.

I can't walk away from this.

From him.

I just… *can't.*

And it may not be perfect, but he's trying, which is more than he's ever done for anyone.

"Wait, so, we're *not* dating?" I ask.

"Not technically, but if you ask me, we don't need the fucking label."

"Does that mean we can see other people?"

He laughs at that.

"Did those words just come out of your mouth? For fuck's sake, Dia, I almost *killed* a guy for touching you."

"That's a no, then?" I tease.

He scoffs. Then his lips are on mine, searching, tasting, devouring. He kisses me in the middle of the school parking lot without a fuck given as to our audience.

This feels like more than a kiss. It feels like he's letting the world know what *we've* known all along. I push to my tiptoes to wrap my arms around his neck, and Finn laces his bicep around my waist, leaning against my car. He pulls me with him, his hands slipping into the back pockets of my jeans possessively.

We must make out for five minutes before we disconnect, equally out of breath and stunned by what just happened.

We really did that.

Now everyone knows.

Our summer fling wasn't just a fling, after all.

I can't wipe the dopey grin off my face when Finn plants a final kiss on my mouth.

"I never answered your question," he rasps against my lips.

Trapped in a daze, I struggle to make sense of his words.

"What question?"

"You asked me once to name one thing I don't hate."

The exact moment I asked him washes over me, the memory wedging itself at the forefront of my mind. It was the night I found him standing in the window. I told him he hated everything.

"Yeah?" I know where this is going, but I'd be mad to stop him now.

"You were right. I do hate everything."

He kisses me again.

Then he says something I know will stick with me long after this moment is gone.

"*Everything but you.*"

Six months later

"I made a deal with the devil without reading it first. Of all his pretty lies, ***I love you*** was the worst."

Twenty

Diamond

"You're going to hell for this." My hand drops between my legs to clutch Finn's hair.

"Good thing I saved you a spot." He laughs against my core and flicks my clit with a stroke of his tongue, spreading my legs wider as he eats me out mercilessly.

I'm not sure how I ended up here. In nothing but a bra with my legs open on the hood of a basketball player's car.

Actually, that's a lie.

I know exactly what got me here.

A text.

Finn: Meet me at our spot before Theo's party. I'm fucking starving.

I knew better than to think he was talking about *food.* After all, we've come to these woods every week for the past six months, and not once did we eat something here.

Well, except *each other.*

"Oh shit, yes. Yes!" My stomach clenches as the pleasure

reaches unbearable levels. Finn groans, his tongue replacing his fingers at my entrance and pushing inside me.

In a perfect world, we wouldn't have to hide like this. I'd be able to tell my parents I did *way* more than watch a dog last summer, and Finn's place wouldn't be a fucking fortress guarded by security twenty-four seven.

I can't blame Mr. Richards for being extra careful. Lexie's murder really did a number on him. If my dog had bled out in my son's arms while I was away, I'd probably hire hard-core security, too.

Some would argue he's doing too much.

Especially considering the dirtbag who killed Lexie was sentenced to three years in jail for attempted murder and possession with intent to sell a month ago. But Finn's dad's made it clear he's not about to let history repeat itself.

It's ironic, really.

Finn went from wishing his dad was home more often to impatiently waiting for him to go away again.

Knowing Lexie died in Finn's arms and Finn didn't even *think* to call him—the cops had to do it—seems to have woken up Mr. Richards as to how broken their relationship truly is.

He's been back in town ever since, trying to reconnect with his son. Let's just say Finn isn't big on the idea of making peace. I think he blames his dad for the million business trips and not being there that summer.

Finn smacks his palms onto his car as he licks me up and

down. My nails scratch at the paint, the sensation of his tongue tearing me apart.

"Careful, you wouldn't want me to ruin Remy." I choke on a moan, and Finn laughs.

"Ruin whatever you want, baby." His mouth clamps down on my clit, and my back arches off the car.

"You never did tell me why you called your car Remy. Is it after someone?" I ask.

"Nah." Finn shrugs. "I don't know anyone named Remy. I just liked the name."

Finn slips two fingers inside my pussy, curling in and out of me furiously. I hope the next time we do this is in an actual bed, but between Finn having basketball practice nearly every day and my parents not knowing about us, stolen moments like these are all we've got.

They don't even know that I have a boyfriend—well, Finn and I don't exactly have the *title* yet, but everyone at school knows we're together.

If my dads found out, they'd probably disown me for lying to them, and I know it's wrong, but I've been pretending that I'm hanging out with Aveena every time Finn and I sneak off to the woods.

"Shit, I'm going to—"

"Fuck yes, baby. Give it to me."

And I do.

I come all over his face before falling onto the hood of his car, crashing back down to earth as my orgasm slowly wanders off. I barely get the chance to catch my breath before Finn shoves his jeans down, grips my thighs, and pulls me closer.

My ass hanging off the edge of the car, Finn frees his cock from his briefs. I gulp at how good he looks. I can't help gawking at his shaft and the veins climbing up his length. We haven't seen each other all week due to his crazy schedule, and I have to admit I've been fantasizing about this.

"They're waiting for us." I chew on my bottom lip. We were supposed to be at Theo's place for a pool party hours ago.

Finn smirks and guides his fist up and down his cock swiftly, positioning his tip at my entrance. "And I've been waiting for this moment all fucking week. *Life's a bitch.*"

The first thrust takes my breath away.

Finn throws his head back with a carnal groan, filling me to the brim.

"I've missed this so fucking much." He stills himself and grabs the back of my neck, forcing my head down to ensure I'm watching as he pulls out completely and thrusts back in.

I moan, my eyes widening when I realize…

He's not wearing a condom.

We've known for months that we're both clean, and even though I'm on the pill, I insisted that we take extra precautions.

"Finn," I yelp as he picks up the pace, fucking me harder and harder. "*Condom.*"

He stops moving on cue and pulls out, his eyes growing in

size as it dawns on him. I immediately wince at the lack of sensation.

"I'm sorry, I—"

I hate myself for lacing my legs around his waist and jerking him to me. We both gasp as his cock slips back inside me.

"Fuck, Dia, I can't…" *Thrust.* "I can't fucking stop." *Thrust.* "Make me stop."

But my body refuses to listen as I shift my hips to increase the friction, willing him to go faster. This feels more intense, more real, more *personal.* I'm so lost in the moment that I nearly forget about the people waiting for us at Theo's.

Until I remember I invited someone I can't disappoint.

Aveena.

I begged her to come to Theo's party when she stopped by my house earlier today. The last thing I want is for her to be alone with Finn's friends while I'm having sex in the woods.

We don't see each other as often as we used to, and I miss her. I just wish I didn't have to feel *ashamed* whenever I want to talk about sex or Finn or parties—basically normal teenager stuff. She always asks me how things are going but looks uncomfortable when I tell her. Maybe her lack of experience makes her feel out of place? Whatever it is, it's made me hesitant to share with her. We're drifting apart, and it terrifies me.

"Crap, we have to go. I invited Vee."

Finn's mouth comes down on mine.

"Mm." He kisses me to shut me up.

"Finn, seriously, we need to hurry. I don't want her to be alone." I bite back a smile, his hot body colliding with mine over and over.

"Just tell her you had dirty forest sex. She'll understand." He leans forward to bite my earlobe. Knowing words won't get me anywhere, I contract my pelvic muscles and clench his cock.

"Oh, fuck." Finn squeezes his eyes shut, gripping my waist as he rams himself faster inside me. He's usually not a minute man. I'm going to have to speed the process along.

"If you come now, I'll let you do it."

His eyes fly open.

He knows exactly what I mean.

He's wanted to try anal for a while, but I had my reservations.

"Your fingers, first. Then we'll see. *Deal?*" I bite back a moan.

I can practically see his wildest fantasies staring back at me. *Yep, that'll do it.* His mouth drops open as images of what he wants to do to me push him closer to the edge.

"Deal." He grabs my throat to kiss me, then pulls away, paying close attention to my face as he gives me everything he has. He was right about one thing. Our sex is dirty and messy, but it's also vulnerable and raw.

Like we're the last people left on this earth.

"Fuuuck." Finn groans, squeezing my throat tighter. He pumps into me three more times before spilling inside me.

I'm going to need a hell of a shower after this.

We're both out of breath as Finn wraps me up in an embrace

I never want to leave. Still inside me, he kisses my jaw and tilts his head forward to whisper something in my ear.

"Everything but you."

My heart swells up painfully.

He makes me so happy.

We've been having the best time these past six months, even with all the sneaking around. We talk every day, spend every weekend together, we party, we laugh. I've been living on a cloud, and while I *am* afraid of falling, when he says things like that, I almost believe I never will.

Everything but you has become our thing, Finn's way of saying I love you without really saying it.

"Everything but you," I croak, and Finn places a kiss on the tip of my nose. My legs are wobbly when he helps me off the car. Thankfully, he catches me before my knees give in and takes the opportunity to kiss me again.

"Okay, now we *really* have to go," I whisper, and he smiles.

Finn reluctantly releases me, then tosses me my shirt and my pants that were collecting dust on the ground. He gives me all of my clothes except my panties.

"Can I have those back?" I stretch my arm out.

"I think I'll hold on to these until you keep up your end of our deal." He smirks, slipping his leverage into his pocket.

Asshole.

I don't bother arguing as I get dressed, grateful for the privacy of the woods. Our spot is in the middle of bumfuck nowhere, near the tree where Finn's parents carved their names all those years ago.

"I'm going straight to Theo's. See you there?" Finn pecks my mouth, and I nod before trailing back to my own car—my parents would find it suspicious if Finn chauffeured me around.

Finn's car disappears down the dirt road by the woods a moment later, and I check my phone for texts once I've buckled up. I have two messages from Lacey.

And one from my dad.

Lacey: WHERE ARE YOU?

Lacey: Theo left to get more booze and I'm stuck with Axel. If you leave me alone with Fletcher The Pig, I'll literally never talk to you again!

A chuckle leaves me.

Is it bad that I've been texting Lacey more than Aveena since the beginning of senior year? Is it bad that I've grown a lot closer to Lacey than my own *best friend*? I do everything with Lacey these days. We party together, go shopping together, we even go to concerts on the weekends.

Vee is so important to me, but she has many triggers—like her hatred for alcohol because of her alcoholic dad—and I don't always know how to navigate them. I tap out of my conversation with Lacey and check the message from my dad.

Gaten: Your brother's coming back into town tomorrow. We're having dinner at the restaurant. Be there at five.

News of my brother's return should make me happy, but Jesse coming back after disappearing for half a year brings me more questions than it does joy.

He just left out of the blue six months ago, shortly after school picked up again. No call, no text, not even a goodbye. My parents said he needed some time away to focus on himself and dig into his past—whatever the hell that means.

I can't help wondering if his ghost act could have something to do with the mysterious secret Brody Richards said he was keeping last summer?

I'd be lying if I said I wasn't relieved to find out Jesse was MIA when Finn and I started to get "serious." I have no doubt Jesse would've snitched on me just to stick it to Finn. He might be back now, but I won't let him ruin the best thing in my life...

Even if it means doing some digging of my own.

* * *

I'm pulling into Theo's driveway an hour later.

My dads ambushed me when I came into the house to shower and wash Finn's cum off me—no classy way to put it. They interrogated me on where I'd been and where I was going for fifteen minutes. I ended up feeding them some story about having spent the day with Aveena.

Then I told them I was meeting some friends to *study* tonight.

They bought it.

Because they trust me.

Because they *love* me.

Meanwhile, I've done nothing but lie to them.

I thought I was going to vomit when Gaten pulled me into a hug and whispered that he was proud of me. In his eyes, I'm their good kid. Unlike my brother and sister who had a special talent for landing themselves in deep shit at my age.

I don't know how much longer I can keep this up. The more I bury the truth, the more disappointed they're going to be when they find out their precious little girl isn't scared of the monster under her bed anymore. Because the only monster she's scared of… is the monster *in* it.

I'm surprised to see Brielle Randall lying on a lounge chair by the pool when I round the house toward Theo's backyard. What is *she* doing here? I thought Xavier dumped her?

It's all everyone's been talking about.

How Brie accidentally exposed her own boyfriend on Snapchat a few days ago. Finn and Xavier thought it'd be a brilliant idea to set off a stink bomb in class last week. Their stupid prank caused the whole school to be evacuated under the pouring rain.

People suspected a gas leak. It got so bad that the cops and fire department showed up. The stink bomb debacle ended with Finn and Xavier being thrown in the back of a cop car.

And it's all thanks to Brie.

Brie decided to record herself when the teacher stepped out of the classroom. She was making pouty faces at the camera with a filter, clueless as can be. Little did she know she'd just caught Xavier showing Finn the stink bomb in his backpack on video.

Finn almost got into a world of trouble over it—they wanted to cut him from the basketball team—but Xavier took the fall, claiming it was his idea. Surprisingly, he was telling the truth. Xavier Emery, a fucking saint, planned a prank *all by himself.* It felt out of character, to say the least.

I put up with Brie hanging out with us all year because she was dating Xavier. Was I foolish to think we'd be rid of the bitch after their breakup? Call me territorial, but I *hate* knowing that she slept with Finn.

I spot Theo, Lacey, and Axel in the pool as soon as I turn the corner. No sign of Aveena or Finn.

"Dia!" Lacey squeals at the sight of me. She hurries out of the pool before I can greet her, nearly tripping on her way to me. I can tell she's a bit tipsy by her drunken giggles but don't mention it. "Where the hell have you been?"

Having sex in the woods.

Lying to my parents.

Making a mess of my life.

Lacey doesn't await my response, trapping me into a hug. I

shriek as her dripping bikini soaks through my clothes. She holds me in place, voluntarily drenching my outfit.

"That's for leaving me alone with Axel," she whispers as we hug, a hint of humor audible in her voice.

"Fair enough." I chuckle.

"Go change into your bathing suit. The water's great." Lacey pulls away to assess me. She glances at my wet clothes and bites back a smile. "Or stay like that. *Same thing.*"

I'm about to ask her where Finn is when strong arms circle my waist from behind, picking me up like I'm weightless. Hot lips plaster kisses all over my cheek, and I laugh, swiveling to look at Finn. He must've been in the house.

"Hey, asshole, what took you so long?" Theo asks Finn, swimming closer to the edge of the pool.

Wait, Finn *just* got here?

"I got lost." Finn's eyes remain fixated on me, and he smacks a long kiss on my lips.

"Where? In Dia's mouth?" Axel snorts, and everyone laughs.

What was he doing the past hour?

I went back to my house to shower, which explains why *I'm* late, but he said he was driving straight to Theo's?

"Love the lipstick, Richards. Which shade is that?" Theo fails to contain his laughter. My eyes immediately jump to the lipstick stain on Finn's collar.

That would be my fault.

Finn is still wearing the same outfit he was earlier in the

woods, so it's not like he drove home to shower and change.

"Your collar." I scoff, but Finn doesn't seem bothered by it in the slightest.

"I'll be back." Finn gives my ass a squeeze over my shorts and sets off toward the house to try and salvage his shirt. He hasn't even been gone two seconds before Lacey calls on me.

"You're still coming to girls' night tomorrow, right?"

Crap, I forgot about girls' night.

Lacey's been bugging me about it for months. Her birthday is coming up, and she invited a bunch of her friends to hang out at her place tomorrow night. It's a school night, which means no sleepover, but she hasn't stopped saying how excited she is for me to meet her out-of-town friends.

"Absolutely." I nod.

I'll just sneak off to Lacey's after the dinner from hell.

To think that at this time tomorrow, I'll be face-to-face with my dishonest brother for the first time in half a year. Most people go to family dinners because they want to spend quality time with loved ones.

But not me.

What I want… is a *confession.*

Twenty-One

Diamond

Dinner is awkward.

My dads and I sit in a leather booth, putting our acting skills to the test as we pretend we're not sharing a meal with a stranger. The worst part is, Jesse doesn't only feel like a stranger.

He *looks* like one, too.

He's changed since I last saw him.

He got a buzz cut, new tattoos, new secrets. He's also pale, exhaustion sucking the life out of his eyes. I don't know where he ran off to these past six months, but it sure wasn't a five-star resort.

"I'll be right back with the dessert menu," our waiter says before walking away.

Dinner was filled with meaningless chitchat and desperate attempts to avoid confronting our real issues. I'm afraid I won't make it through dessert unless I say something.

"Are we seriously *not* going to acknowledge him disappearing for six months?" I address the elephant in the room.

I thought it was awkward before.

I was wrong.

This is what awkward looks like.

Gaten clears his throat, shifting in the banquette and resting his forearms on the table to join his hands.

"Your brother needed some time to himself."

Here we go again.

"What does that even mean?" I confront Jesse directly.

Dave cuts in. "It's complicated."

It would be nice if they let him speak.

"Where did you go?" I push my luck.

Gaten opens his mouth to speak as though he's got rehearsed answers lined up, but Jesse gestures for my dad to let him speak.

"Redwater. I have some friends there," Jesse says.

His explanation triggers my memory, making way for a dark and distant story tucked in the deepest corner of my mind. I remember my dads telling me Redwater is where our foster home was. Where they found Jesse and me when we were kids.

Why would Jesse want to go back? All this town has ever brought him was misery. He spent his entire childhood bouncing from foster home to foster home there.

I'm about to speak again, but Jesse beats me to it.

"What about you, sis? How was that summer job? Anything we should know?" He flashes a knowing smile.

"Kids, please, can we enjoy a nice dinner?" Dave swoops in.

They're lying to me.

They didn't even blink when Jesse mentioned last summer, which begs the question: Why don't they find his comment suspicious? They wouldn't have missed that unless they were wrapped up in trying to conceal their own sins.

"I have to go to the bathroom." I make up an excuse to get away before it gets ugly.

I hide in a bathroom stall for five minutes, contemplating the clusterfuck my life is sure to become if Jesse decides to snitch on me. I almost wish he hadn't come back. Finn and I are happy. We didn't go through *actual* hell for Jesse to show up and mess up everything.

I've just stepped out of the ladies' room when my phone rings. An idiotic grin dislodges the scowl on my face when I see the caller ID.

Finn.

I press the phone to my ear. "Please tell me your night is going better than mine."

I'm careful to hide in the isolated hallway by the bathroom to prevent people from eavesdropping. Finn laughs into the phone, his voice low and raspy.

"Meh. It's all right. You're not naked on the hood of my car." I can practically hear his smirk.

"Trust me, I wish I was." I heave a chuckle. "What are you doing?"

"Thinking about our deal," he teases, his tone thick with lust. My cheeks heat up on cue. I had no idea what I was getting myself into when I agreed to try anal. Now, I'm not saying we're going to go all the way—the stuff looks more painful than this *dinner*, and that's saying a lot. But I did agree to test the waters.

"You're never going to let this go, are you?" I lean back against the wall.

"Not a chance." He scoffs. "God, I can't fucking wait to see you Friday."

I wince at the reminder. We won't be able to see each other until the end of the week—at least, not alone. There's a basketball game this Friday, which means Finn has practice every single night. He's going to be exhausted by the time the big game rolls around.

"This is going to be the longest week of my life," I complain.

"Don't I fucking know it. Remember, we're all meeting at my place after the game. My dad's giving his clowns the night off."

I chuckle quietly. It's about time Mr. Richards realized he was doing too much with the round-the-clock security.

"I'll be there," I assure him.

"You better." I know he's kidding, but I also have no doubt he'd find me and drag my ass to his house if I didn't show up.

The floor creaking startles me.

I stiffen up.

It came from around the corner.

I'm not alone, am I?

"I have to go. I'll talk to you soon."

"Not soon enough."

The words slip out of my mouth before he hangs up. "Finn?"

"Yeah, baby?"

My stomach flips. You know you have it bad when a stupid *nickname* makes you blush.

"Everything but you," I confess.

"Everything but you," he says right back.

Then I hang up the phone and step out of my hiding spot to investigate my possible audience.

No one.

This place is old. It could just be normal building noises. I feel my smile disintegrate as I make my way back to my family's booth. Both my dads are gone, leaving me alone with the one person I didn't want to talk to.

Jesse.

I consider sneaking through the back door—I already told my dads I was going to Lacey's after dinner—but it's too late. Jesse's seen me, and he might not be my favorite person right now, but I can hardly see myself walking the other way at the mere sight of him.

"Where's everybody?" I ask once I regain my seat.

"Gaten got called away to the kitchen. Something about the sous-chef bailing at the last minute. And Dave stepped out to take a call from Charlie's babysitter."

I give a small nod, fidgeting with my fingers underneath the table. I don't say another word and snatch my phone out of my pocket, intending to let the conversation die.

Too bad Jesse has other plans.

"Are you dating him?" he shocks me by saying.

I look up from my phone.

"Who?" I opt for my last line of defense. *Ignorance.*

"Oh, cut the bullshit, Dia. I heard your phone call."

It was him?

"I said, are you dating him?" Jesse hounds.

I have two options.

Play dumb and risk pissing him off more.

Or come clean.

To hell with this.

"So, what if I am?" I lie. Finn and I aren't official, no matter how much I wish we were, but Jesse doesn't need to know that.

Jesse slouches into his seat, rubbing his palms down his face.

"Finn Richards? Seriously? You can't possibly be this fucking dumb, Dia."

It's clear that his goal was to make me feel guilty, to make me doubt what Finn and I have, but all his speech is doing is make me hate him.

"Have you forgotten everything he did to you? For fuck's sake, wake up. He doesn't give a shit about you."

That's when I know I've had enough.

"*He* doesn't give a shit?" I snap a bit too loud, capturing the attention of the couple at the table next to us. "What about *you*? You skipped town overnight and couldn't even be bothered to say goodbye. You disappeared, Jess. You bailed. You don't get to show up out of nowhere and act like a concerned brother."

Jesse's mouth drops open.

He's stunned by my reaction, and I waste no time jumping to my feet before his composure returns and he starts making threats.

"Tell them I said thank you for dinner." I turn to leave.

But I'm not quick enough.

"Dia?" Jesse calls behind me.

I glance over my shoulder despite every nerve in my body telling me to book it to my car.

"I might not be able to fix my own life, but you mark my words, I'm not going to let you ruin yours."

I tear my eyes off him, staring ahead of me as I search my pockets for my keys. Then I feed the growing gap between us by a hundred miles.

"Pretty hard for you to fix my life if you're not a part of it."

* * *

"Never have I ever had sex in a public place." Lacey chortles, grabbing a glittery pillow on the couch and clutching it to her chest.

Is this game lame? Yes.

Does Lacey give a rat's ass? *No.*

I knew when I showed up to Lacey's house to find her puking in the sink with Hadley Queen holding her hair, that this "girls' night" was going to be… well, *memorable.*

I have to hand it to Lacey. It's got to take some serious guts to get drunk on a weeknight. My parents would die before letting me get shitfaced under their roof.

Granted, *her* parents seem to be gone a lot. She doesn't talk about them much, but if the parties she constantly throws are anything to go by, either her folks don't care what she does or they don't stick around long enough to notice.

We cut her off an hour ago, and we've been playing this stupid game ever since.

It's just Hadley, a girl named Astrid, Lacey, and me for now, but there were supposed to be five of us tonight. Lacey keeps talking about how awesome her childhood friend is and how much we're going to love her when she gets here.

Apparently, she used to live in Silver Springs but moved away a while back. It's late, and I'm starting to wonder whether or not I'll get to meet her at all. I might have spent the summer breaking all my parents' rules, but I'm not trying to incur their wrath by missing my curfew.

"I've got one for you," Lacey tells Hadley with a squeal, falling backward onto the fluffy blanket we threw on her living room floor. Hadley forces a smile, but I can tell she's dreading Lacey's brilliant idea.

"Never have I ever—" Lacey points to Hadley with a chuckle. "—made out with a celebrity."

Hadley's cheeks become scarlet.

This seems to be a sensitive topic for her, but Lacey is too fucked-up to care. Uncomfortable as can be, Hadley guides the glass of water in her hand to her mouth and takes a sip.

"Wait, what?" Astrid chimes in. "Oh my God, *who*?"

"Kane freaking Wilder, bitch. They used to be best friends," Lacey blurts. A few lyrics pop into my head as soon as Kane Wilder's name is mentioned.

My sister Catalina and I were full-on obsessed with this guy once upon a time. For what it's worth, I've never met a girl who *hasn't* had a Kane Wilder phase. It makes sense. The guy has the voice of an angel, not to mention he's out-of-this-world handsome.

He mostly does pop acoustic music and writes his own songs, but last I heard, fame got the best of him this past year. I did hear rumors he'd spent some time in Silver Springs growing up. That would explain how he and Hadley met.

"Who's next?" Hadley cuts Astrid and Lacey's fangirl moment short. I don't know what their story is, but I get the sense it doesn't have a happy ending.

"Got one." Astrid glances at Lacey. "Never have I ever been in love with the same guy my whole life."

"Low blow." Lacey scoffs and drags a sip of her ice tea.

I'm not shocked that it came up. Theo's *all* Lacey ever talks about. He's her ideal man, the name she scribbles in her notebooks, her childhood crush and future husband—or so she claims—but he's not interested in her.

At least, not in the way she wants him to be.

She wants breakfast and epic romance.

He wants midnight sex with no strings attached.

"Girl, you have *got* to get over him." Hadley speaks my mind.

Triggered, Lacey groans and covers her face with her hands. "Nope. Not talking about him tonight. I'm way too drunk. I'll start crying."

But she's already getting emotional.

I'm about to pull her into a hug when knocks rattle the front door. Lacey immediately dabs her eyes dry with the back of her hand, rising to her feet. I'm surprised she can even stand considering her blood is ninety-eight percent vodka.

"She's here." She chokes on a sob that's half-sad, half-happy and stumbles over to the door. Looks like I'll get to meet her oldest friend, after all. Lacey swings the door open, revealing one of the most gorgeous girls I've ever seen.

I'm not exaggerating.

Lacey's friend has long, straight black hair, porcelain-white skin, and eyes so blue I can see them from here. She's wearing a black leather top, and her right arm is covered in rose tattoos. A cute lip ring accentuates her cherry-red lips, the unshakable confidence radiating off her making her just as intimidating as she is stunning.

"I can't believe you made it." Lacey squeezes her into an embrace so tight her friend taps her shoulder to let her know she's suffocating her.

"I wouldn't have missed your birthday for the world, Lace."

She laughs, reciprocating Lacey's enthusiasm.

They pull away a few seconds later.

"Happy birthday, rich girl," Lacey's friend teases, and I assume this has to do with some inside joke.

Lacey chuckles, grabbing the girl's wrist. "Come on, I'll introduce you to everyone."

Lacey and her friend stand in front of us seconds later.

"This is Astrid, Hadley, and Dia." Lacey makes quick work of telling her our names. Her friend makes eye contact with everyone, offering them polite smiles…

Until her gaze stops on me.

And her smile slips off her face.

She doesn't speak for a few seconds.

"Tell them your name, dummy," Lacey chuckles, nudging her with her elbow. Then, without tearing her eyes away from me, she says,

"Hi, I'm Remy."

Twenty-Two

Diamond

Finn: Where are you?

Finn: Stop torturing me and get your ass over to my house.

Finn: Pretend like I said something less desperate.

Finn: Also, pretend like I didn't just text you four times in a row.

I've never been one to swoon over a boy's texts—granted, I've never really had a boy blow up my phone like this before—but I can't stifle a squeal as I read Finn's message and jog down the stairs with Aveena.

The basketball game ended hours ago. Vee and I decided to head back to my place shortly after Xavier scored the winning shot. I figured Vee would be less likely to bail on me if we hung out just the two of us before driving over to Finn's house.

We're having a slumber party tonight, which I'm sure has something to do with her agreeing to go to the game and the hangout at Finn's place afterward.

I appreciate her meeting me halfway. I think she's made peace with the fact that in order for us to spend more time together, she has to be willing to spend *some* of that time with the jocks.

We've been eating lunch with Finn and the guys every day for six months, and she's yet to get to know them. It also wouldn't hurt if she made friends with Lacey. I could hardly see myself telling her about the whole *Remy* thing a few days ago considering she wasn't invited to girls' night.

I've been biting my tongue all week, obsessing over the blue-eyed, paled-skin beauty who happens to share a name with Finn's car.

Is it a coincidence?

I thought so, at first.

But I would've had to be *blind* not to notice the way Remy forced a smile whenever she talked to me. It was clear that she couldn't stand me. I tried to convince myself I was crazy until Lacey glanced at me with a devilish grin and slurred, "Never have I ever slept with my boss's son," halfway through the night.

Finn's name somehow got slipped into the conversation, and I *swear* Remy's face changed.

She had that look in her eyes.

Like she was mentally ripping me apart.

The whole thing has made me realize that I don't know much about Finn's past. His mom's accident is pretty much the only window I have into his life before me. What was his relationship with his mother like? Is Finn's envy of Xavier the only reason he and his father drifted apart?

How many girls has he been with?

Did he *love* any of them?

I've been meaning to ask Finn about Remy, but I didn't want to mention it in front of everyone at lunch, so I decided to wait until I got him alone.

I planned to tell him last night, since Lacey told me practice ended early—the cheer squad and basketball team share the gym—but when I texted Finn, he said he had a thing. He was very vague about it, too.

But I didn't insist.

I trust him.

He cares about me. He wouldn't screw me over. I quickly text Finn back before Aveena and I reach the first floor.

Dia: Leaving now.

My trust issues evolve into stone-cold betrayal when Aveena and I walk into the kitchen to find my dads and Jesse seated around the table. There isn't a sound to be heard, the harsh truth creeping under my skin as they stare directly at me.

Dave's eyes are bloodshot with rage, and Gaten's are packed with disappointment.

My gaze darts to Jesse.

His eyes are loaded with guilt.

He snitched on me, didn't he?

"Aveena, sweetheart, can you give us a minute?" Gaten tells my best friend softly.

"Oh, of course." Vee takes the hint.

I glance at her over my shoulder, and she musters a small "good luck" smile.

"I'll be in the car," she assures me before plucking her keys out of her pocket. She's driving us tonight. I know I'm in deep shit from the moment she steps outside.

"What the hell is this? Some sort of intervention?"

Gaten releases a deep sigh. "I'm only going to ask you once, Diamond. Were you or were you not alone this summer?"

If looks could kill, Jesse would have a smoking hole in his forehead right now.

My throat aches. "I…"

There's no point in lying anymore.

"No," I come clean.

Gaten's shoulders sink with relief, as though he appreciates that I didn't lie when confronted, but Dave's eyes tell a completely different story.

I lost his trust.

Worse, I lost his *respect.*

"You sat there." Dave leaps off his chair and charges toward me. He stops inches from my face. "At this very table! Every Saturday for *two* months, you sat there and looked us in the eyes knowing you were betraying our trust."

His anger paralyzes me for a moment.

"I… I knew you would tell me to quit. I needed the job and—"

"You had a job," Dave snaps. "You had *multiple* jobs, Dia. You were dog-sitting left and right, but you gave it all up for the house-sitting gig. You could've left from the moment you found out you were going to live with a boy, but you didn't. Why?"

He's right.

I've been lying to them, but mostly, I've been lying to myself. I told the nagging voice in my head to shut up, that I was only staying because this job paid better than my regular ones, and it was true. At the beginning.

I wanted to make money *and* piss off Finn.

To show him I was here to stay.

Then it became more.

It became about figuring him out. Cracking his chest open and making sure he had a heart. I stayed because I wanted to see into his soul. I stayed until I didn't want to leave.

"Why?" Dave urges a few seconds later.

A tear traces down my cheek and dies on my mouth as I whisper, "Because I love him."

Gaten can't bring himself to speak, but Dave? He couldn't

care less about my confession. If anything, he must find it funny because he lets out a bitter scoff.

"Give me your phone." He stretches his arm out toward me.

"W-What?" I stammer.

"You heard me. Give. Me. Your. Phone," he stresses.

He can't be serious.

"Why?" I step back.

"Because you can't be trusted with it. Just like you can't be trusted to stop talking to this boy. You're not giving me a choice," he insists, driving his palm closer to my face.

"What does *that* mean?" I spit, slipping my hand into my pocket as if to protect my phone and freedom.

"It means we were wrong," Dave scolds. "We've been treating you like an adult. We've been *trusting* you like an adult, but you're just a kid who doesn't know what's good for her."

"You mean him, don't you? *He's* not good for me?"

They don't know a thing about him.

They don't know he's the kind of person to set the world ablaze for the people he loves. They don't know he would've gladly given his life for Lexie or his mom. Or that there's a huge heart hidden behind years of trauma and bad attitude.

"Dia, give him the fucking phone," Jesse barks, and his intervention sets me off.

"You." I point a finger at him. "You've got some nerve pitting them against me for lying when you've done *nothing* but keep secrets. Where were you these past six months, huh? Better yet, why did you stop being friends with Brody Richards? You're full of shit, Jesse." I steer my focus onto my dads, who seem completely clueless as to how they should handle this situation.

"Don't even get me started on you two. You never talk about my birth parents. What happened to my mom? You never told me how she died. You never told me *anything*."

My dads are stunned, but the guilt ripping across Gaten's gaze confirms my biggest fears.

My palm lifts to my mouth. "Oh, God, is she even *dead*?"

Gaten's eyes glisten with tears, and he moves closer to me. "Dia, please—"

"Please what? Don't make a scene? Don't ask about my mom? What about my *dad*? Can I talk about him, or is he off-limits, too?"

No one speaks for long seconds.

Until my brother mutters, "Guys… it's time."

"Time for what?" I search my parents' eyes for a hint.

Gaten and Dave exchange glances.

Then Dave shakes his head in disagreement.

What just happened?

"You won't tell me? Fine. I'll figure it out on my own."

I can't control my limbs as I tear through the kitchen in a fury. I've just placed my hand on the doorknob when Dave's voice rings out in the kitchen.

"Dia, don't you dare walk out that door—"

But I'm already gone.

* * *

Aveena and I drive up Finn's driveway twenty minutes later. I haven't shed a tear or said a word about the fight with my dads since I climbed into her car. She doesn't suspect a thing. Not because she's a bad friend, but because I'm surprisingly good at pretending like my whole world isn't falling apart.

As if today wasn't awful enough, I just saw Brie and Xavier making out on Lacey's Instagram story. I can't believe he invited Cruella tonight when he very *publicly* dumped her at Theo's pool party a few days ago.

"Seriously?" I blow out a breath at the nauseating video of Brie and Xavier on my phone.

"What?" Aveena questions.

"Well, that didn't take long." My first instinct is to slip my hand into my bag and pull out the hairbrush-shaped alcohol flask Lacey made me buy. We used it to sneak booze into a concert a few months back.

I filled it with tequila from my parents' stash when they weren't looking. I judge myself for trying to drink my pain away from the moment I uncap the bottom.

And if the look on Aveena's face is any clue?

She's judging me, too.

I make up some excuse about needing a drink since we're going to be spending the night with Brie, and she doesn't argue.

Meanwhile, I'm dying inside.

Vee parks the car in Finn's circular driveway, her disapproval for my drinking habits stamped across her forehead. Next thing I know, I'm leading the way to Finn's backyard. He texted me that they were out on the trampoline.

Aveena follows suit, her footsteps hesitant and slow, but all I can think about is losing myself into Finn's arms. I want him to take me to his room, strip me naked, and fuck the guilt out of me. I want him to save me, the way I saved him that night on the bridge. Finn Richards is the hill I want to die on, to hell with the consequences.

We turn the corner to see Finn, Brie, Lacey, Xavier, Axel, and Theo hanging out on the trampoline. The boys are chugging beers while Lacey and Brie giggle like five-year-olds. No surprise there—I could smell weed all the way from the driveway.

Finn's eyes flare when he notices me.

"Ladies, just in time," Axel comments as we approach them.

Finn doesn't give me a chance to come to him, immediately pushing to his feet to meet us by the pool. My lungs shrink in size and capacity when he stops inches away from me and leans forward to whisper in my ear, "I believe we have a *deal* to get back to."

I don't know what the hell it is about his voice, but shivers erupt all over my body, my heart rate quadrupling as his breath brushes against my earlobe.

Shit, I can't leave Vee.

I shoot a glance toward Aveena as soon as he pulls away. I

expect the look in my best friend's eyes to be ridden with panic, conveying a clear "don't you dare leave me" but find a rather accepting grin on her face.

"Go," she encourages.

I assess her features for a moment, a grateful smile on my face as I ponder my next move. But Finn's heard more than enough, capturing my hand into his and taking off in the direction of his house.

I'm not sure how we wind up in his bedroom, but I embrace my shrouded thoughts, my hands flying to his hair when Finn's mouth crashes against mine.

Fuck. To. The. Yes.

I shriek when my back hits his mattress with a thud, and Finn laughs, climbing on top of me to muffle my shock with a hot kiss. We never once talk about what's going to happen, grasping at each other's clothes desperately. It's been a whole week since the last time we were alone, and it shows.

Our shirts are the first to go, but his cock begs to be freed, protruding from his pants. I shift my hips against his, eating up his groans when his thumb grazes my nipple over my bra.

He's about to fling my bra over my head when his phone rings. This isn't the first time someone's called him while we were doing the deed. He's never let that stop us before, so you can imagine my surprise when he releases an irritated groan and disconnects from my mouth.

He looks like he's in pain, like it kills him to do this, as he exhales. "I have to take it."

I'm shocked, to put it mildly, but tell myself this call has to be important for him to leave me hanging.

"I'll be right back." He anchors torturous kisses up and down my neck.

He's quick to grab his phone on the nightstand and exit the room. His footsteps sound down the stairs. *Red flag*, my brain screams. Why wouldn't he just pick up the phone in front of me? Why would he need to go downstairs?

My doubts retreat to the back of my brain when I spot a dusty wooden box neatly placed on Finn's desk. It looks old, a visible crack embedded in the lid. I'm willing to bet it hasn't been opened in years.

It's calling my name, tempting me to take a peek. You'd think I would have learned my lesson after sneaking into Finn's mom's office last summer, but nope, I still move off the bed and make a beeline for the mysterious box. I open it, expecting to find, well, *anything* but this.

In the box are letters.

Hundreds of them.

All dated from three years ago.

Did Finn write these?

I recognize his clumsy handwriting from the many notes he left for me last summer. According to the dates, he would've written these when he was fifteen.

I keep glancing toward the door as I reach for one of the

wrinkled letters. Then I unfold the piece of paper, sit on the edge of his bed, and start to read.

Dear heart...

You're a fraud.

Do you know how many dumb fucks actually believe you can *feel* things?

They think you're so great, in control of our emotions, but you're just a vessel. Pumping blood into our bodies and hogging the credit for every love story ever written.

The brain is really the one doing all the work, and the worst part? Even though I know you don't feel shit, when my mom disappeared underwater, it hurt in my chest.

That's right, in my chest.
Not my brain.
What the FUCK is that about?

I should tell you I didn't want to write you this letter. Good thing this is the last therapy session my dad will ever drag my ass to.

The lady with the glasses has officially declared me a "lost cause." She told Dad to call her when I decide to help ***myself,*** and that, until then, there's nothing she can do for me.

She did insist I write one more letter for my last session, though (I swear she gets a kick out of torturing me). First, I had to write a letter to my dead mother, and now I'm writing a letter to a goddamn *organ.*

I know what you're thinking. Maybe *she's* the one who needs help.

Anyway, I'm not sure what else to say, heart. The point of the exercise was to pinpoint how I feel about you and I think I've made myself pretty clear. But, just in case I didn't, here's a recap...

Dear heart,

I hate you.

-Finley

A smile preys on the corners of my lips as I read fifteen-year-old Finn's words on repeat. I may not know much about his childhood, but this… his letter… it helps me see into a world he's kept tucked away for most of our relationship.

This is what his life looked like. After his mom died, she left behind a broken, reckless teenage boy whose survival depended on finding someone to blame.

And when it wasn't himself, it was his own *heart*.

"Am I bothering you?"

My heart somersaults when Finn's deep voice travels across the room. Chances are, he's been watching me infringe his privacy for five minutes, but I still try to cover my tracks and stash his letter under my thigh. He cocks an eyebrow at my reaction, a smirk stretching his beautiful lips.

He scoffs. "Subtle."

Flushed, I pull the wrinkled letter out from underneath my thigh, exposing my sin with a cringe. "Was worth a shot."

Finn heaves a quiet laugh in response, stalking toward me and plopping down on the edge of the bed next to me.

"How much did you read?" he questions before reaching for the letter in my hands and trapping it into his fist.

"All of it," I admit shamefully.

He nods.

"I didn't know your dad dragged you to therapy."

"Yep." He blows out a breath. "Every Friday from fifteen to sixteen. Worst year of my fucking life."

I watch him trail to the trash can by his desk, ball up the

letter, and throw it away.

"I found the box under my bed when I was cleaning my room," he explains.

I know exactly what he's referring to.

It wasn't too long ago that he was wrecking this very bedroom with a baseball bat. Lexie had just died in his arms a few hours prior. It took him *months* to clean up everything and replace what he broke.

"I'm not sure why I kept them." He shrugs, picking the box off his desk for a closer look. "I always told myself I'd burn those letters to ashes but never got around to it."

He doesn't look at me when he says it.

He's lying.

I'm willing to bet the letters made him feel connected to his mom somehow. And he'll never admit it, but he kept them because he cares. He cared too much then, and he cares too much now.

Finn was a mama's boy through and through. I used to think my parents were superhumans, too. Sad to think my dads might never look at me the same way again…

My recollection of the harsh words I exchanged with them before coming here chips away at my composure. I wasn't supposed to let it get to me. I was supposed to let Finn screw my brains out and forget about the bonds I just broke, but my eyes steam up despite my best efforts.

I focus on keeping the sobs at bay and get off the bed,

turning my back to Finn as I pretend to pace around the room. Envisioning the *brutal* disappointment on my parents' faces coaxes tears from my eyes, and I start to cry silently.

Only, I must not be as silent as I expected because Finn catches on immediately.

"Dia?" he calls.

Stop fucking crying.

"Dia? Talk to me."

I choke on a sob a moment later and feel Finn's imposing presence behind me. He tries to walk around me to take a look at my face, but I whip it away from him, grasping at the little pride I have left. Finn lets out a growl of irritation, grabbing my cheeks and steering my face toward him.

You'd think I slammed a sword through his chest when he sees my glistening eyes. There's a mix of sadness and rage festering in his gaze, and it isn't long before rage wins the war.

Finn's fists close into tight balls. "He's fucking dead."

I blink at him through confusion and a thick veil of tears. "Who?"

"Whatever pathetic fuck put tears in your eyes." He releases my jaw. I crack a small smile, his overprotective side bringing warmth to my thawing heart. He might sing a different tune if he knew the "pathetic fucks" in question are my parents.

"That would be my dads." I wipe one of my cheeks with the back of my hand.

Finn's features display his worries, but he doesn't say a word, waiting for the story's conclusion.

I inhale a sharp breath before continuing. "*They know*. About last summer. They found out I've been lying to them."

"Shit." He sighs. "How did they take it?"

I sniffle. "What do you think? They flipped out. They don't want us seeing each other anymore."

Color drains from Finn's face, his jaw muscles twitching and his shoulders contracting as though he's assessing a life-or-death threat. He doesn't like the idea of my parents keeping me away from him, that's for sure. I anticipate a rash reaction but get a deep, calming breath instead.

"What did you tell them?" he asks, leaving me in awe of his self-control. I'm glad he didn't make it about him.

In that moment, as I look into those gorgeous hazel eyes, I want to tell him the truth. And the truth is that… these past six months have been the happiest of my life.

"I told them that I'm in love with you."

Finn's mouth drops open.

I said it too soon, didn't I?

What if he doesn't feel that way yet?

Shit, shit, shit.

"Oh, God." I back away. "I don't know why I said that. I just—"

My heart nearly liquefies when Finn's fingers curl into the belt loops of my jeans and he yanks me to his chest. His mouth smashes against mine with such pressure that I have to grip his shirt for balance.

He doesn't say "I love you" back. At least, not with words. He says it in the way he seeks my tongue, deepening the kiss until we're both gasping for air.

He says it in the way he wraps his hands around my waist, guiding me down onto his lap as he takes a seat on the edge of his bed. I'm straddling him before I know it, digging my nails into his scalp and pulling at his hair as I grind on him relentlessly. His cock is rock solid, throbbing in his pants, and I feel high on the look on his face.

The lust, the desire, the *hunger*.

I taste his need for me when he groans inside my mouth, his fingers unclasping my bra. His mouth latches onto my stiff nipples less than a second later, his hands traveling up my ribs and cupping my breasts as his tongue twirls around each tip.

"You're the only fucking thing that matters to me." Finn disconnects from my breasts to mark my neck with purplish wounds. "I'd die for you, Dia. I'd *kill* for you. Tell me you know that."

His teeth continue to brand my skin with traces of him. He kisses my neck like his hickeys are his insurance policy. His way of making sure that I'll never leave.

That I'll never *forget*.

I see his Adam's apple bob when I detach myself from him and slip out of my jeans before settling back onto his lap in my panties. His eyes flare when I start to play with his belt. His mouth finds mine again for a hot, messy kiss as I'm pulling his cock out of his briefs.

I spit inside my hand and work his shaft fast and hard, looking him dead in the eyes as I do.

"Dia…" He closes his eyes, sounding irritated.

Enjoy it. It might be the last time.

My lungs bail on me when Finn's eyes snap open.

I only realize I said that out loud when I see the look of anger on his face. He replaces my hand on his cock with his, his available hand jerking my gray panties out of the way as he positions himself at my entrance, making sure that I'm ready with two fingers. He grunts at what he finds between my legs.

"Don't think for one fucking second that I give a shit what your parents say. They'd have to ship you off to a deserted fucking island to keep me from you, you got that?" He drills the words into my brain. "Even then, I'd find you. *Always*."

Then he squeezes inside me without a condom.

His size stretches my walls to the limit as my forehead falls against his. It's been a week since he was inside me, and I might be on the pill, but we're still being incredibly unsafe. I can't help sinking my fingertips into his shoulders to lift myself up and slide down again.

"Fuck yes." Finn pumps his hips into me, matching my tempo and watching my every move as I bounce up and down his length. I can feel him deeper with each stroke, and I moan so loud it doesn't even sound like me.

"More," I whimper.

"Take it, baby. I can handle it," Finn assures me, his hands flying to my ass cheeks and squeezing. He makes me jump on his cock, our mutual efforts quickly becoming too much for me.

"Oh, God." My fingers dip between my legs, the pleasure reaching unparalleled levels as I play with myself without a sliver of shame. Finn can't seem to tear his eyes away, his jaw flexing as I flick my clit in circles.

He shocks me by rising off the bed. My legs close around his waist instantly, my stomach clenching as he fucks me while standing up, hands smacked on my ass cheeks for support. I pick up speed with every thrust.

"Fuck, Dia, slow down," he says, his voice a guttural plea.

"I thought you said you could handle it," I tease, rocking my hips harder.

A wicked smile playing on his lips, he arches an eyebrow. "Not sure I like your attitude, Gem."

"Yeah?" I lean forward to bite his earlobe. "What are you going to do about it?"

I shriek when Finn pulls out of me without a warning, carries me to the bed, and pins me facedown against the mattress. My nails claw at the sheets from the moment he drives himself inside me from behind.

"Yes!" I cry out, backing up into his pelvis and making him groan. Finn resumes fucking me into the mattress until I can hardly speak.

"What? No snarky comment?" he taunts, gripping my waist as he rams himself inside me. "Where did that smart fucking mouth go?" He slaps my ass as punishment, making me flinch, and I damn near fall apart when I feel his thumb circling my asshole.

"Finn?" I tense up.

"Relax, baby."

Then he's pushing his thumb into my asshole. Just a tad. I don't even think it's fully in, but it's enough to drive me completely insane.

"Oh, God." I whimper into the sheets as he starts to finger my ass. It hurts a smidge, but his arm snaking under me to find my swollen clit allows for a change of sensation. Finn rubs me in strong and speedy circles for a few minutes, his thumb and cock stretching both of my holes over and over.

An earth-shattering orgasm overtakes me in a matter of seconds.

"There she is." I can practically hear his victorious smirk as I squirm beneath him. "Milk my cock. That's a good girl."

His dirty talk tips me over the edge, and I come undone, roping Finn into an orgasm of his own. His thrusts become sloppy and demanding as he twists my hair around his fist and moves in and out of me furiously.

He's unloading inside me a split second later. I'm stuck in a daze, in a far, faraway land where I can't be reached when he pulls out, lies back on his bed, and ushers me into his arms.

We stay like that, sweaty bodies pressed to one another, for over thirty minutes. We kiss, we laugh, we relish in the aftermath of our orgasms. It's almost perfect.

Almost being the keyword here.

"Not to ruin the moment, but I smell like semen," I whisper into his neck, and Finn lets out a breathy laugh.

"I'll get our shower started." He kisses my nose and pauses. "*Everything but you*," he says before rising off the bed and throwing on a pair of sweatpants.

"Everything but you," I reply.

My gaze shadows him inside the bathroom connected to his room, a big, dopey smile on my face. He's just disappeared inside the bathroom when I decide to check my phone.

I spot it on the floor, next to my clothes. I have three messages from Aveena. And two from a number I don't recognize. Curious, I tap the stranger's messages, my eyes skimming over the most horrifying words I've ever read in my life…

Unknown Number: This happened last night.

Unknown Number: I'm so sorry.

There's a video attached in the conversation.

And the thumbnail?

The thumbnail is my worst nightmare.

Twenty-Three

Diamond

The screen is black, the distant buzzing of silence all I can hear when I click on the video and wait for *something* to happen.

There's nothing.

No sound.

No image.

Shocker.

Unknown number, sketchy messages? I knew this had to be a prank from the moment I unlocked my phone, but I could've sworn I'd seen a shirtless Finn in the thumbnail of the video?

Nah.

Get real, Dia, it can't be him.

He'd never do that.

My gaze drifts from my screen to the bathroom. I hear the shower running and Finn's muffled voice on the other side of the door. Is he on the phone? This is the second mysterious phone call he's received today. Who's calling him all the time?

My overthinking comes to a screeching halt when I notice movement in the video. The phone recording this is resting on a bed, pointing toward a wall. I squint, discerning what seems to be a desk? Then a creaky noise begins grating on my ears.

It sounds like…

A squeaky mattress?

The camera starts to move back and forth, matching the squeaky noises. Then I hear a girl moan.

This is a sex tape.

I'm this close to chalking it up to a "wrong number incident" when the walls of ignorance I was hiding behind crumble around me. My palm flies to my mouth as I look ahead of me and realize…

I've seen that desk before.

I'm afraid I might throw up, but I can't tear my eyes away from the wooden desk next to Finn's bed.

This was filmed here.

This is Finn's bedroom.

Fingers with black nail polish slide into the frame, gripping the sheets. The moans intensify. The female hand grabs the phone and lifts it up to reveal a scene that reaches into my chest and shoves my heart out of my body.

The video doesn't show the *deed*, but it shows a girl trapped underneath a muscled torso, a guy's face buried deep in her neck as they fuck like animals.

But it's not just any guy.

It's *my* guy.

My Finn…

And the girl?

The girl is Lacey's friend, Remy.

The navy blue pillows in the background of the video knock the air out of me. I glance down, tears soaking my face in an instant. I'm sitting on the exact bed where they did it. The bed where Finn told me he'd die for me not even thirty minutes ago.

Oh my God.

Finn was awfully secretive yesterday. He wouldn't tell me why we couldn't see each other when basketball practice ended early.

This…

This is why…

He was with her.

He's probably on the phone with her right now.

I don't know anyone named Remy. The words Finn said to me in the woods dagger me in the chest. *I just liked the name.*

"Fuck, Rem, you're so tight," Finn grits out.

I'm crying so hard I can hardly breathe.

Remy's piercing blue eyes lift to the camera, staring me dead in the eyes and taunting me. "Promise me you don't care about that bitch."

Finn laughs a gravelly laugh, drawing his head out of her neck and saying, "I don't care about that bitch. It's always been you, Rem."

He pauses.

"*Everything but you.*"

That's what kills me.

Three little words are all it takes to murder a part of my soul. I recognize his groans. He's going to come. I know because it used to be me. I've been the girl in the video. Now I'm just the idiot who fell in love with a monster.

Finn pins both Remy's arms on each side of her head as he finishes, and the black stones clasped around his wrist cause irreversible damage to the shriveled-up, cold vessel in my chest.

He's wearing the bracelet I made him.

* * *

Finn

"Stop fucking calling me when she's here," I spit into the phone, the clattering of the shower on my left doing little to muffle my voice.

This bitch has no sense of timing, *whatsoever.*

She pulled the same shit last night when I was walking out of basketball practice. I swear she has some sort of sixth sense for picking the worst moments to call.

I've just shoved my phone into my pocket when I hear a woman moan. It's faint enough that I convince myself I imagined it. Until it happens again.

Louder.

Clearer.

I swivel around, sneaking a peek toward the bathroom door. It's open an inch, the noise coming from my bedroom. I swing the door open without a second thought. I walk out of the bathroom to find Dia sitting on the edge of my bed, all dressed, her back facing me.

I scoff. "Porn, huh? This your way of telling me you're ready for round two?"

But Dia doesn't laugh.

She doesn't even *move*, staying disturbingly still with her head hanging low. Her phone lies flat on her lap, her eyes fixated on the screen.

"Dia?" I assume she didn't hear me.

Still nothing.

"Dia?" I repeat.

Okay, this is weird.

"Baby, what's wrong?"

She doesn't acknowledge my existence, her lack of a response starting to freak me the fuck out. My patience runs out fast enough, and I cut across the room to meet her. She doesn't even glance up when I stop before her.

She looks like she's in shock, her eyes ghostly, her makeup smeared down her flawless face. The moans grow louder and louder the closer I get to her.

What the fuck?

"What are you watching?" Fear grips my insides. I don't wait for her to return to the land of the living and pick the phone off her lap to see for myself.

Then I immediately want to die.

I want to tear my own throat out, peel off my own skin, make myself bleed for the atrocity on her screen.

The video shows Remy, clawing at my back, her mouth open as I fuck her brains out. It never ends. It just goes on and on, filling my throat with rage and panic.

"That's what you were doing." Dia's croaky voice is gutting. "Last night. That's why you were busy."

No.

No.

Fuck.

"It's her, isn't it? The person you're always on the phone with."

I don't even get a chance to reply before she's pushing to her feet and snatching her phone out of my hands.

"Dia, wait, please," I word-vomit, but it's too late. It feels like the air is thinning in my lungs as I watch her swing my bedroom door open.

Then she runs.

She gives up on me.

As she fucking should, but it doesn't stop me from throwing on the first T-shirt I can find and chasing after her. I run like a goddamn track star, shadowing the only good thing in my life down the hall and nearly breaking a leg in the process.

"Dia, wait!"

Pathetic.

So pathetic.

She gets to the stairs before I do and doesn't waste a second bolting to the first floor. I'm so agitated I almost consider sliding down the banister like they do in the movies—anything to catch her before I lose her forever.

"Vee. Car. Now!" I hear Dia tell her best friend, who happened to be in the kitchen. The front door slams, and I lose it, my sight becoming blurry. I can't think. I can't breathe. The only thing that matters is stopping her. Getting her to listen to me. Everything else fades away, including the truth.

The truth being that she's right.

I *did* betray her.

Even if it's not in the way she thinks.

I barely notice Xavier standing in the kitchen when I rush to the door. He's watching the scene unfold with a million question marks in his eyes, but I don't give two shits right now.

"Dia!" I choke on an embarrassing plea as soon as I'm out of the house.

Fuck you, heart.

I knew I was right to hate you.

I see Dia climb into Aveena's passenger seat as I'm closing in on them like a professional stalker. Aveena hurries inside the vehicle, and I hear the click of the door lock just as I halt in front of them. *Locking the doors was a smart move.* I definitely would've swung the door open and dragged Dia's ass out of the car.

Aveena begins to drive away.

Then I panic and jump in front of the car without a care about my survival. Thankfully, Aveena slams the brakes at the last minute. Dia can either hear me out or have her friend run me over. *Her choice.*

My baby is sobbing in the passenger's seat, and I'm almost tempted to let Aveena hit me with her car.

I deserve it.

I deserve all of it.

"Dia, please." I stare her dead in the eyes through the windshield. The window on her friend's side is open, and I know she can hear me. "Don't fucking do this. Just listen to me."

In response, Dia severs the eye contact and glances at Aveena before saying, "Drive."

Aveena pushes the gear into reverse, and I rush to the passenger-seat window before they can take off. I slam my palms to the glass, fully aware that I look like a psycho.

I can't help it.

I can't just let her go.

"Dia, look at me. Just fucking look at me. Please." I start to tear up, sounding like I swallowed a chunk of fucking glass. She won't even spare me a glance, avoiding my eyes and covering part of her face like she can't *stand* to look at me.

Aveena's expression reeks of pity, and I cringe.

This is what I've become, huh?

A lovestruck puppy people feel *sorry* for?

My brain clings to the word "love."

That's right.

I fucking love her.

I'm in love with the girl I once swore to destroy.

And if she's going to leave, she should know that.

"Diamond, I love you," I croak, pressing my forehead to the window. For the first time since she got into the car, she hears me. She hears me and looks up.

"I fucking love you, Dia. I do. Just give me a chance to explain. Just… Please."

Her features twist in shock. Like she can't believe I just said that. I wish I'd said it earlier. Back when she first told me she loved me. I wish I didn't have to use my love like a weapon to keep her.

But I'm selfish.

Let's be real, *I'm a piece of shit.*

I'm the guy who ruins everything she owns and lies.

I'm the guy she has to lift off a fucking bridge in the middle of the night. But mostly, I'm the guy who borrows money from a criminal to hire a private investigator.

The guy who would cross *every* line imaginable to get rid of his house sitter...

What kind of person hires a PI to dig into someone's past and wreck their future? What kind of person takes sketchy phone calls from the woman he hired and hides it from his girl?

I wasn't with Remy last night, but I can't tell her that.

I can't tell her that without *also* telling her that her entire life is a lie. That her perfect little family didn't want her. That they never even confirmed her mom's death or that her dad is the kind of monster they write about in history books…

I can't tell her the truth. Not without exposing their sins. And I can't open up to her. Not without showing her a police report that will completely *destroy* her.

Dia doesn't reply for long seconds.

I can tell I'm getting to her, but will it be enough?

"Tell that to your whore!" Dia belts at the top of her lungs.

Aveena pumps the gas before I can blink, forcing me to leap out of the way. Axel, Theo, Brie, and Lacey flock to the front of the house a moment later, asking me what the hell happened, but I can't form a sentence. All I can do is stand there, watching the girl I love disappear from my life…

Taking a piece of my black, selfish heart with her.

Thank you so much for reading Dear Heart, I Hate you!

Dear Heart, I Miss You (Book 2 in Finn & Dia's duet) is releasing on **May 20, 2022.** PRE-ORDER YOUR COPY NOW!

Please consider leaving a review for **Dear Heart, I Hate You** on Amazon if you would like me to write more books in the Easton High series (Theo & Ashley, Catalina & Mal, Kane & Hadley)

Reviews allow authors to keep writing and let us know a series is worth continuing!

Connect with me:

Want to stay updated on my next releases?
www.eliahgreenwood.com/subscribe

Want previews of my next books?
Instagram: @eliahgreenwood

Want to see my cover reveals early and get exclusive excerpts?
Private readers group: Eliah's Rule Breakers

Also by Eliah Greenwood

Dear Heart, I Miss You (Book 2 Finn & Dia, Releasing May 20, 2022, Available for Pre-order)

Dear Love, I Hate You (Book 1 in the Easton High series. Standalone)

The Rules Series

Unwritten Rules (Haze & Winter, Book 1 in the Rules series)

Unspoken Rules (Haze & Winter, Book 2 in the Rules series)

Unbroken Rules (Haze & Winter, Book 3 in the Rules series)

About Eliah

Eliah Greenwood is a Canadian author, who started her writing journey on the internet at the age of fifteen. When her debut gathered 35,000,000 reads online, she decided to publish the series that set so many hearts, including hers, on fire. When she's not writing and screaming at her computer screen, you can find her binge-watching her favorite TV shows on repeat or reading in a warm blanket. She is currently working on her sixth book.

Acknowledgements

First and foremost, I want to thank Amanda Anderson (@allaboutthatromance & The Last Chapter Bookstore) for keeping me sane. As always, you were the first to dive into Finn and Dia's story and you are, without a doubt, the reason I pushed through and finished this book. I am so grateful for your friendship and can't wait for you take over the world.

To Rachel Grant, for being a dedicated fan since my first book and sending me the **best** voice memos when I need it. I love you.

To Michelle Lancaster, (@lanefotograf): thank you so much for giving me the best Finn. You are talented beyond belief.

To my editor, Sandra from One Love Editing, who always finds ways to squeeze me into her schedule at the last minute: thank you for sliding into my private messages when I'm feeling down about my writing and knocking some sense into me. Forever grateful for you. To my readers, new or from the OG Wattpad gang: a huge thank-you and a big hug. I know this book would be nothing if it weren't for your willingness to give it a chance. You are the reason I get up in the morning and your support means the world to me.

To my street team for *Dear Heart, I Hate You*: I couldn't do this without you. To my family and author friends, I don't think you understand how crucial you are to my process. This job tends to feel lonely but thanks to you, I'll never be alone.

Last but not least, to the amazing book community that welcomed me with open arms. I'll never forget it.